A FIERCE ARCHER

Clan Ross
Book Six

Hildie McQueen

Dragonblade Publishing, Inc. is an imprint of Kathryn Le Veque Novels, Inc.
P.O. Box 7968
La Verne CA 91750
ceo@dragonbladepublishing.com

Produced in the United States of America

First Edition April 2021
Print Edition

ARE YOU SIGNED UP FOR DRAGONBLADE'S BLOG?

You'll get the latest news and information on exclusive giveaways, exclusive excerpts, coming releases, sales, free books, cover reveals and more.

Check out our complete list of authors, too!

No spam, no junk. That's a promise!

Sign Up Here

www.dragonbladepublishing.com

Dearest Reader;

Thank you for your support of a small press. At Dragonblade Publishing, we strive to bring you the highest quality Historical Romance from the some of the best authors in the business. Without your support, there is no 'us', so we sincerely hope you adore these stories and find some new favorite authors along the way.

Happy Reading!

CEO, Dragonblade Publishing

Additional Dragonblade books by Author Hildie McQueen

CHAPTER ONE

THE PEACE OF winter didn't last long. Spring brought with it sunshine and danger. While Ewan Ross struggled to decide what his future entailed and what was best for the advancement of Clan Ross, he remained with Clan Fraser. The keep was two days' ride south of Ross Keep, which helped with the current alliance between the clans.

They were in Laird Fraser's study, a routine of each day before the leaders went out to speak to all the guards.

There was a knock on the door frame and a man entered.

"Laird, I was on patrol at the border with Mackenzie lands. A farmer and his family have been attacked. Four of them are dead. Every one of them cut through," the guard's voice broke as he informed them.

"Which family?" Laird Fraser asked, his expression tight with restrained anger.

The guard let out a long breath. "Thomas Lewis, his wife, and two sons. There was an infant as well, a girl. We took the wee one to a neighboring family to care for."

Keithen Fraser, the laird's son, jumped to his feet. "We must declare war on the Mackenzie! Ye know they are responsible."

"Lewis was a good man. He worked hard to ensure a good life for his wife and bairns. What reason could anyone have to kill him?" the laird stated.

The guard shook his head. "We asked the neighboring farmers. One reported to have seen men riding through. A group of five or six. They did not wear distinctive tartans but were described as menacing."

Although it could not be proven that the people who died were killed by a Mackenzie, no one else in the region had reason or was capable of such savagery.

Always infuriatingly fair, Laird Fraser motioned for Ewan, Keithen and Broden McRainy, a guard, to come forward. "We will do nothing until there is proof. Go out with four men each. Scour every inch of the border until ye find something to prove who was responsible."

Laird Fraser banged his fist on the table. "Bring me back something."

Within the hour, the men were divided, each of them assigned four of the best scouts and warriors. Ewan and his four men raced northwest of the small farms, where families had been massacred.

They rode hard until reaching the closest Mackenzie border and pulled their horses to a stop. Looking to each of the men, he directed them in which direction to continue. "Each of ye, ride until the sun is directly overhead and then return here. Keep yer eyes open for any sign of recent travel, blood, torn clothing. Anything."

News of attacks on other people of clans in the surrounding area had been reported consistently. Although everyone suspected the new Mackenzie laird, there was little proof, as the attackers ensured there were no survivors to bear witness.

Upon the death of the last two Mackenzie lairds, a new seemingly benign leader, named Atholl Mackenzie, a nephew of the first late Mackenzie, was given the lairdship. The man, who remained single, although with a reputation for ruining many a lass, had met with Laird Fraser recently. He extended promises of goodwill. However, in the passing months, it was becoming more and more evident that he was as power thirsty as his predecessors.

The senseless killings were meant to bring clans to war with one another, a tactic that, thankfully, had only caused small squabbles so far. Almost every laird suspected Clan Mackenzie, and not one another.

It made little sense that the Mackenzie would target Clan Fraser. With newly acquired alliances with Clans Ross and Grant, they were not an easy mark. There was also the fact that just a day's ride away, another large Clan Fraser lived.

Keithen Fraser, the laird's son, had married Ava Mackenzie the late laird's only daughter. It was a marriage that had been negotiated by the lairds in an effort to come to a truce following battles. However, the relationship remained tenuous at best. And now, the new Mackenzie demanded a new public pronouncement, one way or another.

Being that Laird Fraser's son, Keithen, was married to the late Mackenzie's daughter, Ava, any kind of pronouncement was superfluous. Except for the fact that the Frasers and Mackenzies had never truly been on friendly terms.

Perhaps it was because of the lack of formal terms that now a farmer and his family had been attacked and killed. It was that innocent people who had nothing to do with quests for power often paid the price.

Hours later, all of the warriors met back at the farm. None of them had found any clues that stood out.

"How can it be that we found nothing?" Ewan asked, frustrated.

Broden shrugged. "It could be the attackers traveled southwest to throw us off their tracks."

"Or that we are mistaken, and it was not the Mackenzies, but others," Keithen suggested. "It could be they expect us to not come after them and all of this has nothing to do with the Mackenzie."

"That is why two groups are scouting the eastern areas. We will find something. Once we do, whoever is responsible will pay." Ewan frowned toward the small house and its land. "They did nothing to deserve such a horrible end."

Broden met his gaze. "It is usually the innocent that pay for warring people in power."

"True," Keithen replied grimly. "We should search the home and surrounding area. Keep your eyes open."

They dismounted and walked around, searching for any clues of who was responsible. Ewan scanned the area, from the newly dug graves to the corrals where the few livestock the family owned were grazing.

"Ye both can return to the keep," Broden told them. "The day is ending. My men and I will ride out to the neighboring farm and ask the farmer to come over here and take care of the animals. Hopefully soon, the laird will grant this land to someone."

The sun was falling as an exhausted Ewan rode back to Fraser Keep. Instead of taking the usual route back to Fraser Keep, he detoured into the nearby woods that marked the border between Mackenzie and Fraser lands.

If the attackers had not wanted to be seen returning to Mackenzie lands, it was possible they stayed on Fraser wooded lands before crossing into theirs.

The birds silenced as he rode past, a giveaway to others of his presence. A crack, like a branch breaking, sounded and Ewan listened intently. But soon thereafter, it was silent again. It could have been a wild beast or the wind, he supposed.

Ewan dismounted at seeing a broken branch. It was newly broken. Someone had just been through there.

Again, he considered, it could have been a wild beast.

At the sound of a primal growl, Ewan whirled. A man on horseback crashed through the trees.

Ewan went for his sword, but it was with the horse, and the at-

4

tacker blocked the way.

A red birthmark covered half of the man's face. Ewan's blood went cold as he recognized the man he hated with all his being.

The marked man was the lead guard for Laird Mackenzie and the one directly responsible for the vicious attack on Catriona McKay, the woman he cared for deeply.

Fury swept through every inch of his being. Not only was he finally face-to-face with the man he'd been hunting for months, but it was impossible to get to his sword.

The man held up his sword, a cruel twist to his mouth. "Ye will die today."

"Who are ye?" Ewan called out, hoping to distract him. "I am sure ye do not know who I am."

The man sneered. "Oh, but I do know ye. Ye are an archer, perhaps the one who killed my laird."

It was impossible for the man to know anything about it. No one knew he'd been the one to shoot three arrows into the bastard. Then again, he'd given away his gift of archery at the last competition. The small tournament had been at the Fraser Keep and attended only by those close to the family.

So, the fact remained. Someone had told this man.

The warrior charged forward and Ewan dove to the ground. He would not be able to keep the man at bay unless he sheltered behind trees.

Scrambling to his feet, he ran for the nearest tree only to stop at the unmistakable sensation of a blade plunging through his body. He gasped when pain erupted and unable to remain upright, he fell face-first onto the forest ground.

"YE ARE FORTUNATE to have survived." Catriona's face came into focus and Ewan Ross wished with all his might that it were possible to lift his hand and caress her cheek. Her amber brown eyes pinned him for a moment before she turned away. "He's awake."

He tried to lift his head to see who she spoke to, but no matter how hard he tried, no part of his body responded. Twice, Ewan tried to ask for something to drink, but the only sound he made was a croak.

"What is it? Are ye in pain?" Once again, Catriona peered down at him. "I'll get ye some water."

Moments later, she lifted his head and tipped a cup, allowing the precious liquid to flow down his parched throat. He drank greedily until every drop was gone. "Thank ye."

"Laird Fraser asked to be informed as soon as ye were awake." She turned away and went to a table and began mixing items with a pestle. "A maid will return shortly to care for ye. I have been helping the healer with yer care."

It was a struggle to keep his heavy eyelids open, but he managed to. "What happened?"

Catriona's head whipped up and her mouth fell open. "Ye do not remember?"

All he could recall was the last meeting with Laird Fraser, where they'd decided to go to a farm after an entire family had been killed, except for a bairn. Laird Fraser wished for them to find proof of who was responsible.

He also remembered that they suspected the slayings were ordered by Clan Mackenzie.

Had he ridden out that day? With whom had he gone?

"I do not remember anything other than leaving to go in search of attackers. How long have I been back here?"

Moving closer to the bed, she lifted the edge of her apron and wiped her hands. "Three days. Someone cut ye through in the forest, near the border between our land and that of Laird Mackenzie."

"Who found me?"

Catriona disappeared from sight to be replaced by a man.

"What were ye doing on Mackenzie lands?" Laird Fraser's face was contorted in rage. "Ye and the rest of the guards know better than to travel into Mackenzie lands."

Ewan grimaced when he shifted, as even the slightest movement brought discomfort. "I do not recall going to Mackenzie lands."

"Ye were found by hunters. Ye're very lucky."

"I cannot remember."

Laird Fraser frowned. "Ye separated from the four that went with ye. They said ye ordered them to ride back here without ye."

Since Ewan had only come to live at Fraser Keep for a little over a season, he was not familiar with where, exactly, the land borders were. In the past when he'd traversed into Mackenzie lands, it was with a plan in mind.

"If I was across the border, perhaps I was following who I thought responsible for the killings."

"When ye can ride, it may be best for ye to return to yer clan. If the Mackenzies think ye are dead, it may serve to our advantage."

When Laird Fraser left, the room was eerily silent. Ewan tested his limbs, first one leg, then the other. He wiggled his feet and then flexed his hands. Then he repeated each movement once more, just to be sure and blew out a relieved breath that they moved as he commanded. Although it was painful, he shifted and attempted to sit up. It proved impossible to lift himself up, much too painful, so, he gave up and fell back onto the bed with a loud groan.

Why could he not remember anything? It was as if a fog had fallen over the events of the day he was injured. If he'd seen someone, it was possible whoever it was had attacked the farmers. If only he could see the face.

Sliding his hands down his torso, Ewan discovered his entire midsection was bandaged. He'd been wrapped from lower chest to stomach. The cloths were hard from dried blood. When he pressed gently, inch by inch, he found a long wound, just under his right ribcage. He'd been lucky to have been left for dead and that whoever attacked him had not thrust into him another time.

The back of his head throbbed. Reaching back, he felt a large lump. Whoever had sliced him through had obviously attempted to finish him with a blow to the head.

Indeed, he was damned lucky to be alive.

Keithen Ross, the laird's son, entered. Wearing a heavy tunic and dark trews, the tall man lowered to a chair and crossed his stretched legs at the booted ankles. "We keep our healer busy," Keithen said with a chuckle.

"Where is the healer?" Ewan asked. If he could get some of the healer's tonics, it was possible he would be able to sit up.

"Seeing to an injury. One of our guards fell when lowering from the wall and broke his leg." Keithen studied him for a moment. "Father tells me ye cannot recall what happened."

"Tis true, I do not remember anything past speaking about going out to the farm. Yer father has asked that I leave as soon as I recover." Ewan grimaced as a wave of pain seared across his midsection. "I will leave, but I require a bit more time. I have something to finish."

"I suspect ye have already accomplished more than we know or suspect," Keithen said and Ewan felt a cold trickle travel down his spine. The man continued. "What else, or should I say who else is on yer list?"

Both he and Keithen had sought revenge against the same group. Those that Keithen had not felled, Ewan had. Together, they'd killed almost every member that had been on duty when both Lady Fraser and Catriona McKay were taken.

Although Keithen had a more understandable reason, Ewan felt just as justified. If asked why he wished to kill them to the detriment of his own life, Ewan could not justify his actions fully. But he hated any kind of mistreatment. He always had.

On the other hand, no one would question Keithen.

One guard in particular, the one with a red birthmark across his face, was the only one that remained alive. He was the leader, the main one who'd raped and beaten Catriona. The bastard and the group of guards he commanded had mercilessly tortured the defenseless woman.

They'd left a shell of what she'd once been, filled with shame that was not justified.

No, he could not justify his actions, other than to admit that her plight had torn through him. One look at her and his entire soul ached for her. If there was such a thing as the calling of one soul to another, it had certainly happened when he'd first set his gaze on Catriona. That she'd been hurt in such a horrible manner was not something he could allow to go unpunished.

Something about her pulled at him. Although he was not ready to invest too much thought in what exactly he felt for her, it went without question that Catriona was a woman of worth.

"Ye and I have a common enemy. We are united in this. However, ye do not have the same reason I do," Ewan finally replied.

Keithen studied him for a long moment. "I suppose asking yer reasoning is of no avail?"

Ewan shook his head. "The reasons are my own."

"Why did ye kill Laird Mackenzie?" Keithen asked.

Struck silent, Ewan inhaled deeply, attempting to keep any expression from his face. "Why would I kill him?"

Keithen straightened and leaned forward. "It is said that the men who shot Laird Mackenzie had to have a special talent. The three arrows that fell him were loosed so close together, it was as if the archer had practiced this special archery skill for a long time."

Silence stretched for several seconds. It was on the tip of his tongue to deny it but, instead, he blew out a hard breath. "I did what ye and the other clan leaders couldn't. No one would suspect or blame me. A clan war will not come yer way because of it."

"It was not yer place," Keithen pronounced. "If anyone should have killed the bastard, it was me."

"And ye surely would be dead as we speak."

"It is a miracle I am not." Keithen was right. He had been captured by the late laird's son and hung for the killing. However, Clan Ross had arrived just in time to save his life. Keithen's sister, also an accomplished archer, had pierced the rope with an arrow.

Just then, the healer entered with two maids. One carried a bucket of steaming water, the other a stack of clean linens.

Without preamble, the older man pinned him with a hard look. "Ye lost a lot of blood and are certainly with luck." Gray hair pulled back into a queue and a pristine tunic, he moved to the bed and lifted the blankets.

The healer motioned the maids closer and instructed one to soak the cloth wrapped around his midsection so it would be easier to remove.

The hot water seeped through Ewan's bandages with a soothing affect. He wanted to relax but suspected the bandage removal was going to be painful. The ripping off of the bandaging was uncomfortable, but he managed to keep from making too much noise.

As the healer cleaned his wounds, Ewan was shocked at how long the piercing appeared. However, it was healing nicely. His midsection was rewrapped.

"The wound to the back of yer head is what worries me," the healer explained. "I wish to see what happens when we help ye to sit."

With Keithen's assistance, he was helped to sit up and, immediately, the room swayed and his vision blurred.

Closing and opening his eyes to clear his vision, Ewan let out a deep breath to keep from becoming nauseous. Refusing to look at the healer, Ewan concentrated on the wall opposite the bed, but his vision continued to be blurry. "Something is wrong with my eyesight."

The healer shrugged. "I expect everything will return to normal after ye heal properly." The man leaned forward and looked into Ewan's eyes. "They appear fine."

Keithen waited for the healer to leave before speaking again. "My father did inform me that he wishes ye to return to yer clan."

The decision was not surprising. Upon learning that he'd been the archer to kill the late Mackenzie, it was imperative Ewan leave. The last thing the Frasers needed at the moment was to be involved in another conflict.

It was doubtful, in Ewan's mind anyway, that the new Laird Mackenzie wished to battle. The man, however, was no doubt behind the efforts to bring conflict between smaller clans and the Frasers.

Ewan let out a breath and nodded. It was his fault for showing off during the archery competition. When he'd shot three arrows at once, those that were aware of how Laird Mackenzie had been killed immediately suspected he was the assassin.

Could it be that one of the people who'd been at the tournament had purposely attacked and attempted to kill him? It frustrated Ewan not to recall what happened before he was found left for dead.

"Get some rest," Keithen said and left.

Ewan slid from the bed and pulled clothes from his trunk. At seeing his tunic, neat stitches where a tear had once been caught his attention.

For some reason, Catriona had insisted on being the one to mend his clothes. She'd asked to do it and he'd made sure to bring her an article of clothing weekly. It had become the only time he could see her alone without the lass avoiding him.

Not that he blamed her for being wary. After all, the poor woman had been through a horrific ordeal. There was little doubt in his mind that Catriona was changed for life. Whoever she'd been before he'd met her was forever gone. A pity, as he'd heard she was a lively creature who was quick to smile and pass out advice.

Moving slowly through the pain, he dressed and then stood still for a moment as the room once again swayed when he straightened.

After taking a few shaky steps, Ewan managed to keep from becoming dizzy. Although his vision remained a bit off, he could see well enough to make his way out of the small room he'd been given by the Frasers.

It was time to find out what happened the day he'd been injured. If he heard the exact details from one of the guards, hopefully, it would prod the memory.

"What do ye plan to do?" Broden asked him when he walked out to the great room and lowered to a bench. "Return north or back to Uist?"

It was the question he'd been asking himself since he'd spoken to the laird. "I am not sure as yet. It is probably best that I return north."

His cousin, Laird Malcolm Ross, would put him to work and allow him to provide a good life for himself. As much as Ewan detested the idea of asking for help yet again, he wasn't ready to return to Uist.

"Ye are not ready for work as yet," Broden said, studying him with a flat expression. "Whoever cut ye, did not like ye at all."

"Tell me what happened," Ewan said. "I do not remember anything of that day."

Broden nodded. The man was almost as tall as him, but slimmer. The warrior had seemed to dislike him since Ewan's arrival. However, at the moment, Ewan didn't have time to figure out why.

As head guard, Broden didn't treat him any differently than the others, and yet Ewan sensed that the man did not care for him in the least.

"We rode out to the farm," Broden said as he walked toward the guard buildings and Ewan fell into step beside him. It hurt to walk, but he managed to keep up. Admittedly, Broden walked slower than usual.

"Each of us rode in separate directions and returned to the same spot at the sun being directly above. After looking about the farm, my group and I headed to a different farm. I was told by yer guardsmen that when ye all were heading back here, ye took a different route."

"Did I give an explanation?"

Broden's grayish gaze met his. "Not to me, or anyone else. No one was aware of yer new path until ye were brought back here by the hunters."

As the head guard had retold what had happened, small pictures formed in his mind. Perhaps the healer was right, and both his memory and eyesight would return to normal as he healed.

They'd come to a stop and Broden motioned toward the keep. "Ye look about to drop. Return to the keep. I do not have time to tend to ye."

Although annoyed at the man's tone, Ewan turned away and trudged back to the keep. Once he sought a meal, he would return to bed and rest. As much as he hated idle time, Ewan was well aware that rest was the best healer.

Just as he entered the great room, he noticed several women sitting around a table at the far end of the room. Immediately, he knew Catriona was among them. Whenever the woman was out of her bedchamber, she sat at the same table. Positioned beside the fireplace, it was warm there, and protected by two walls. No one could approach the table without being seen.

The men knew better than to approach her, although some had done so without issue. However, one time, a man had approached and Catriona's reaction had been alarming. The man, who'd been a visitor, remembered Catriona from childhood and had neared to greet her. A startled Catriona had fallen to the floor and, while screaming, had scurried to the corner next to the fireplace where she'd cowered. It had taken the laird's wife a long while to coax her to move and get her away and to the safety of her bedchamber.

It was days before Catriona had emerged once again.

When Ewan lowered to sit at a nearby table, he felt the gaze of the women. Ignoring the pointed looks, he waved a servant over and asked for food.

"What are ye doing out of bed?" The slight hoarse tone in Catriona's voice was like a soft balm to his entire being. That she'd walked over to him was stunning. He looked past her to the table to confirm his reaction. Four sets of rounded eyes met his.

"I am hungry. Once I eat, I will return to bed," Ewan replied, forcing an annoyed tone to his response. "Besides, I am not sure I can stand up right now."

He didn't look directly at her, not wishing to alarm her. Instead, he bowed his head. In truth, the pain was growing increasingly worse. "Perhaps someone should help me to bed," he grunted.

"Young man." Lady Fraser neared. "Whatever are ye thinking to be out and about so soon after being cut through? Ye must go to bed at once."

"He cannot move," Catriona replied for him. To Ewan's shock, her hand pressed to his forehead. "He is feverish."

Lady Fraser tsked. "Of course, he is. The wound is fresh...and bleeding."

Ewan looked down to find that blood had seeped through the fabric of his tunic and he moaned. "This is one of my new tunics."

"Up with ye," Catriona said as he was lifted from the chair by guards who'd probably been motioned forward by Lady Fraser.

At the movement, he cried out in pain. The room swayed and he gulped in air. It was as if the breath were taken from his body and he could not take any in.

"Call the healer," someone said. The lack of ability to breathe took precedence and he concentrated on not passing out when pain ripped through his body as the guards carried him to a bed.

TIME PASSED, WHETHER quickly or slowly, Ewan had no idea. Voices and faces came in and out of focus until he finally gave up trying to recognize what was happening. Feverish, he went from shivering to being so hot that he begged for water. Ewan recognized he was very ill and prayed that he would live.

Then everything stopped. Perhaps a day had passed, or even two, he wasn't sure. What he did know was that seeing the beautiful woman standing at the window peering out was the loveliest scene to wake to.

"Ye almost died," Catriona said as if sensing his gaze. "Perhaps this time, ye will remain abed until the healer gives instructions otherwise."

As much as he wanted to argue the point, Ewan decided it wasn't the time. "What day is it?"

"It has been five days since the day ye were found, and two days since ye acted so foolishly and left yer bed."

Two days. Ewan blinked, noticing that his eyesight was normal. One good thing had come from being asleep for two days. Hopefully, it also meant his memory would return.

He let out a breath, grateful that it brought only slight pain. Not only that, but that he could breathe easily.

"Why are ye caring for me? Ye should not fret, a servant can care for me." Ewan hated to say the words. As much as he wished to spend time with her, he didn't want to be responsible for doing or saying something that would bring her more distress.

"Tell me, why did ye kill Laird Mackenzie?"

CHAPTER TWO

C ATRIONA WAITED, KNOWING that Ewan was scrambling to come up with a reply. She had so many questions. Why had he killed the Mackenzie? Why did he remain there at Clan Fraser when he had no reason to? Also, his family was on the Isle of Uist and yet he lived either at the Ross' to the north or at Fraser Keep.

As much as she detested to be near any male, there were a few, in actuality, who didn't bring her distress. Laird Fraser, Keithen, Broden and the healer. All of these men she'd grown up knowing her entire life. It was different with Ewan. Although she wished to flee each time he was nearby, she fought against it. Something about him called to her on a very basic level. It was as if they had shared a common experience before. In actuality, she'd only just met him. Nothing about what she felt when she was near him made any sense.

It was doubtful someone like Ewan Ross could begin to understand what she'd been through. She doubted that even if a man witnessed it happening to someone they cared for, it would never possibly be the same as actually experiencing it.

And yet, there she stood in front of him, wanting to know answers to the questions that had been swimming around in her mind for weeks.

"Why do ye think I killed him?" Ewan's deep voice cut through her thoughts. "I had no relationship or interaction with the man that would make me wish to kill him."

Catriona pinned him with a direct look. Upon his hazel eyes meeting hers, the urge to flee became hard to resist. And yet she planted her feet firmly and looked away for a moment so that she could speak freely.

"It was clear at the archery competition. Several of the Frasers commented on the fact that the late laird had been pierced by three arrows that had hit him simultaneously." Once again, her eyes met his gaze but she quickly looked away. "Ye can shoot three arrows at once with extraordinary precision."

When she lifted her gaze back to him, his eyes were closed tightly, as if he was trying to avoid pain. "I cannot answer yer question. Why won't ye and yer people just be glad it was done?"

"The motive. What reason would ye have to do it?" Catriona persisted. "Tell me."

The man had been cruel. He had killed hundreds of innocents without cause. There were hundreds of reasons anyone would wish him dead.

"Whoever killed the laird did the world a favor. The man was cruel to hundreds and deserved death. Should there be a clearer reason than the devastation and overtaking of small clans by killing, pillaging and destruction?"

She would not be deterred by what he said. There was truth in the words. However, like him, Catriona understood that there were always consequences, no matter how good an action was.

"Ye, however, were not a victim of any of those things. Which brings me to consider that perhaps there is another, more personal reason."

His sharp inhale told her that she'd hit a sensitive spot. Sensing he would either admit to doing it or stop talking, Catriona decided it was best to ask one more question.

"Admitting what ye did will stay between us. I cannot explain the need to know, other than I detested the man with all my being and although his death does not erase...things...it helps me feel vindicated."

When his eyes lifted to hers, they'd darkened. "There isn't a better answer to why than that. The vindication ye and the other victims need."

"So, then ye consider yerself a champion of the downtrodden?"

"I like the sound of it," he replied flippantly. "However, I have not admitted to being who killed the late laird."

When he closed his eyes this time, she left the room. It was best to give him time. The conversation was not over. She needed to find out why Ewan Ross had killed the late laird. The reason was important. Not only because she wanted to be appreciative to him, if he was indeed who killed the man, but also because she hoped it would help her move forward.

Upon entering her bedchamber, Lady Fraser entered right behind. Since they'd both been taken by Clan Mackenzie and kept as captives, Catriona and the laird's wife had become especially close. Catriona had grown up spending more time at the keep with the laird's daughter, Esme, than with her own family. Often, her parents come for meals, just to see her as she often refused to return home, fearful of missing her friends.

During their capture, Lady Fraser had been treated well, unlike her, who'd been sent to the dungeon. The laird had instructed the guards to do what they pleased with her. Catriona shuddered, willing the memories away.

"Darling," Lady Fraser said. "Do ye feel up to traveling to the village with me tomorrow? Flora is set to return, and I thought it would be a good outing. We can fetch her and perhaps pick up a few things at the village square."

Since her horrible abduction, Catriona had only ventured as far as the flower field outside the walls. Accompanied by other women, it had helped ease some of her anxiety. The thought of traveling to the village made her wary.

"What if someone stops us along the way? I am not sure that it would be a good idea to travel together. Someone could..."

"Nothing of the sort will happen, Catriona. It is time for ye to visit yer family. Time for ye to face things. Ye cannot expect to spend the rest of yer life cowering in here." She motioned around the room.

In her heart, Catriona agreed wholeheartedly with Lady Fraser. Ever so slowly, she nodded. "I will try. Ye are right. It has been many days since I have seen my parents and my sister. I will go with ye."

Lady Fraser clapped. "That is good news, dear one."

⟫⟫⟫⟪⟪⟪

CATRIONA WAS THANKFUL for the security of the closed carriage as they traveled to the village.

Despite her initial trepidation of traveling, she was excited to see her family. It would be a treat to see them all at the same time. Although her sister and mother had often visited, her father rarely came to Fraser Keep. His work running the mill kept him and his workers busy for most of the year. When he wasn't milling the grain, he dispensed and sold grain for the rest of the seasons.

"Once we deposit ye at yer family home, I will go to the market, see about Flora and then we can return to the keep. If ye wish to remain longer, ye can send word to the coachman," Lady Fraser said with a pleased smile playing on her lips.

Considering she wished to spend time with her family and still afraid of any reactions that would bring them to worry, Catriona decided it was best to keep the visit short. "I will not be staying. Once ye are ready to return, please stop by for me. I am afraid to remain too long and..."

"No need to explain," Lady Fraser said. "Tell yer mother I will come inside for a visit once I return for ye."

Catriona peered out to see that they'd arrived at her house. The structure was the same and yet it seemed so small compared to where she'd been living for the past year. The sight of her childhood home gave her comfort.

Immediately, her mother rushed out through the front door to greet her.

"Dear daughter, I am so happy to see ye," her mother said, hugging her tightly and ushering her into the house. Once Catriona settled in the kitchen, her mother turned to look out and motioned for a young lad to come near.

"Go to the mill and ask my husband to come at once. Tell him Catriona is here. Then go and fetch Audra. Tell her to come and bring the babe." Her mother spoke quickly, barely catching her breath. "Tell my husband to bring flour."

Excited at the prospect of earning a coin, the boy raced off, closely followed by a dirty, hairy dog of questionable breed.

Once again, her mother hugged her close. "If I'd known ye were coming, I would have cooked one of yer favorite meals. All I planned to make today was a simple stew."

"I adore anything ye cook, Mother," Catriona assured her. "My visit will not be long today. It is my first time leaving the confines of the keep. I will only be here for a part of the day. I must return with Lady Fraser."

"Does this mean ye are getting better? It must be or else ye would not dare venture out." Her mother caressed Catriona's face and pressed a kiss to her forehead. "My dear girl, how I have missed ye."

Tears welled in her eyes and Catriona blinked them away. How could she tell her mother that she wasn't the same person? She would never again be the carefree woman who'd gone to visit the Frasers that day so many months ago. Instead, she attempted a smile. "I miss ye as well. I hope to come visit often, now that I see I can without incident."

"Good. Ye must spend time with yer sister. Now that she has the new bairn, she seems to be constantly at her wits' end."

Her sister, Audra, was ten years older than Catriona and had been married for six years. Despite the difference in their ages, they'd been close until Audra left home. Now with five children, it was comical to see her once calm and orderly sister constantly frayed and barely kept together.

"Does she require help?" Catriona asked. "I thought Geoffrey hired a nursemaid," she said, referring to her sister's wealthy husband.

Her mother shrugged. "I hate to admit that my grandchildren are quite disorderly. They run nursemaids off rather quickly."

The door opened and her father barged in with a wide grin directed at Catriona. Although he neared, he did not move close enough to touch her. Catriona hated that he had to be so cautious, but the last few times he'd visited, she'd had a hard time allowing him close.

"It has been several weeks since I've seen ye. I am sorry for not coming, but ye know this is the busiest time at the mill."

Catriona moved to him and leaned against him. Immediately, the familiar woodsy scent of her father filled her senses, making her feel secure and safe.

"May I hug ye?" her father asked in a soft voice.

"Aye." Upon her response, his arms circled her, and Catriona let out along breath at her lack of an adverse reaction.

Moments later, the sounds of children and a loud shrill wail made Catriona flinch.

"Stay here. Don't ye dare come inside, ye hear me?" Audra screamed. Then she walked in with a bairn on her hip and another two attached to her skirts.

"Dear sister, I am so happy to see…" Audra stopped talking and looked down to the silent children grasping her clothes. "I'm…sorry, I didn't mean to bring these two inside."

"It's fine," Catriona said, nearing and taking the babe from her sister. "Finally, a girl."

Audra sighed and went to the table. She peeled one of the two boys from her clothes and placed him in a chair. The one remaining at her side clutched her leg. She tugged him off, but he managed to reattach himself. Finally, she gave up and blew out a breath. "Ye feel better then?"

"A bit," Catriona admitted as she swayed with the babe in her arms. "I am striving to move forward as much as I can. Although, at times, I am still very fearful."

Her parents exchanged worried glances. Her mother began pouring drinks into cups and placed them in front of each of them.

The awkward silence made Catriona realize her family wanted more answers that she wasn't prepared to give. Not because she didn't want to, but because she wasn't sure what the future held.

"I plan to remain at the keep for now. I am helping with mending and such for the additional guards who came from Clan Ross. Also, it helps to be with Lady Fraser."

"What of yer life outside remaining cloistered?" Audra began, but then stopped. "Forgive me, I have no right to ask."

"Ye have every right," Catriona replied, reaching out to clutch her sister's hand. "I wish I knew the answer. I am not sure it is possible for me to ever have a normal life again. Although I do wish it, I just can't."

Her mother sighed. "Ye need time. I believe ye will get through this. Ye are very brave to have come here today."

The rest of the day went quickly. There was only one time that Catriona became anxious. Someone knocked on the door, a man calling out that children had let his chickens out. The irate man demanded Audra control the boys. Both her mother and Audra rushed out to call the boys, who ran in circles, scaring the birds away instead of helping to collect them.

Catriona watched from the window as her mother and sister managed to find the birds. While she was distracted, the toddlers left behind had come up to her and were now clutching her skirts. One was sucking his thumb and the other was staring up at her.

After promising to find ways to see each other more often, Audra and her brood left. Her mother let out a breath and leaned back in a chair. "Audra needs help. Perhaps she should hire an older, stricter governess for the boys. They need a firm hand."

Despite feeling overly tired and ready to leave, Catriona helped her mother clean and prepare supper. Just as she sat down to rest, Lady Fraser arrived.

Her mother and Lady Fraser exchanged pleasantries. It was obvious by their conversation, they saw each other often. Apparently, every time Lady Fraser came to the village, she stopped by for a visit.

"I will come to visit ye in a few days," her mother said as they hugged goodbye a little while later. "I will bring back some of the mending to do here. There are far too many guardsmen for ye to be the only one doing the task."

"One of the maids also helps, but we could certainly use another pair of hands," Catriona assured her. "I look forward to yer visit, Mother."

As soon as they arrived back at the keep, Catriona immediately sought the refuge of her bedchamber. When asked, she refused an invitation by Lady Fraser and Ava Fraser, Keithen's wife, to come to the sitting room. She preferred the quiet and stillness of her own private space.

It had been a huge undertaking to leave the keep after over a year. Despite the joy of seeing her family and doing her best to pay attention to their conversation, it had been tiring pretending to be well.

The longer she remained in the prison of her own making, the more power she gave to the animals who'd attacked her. And yet, the night terrors and the flashes of the horrible days in captivity remained clear and present.

Letting out an annoyed groan, she tore her clothing off with shaky fingers. Then placing one foot in front of the other, she slowly approached the tall mirror. Her entire body shook when she reached for the cloth draped over it, and before she could change her mind, Catriona tore it away.

At first, all she looked at was her face. She noted that the hairstyle she wore, a braid wrapped around her head, was not particularly flattering. Forcing her gaze to travel down, she noted the first mark that had not been there before. Puckered skin at the base of the right side of her neck. A bite? Or perhaps fingernails had dug into her skin there. How could she remember every single time she'd been hurt?

Moving away from the mark, she looked to her chest next. Had her skin always been so pale? No, she and Esme had often laid out next to the creek and sunned themselves. Sometimes, they'd removed all their clothing, except for their shifts to allow the sunshine to kiss their bare skin.

On her left breast was another mark. This one was clearly a bite mark. Catriona's breath caught and she looked away, attempting to calm the sudden lack of air. If she was to become stronger and push it all to the past, then every single mark would be seen. Once that was completed, she would be able to forge forward.

She remembered exactly what happened when looking at the third mark. This one was a healed cut that ran from just under her right breast to the side. One of the guardsmen had cut her with the tip of his dirk when she'd kicked him.

Neither their faces nor their voices did she attempt to recall because they did not deserve any space in her mind. Then turning away from the mirror, she looked over her shoulder. Remarkably, there wasn't any other scarring.

Once again, Catriona faced the mirror and scanned herself. The only other scar was on her left knee. Her lips curved at noting the jagged old scar that her mother had sewn together after she'd fallen out of a tree at ten years old.

Keithen had chased her and Esme with a dead rat.

He'd gotten a proper spanking for it, much to her and Esme's delight. When he'd walked past them rubbing his bottom, they'd followed after him, taunting him until he'd ran and hid.

Once again, Catriona looked back up, meeting her own gaze for a long moment. In her mind, she had conjured up a badly scarred and disfigured body. In reality, the worst of it was inside. Those scars would remain for a long time.

Just as she pulled on a soft dressing gown, Flora, her companion, entered. In truth, Catriona felt it was silly of Esme to have hired someone to care for her needs. She was, after all, just a simple village girl. However, because of her close friendship with the laird's son and daughter, she'd always been considered family.

As grateful as she was for Flora, as of late there was little she needed the woman to do. Since recovering from her injuries and debilitating fear that had plagued her the weeks after her release, Catriona was able to do well for herself.

But she would not send the woman away. Flora's husband had been killed by the Mackenzies and the woman needed to work in order to support her child and mother.

At first, Flora had remained at the keep, living there while her mother and infant son remained in the village. Now, she'd moved back to her home in the village and only came to stay at the keep during the day.

"Are ye about to bathe?" Flora asked at noticing her clothing strewn about the floor.

The woman began collecting the clothing and Catriona allowed it, knowing Flora needed something to do. "Yes, but then I realized I'd not asked for heated water and the tub to be brought."

Flora shook her head and smiled. "I will see to it."

"Thank ye," Catriona replied as Flora hurried out, her strides sure and purposeful.

Once alone, Catriona went to her sewing basket and pulled out a torn tunic. Immediately, her mind went to the owner, Ewan Ross, who was currently recovering from a horrible injury.

She let out a sigh recalling the handsome face. One day, after noting that most of the tunics he wore had tears or had unraveled at the sleeves, she'd surprised him and herself by insisting on mending the clothing. He'd readily agreed. He was thankful, he'd said, not to have to worry about his arms going out the wrong holes.

Catriona was not about to fool herself into lying and saying that she mended his garments out of pity. The truth was that she found Ewan Ross to be the most alluring man she'd ever set eyes upon.

Since she was very young, she'd convinced herself that she was in love with Keithen. Even now, she found him very attractive and she loved him. But the love she felt for Keithen Fraser was a sisterly one. She could finally admit it. Now that Keithen was happily married, Catriona was glad for him.

As far as Ewan Ross was concerned, what she felt for him was so very different. The attraction to him was almost primal. Every part of her came to life at his presence. It was as if her body recognized his and demanded nearness.

The thought of intimacy paralyzed her with fear. No matter how much her body demanded his touch, it saddened her to know nothing would ever come to be between them.

CHAPTER THREE

D ESPITE GLARES FROM the healer, Ewan made it a point to attend last meal. If he could walk, there was no reason to remain cloistered in his room. If he was to leave Clan Fraser as soon as he was able to ride, then he needed to make the most of his time while there at the keep.

A maid hurried to him, placing a trencher in front of him along with a tankard filled with ale. He drank greedily, realizing he was more thirsty than hungry.

The meal was simple that day, lamb in juices with a few root vegetables. The freshly baked bread, however, melted any resolve to not eat much, as it begged to be slathered with freshly churned butter.

"Do ye require anything else?" The serving lass leaned forward, allowing him a perfect view of her ample bosom. She was pleasant to look upon, with bright red hair and a button nose. Her gaze locked on to his lips and hers curved at noting she'd gotten Ewan's attention.

"Thank ye, nothing else at the moment." He'd not necessarily turned her down and, yet, he wasn't sure any kind of intimacy would be prudent in his current injured state. If Ewan was to be honest, as much as he enjoyed bedsport, in the last weeks, he'd not taken any offers from willing lasses.

Movement caught his attention and he looked across the room. Catriona watched him, her brows lowered and lips pursed. Was it possible that the beauty was bothered that he'd been approached by another woman? As much as he hoped so, Ewan doubted she cared one way or the other. In his dreams, she would be irritated enough to confront him, only for them to end up kissing and tangled in bed.

With a soft chuckle, he lifted his cup in her direction with a slight bow of his head. Her eyes widened and she quickly looked away.

"Whose attention are ye seeking?" Keithen lowered to sit across from him, blocking his view of Catriona.

Ewan chuckled. "Someone who barely pays me any heed."

"Seems the way it is, Friend. Women are complex creatures."

The lamb was good and Ewan ate his fill. Noting it was only he and Keithen at that end of the table gave him freedom to speak. "I remembered something, and it is not pleasant. I know who attacked me and why."

Keithen looked around and spoke in a low tone. "Who?"

"Not here. It's best I am not overheard."

"Very well," Keithen said and then changed the subject. "Have ye decided where ye're going to go from here?"

Ewan nodded. "I will return north to my cousin's lands. There is much to do there to keep me busy."

"What of Uist? Will yer father not insist ye return?" Keithen asked.

When his face hardened, Keithen gave him a quizzical look.

Ewan pretended his injury caused discomfort and thus the grimace. He touched his midsection gingerly and then blew a breath out.

"I am the fourth born son, there is nothing for me to do there other than guard. There haven't been any threats against our clan in the entirety of my father's life. My father agreed with my departure."

"What about the Norse? Have they never threatened?" Keithen was curious about the state of affairs in other regions. Ewan understood.

"We are on friendly terms with the ones that do come to Uist. Some have come to meet with my father to propose trades and such. There is actually a small village of Norse on the northernmost portion of the Isle."

"Interesting," Keithen said. "I can see why ye wished to leave. Boredom is not good for someone born to be a warrior. I will remind ye that for many years, my clan also had peace. Never forget that things can change from one day to the next."

Ewan grinned at his friend. "And now ye find yerself married to the enemy's beautiful daughter."

"Aye, and very glad for it," Keithen said as he looked to the head table where his wife, Ava, sat.

Later that evening, Ewan joined Keithen and Broden in the laird's study. Although Laird Fraser remained distant toward him, the man was anxious to hear what Ewan had to say.

He let out a breath. "The man who attacked me was one of the Mackenzie's guards. He stated that he wished me dead because he believed I killed the Mackenzie."

Everyone exchanged looks at his statement.

"Aye, I did it," Ewan stated. "Ye are aware."

"So ye finally admit to doing it?" Laird Fraser asked. "We all did suspect."

Ewan wanted to groan at his actions on the day of the tournament. He looked to Keithen. "Yer wife knows then?"

"She's not come out and said it, but I think she suspects."

The laird motioned for him to continue. "What was the guard doing there?"

"Skulking about. I believe because it was he and whoever was with him that attacked the farmer's family."

"To what end?" Broden asked, frowning. "They have little to gain from a battle against us. If anything, they have more to lose."

Everyone went quiet considering the reasoning.

Finally, Ewan decided to give his opinion. "It could be whoever is responsible, be it the Mackenzie or not, hoped ye would blame another clan, perhaps a smaller one and begin warring with one another."

"There have been similar attacks to both of them. That is enough of a reason for them to retaliate, thinking it was us who are responsible," Laird Fraser noted. "And yet, that the Mackenzie guard was about does not mean it was them who are responsible."

"As much as I would like to blame them, I have to agree with father," Keithen added.

"How can we ever find proof?" Broden asked.

An idea struck and Ewan straightened. "Meet with the other lairds. Perhaps it will be easier to find the truth if ye work together."

Laird Fraser looked at him and nodded. "I believe I will."

Messengers were dispatched and Ewan left the laird's study needing to rest.

HIS MIDSECTION ACHED, the discomfort growing with each step he took. Holding his arm over his stomach, Ewan walked through the great room toward where his room was.

"Do ye require help getting to bed?" The maid from earlier appeared from the direction of the kitchen.

Ewan could barely stand up straight. The idea of any kind of lovemaking made him cringe. "Although it's a tempting offer, I must refrain."

He turned away, but the woman was persistent, her hand on his arm. "Ye do not have to do anything," she purred, a curve to her lips.

"He said no." Catriona appeared at the end of the corridor. "Go see about yer tasks," she snapped and glared at the maid, whose eyes widened and cheeks flushed with consternation. "Yes, Miss."

As the maid scurried away, Catriona frowned up at Ewan. "Ye must learn to be firmer. If ye are not interested, make it clear."

"Thank ye for coming to my rescue," Ewan said. "Do ye know if the healer is about?"

Immediately, she pinned him with a direct look. "If ye are hurting, it is because ye have not remained abed as the healer insisted. Come, I will help ye to lay down and then see about fetching the healer."

Catriona walked with him into his bedroom, and Ewan almost chuckled at the thought that he'd turned down one lass, and now another, much lovelier and not at all with any intentions in mind, walked beside him.

"Give me a moment," Ewan said, standing next to the bed. "I have to prepare myself to lower to it." It would not do to embarrass himself by crying out in pain when lowering to the bed.

"I'll help." Catriona neared and untied the strings at his throat. Then she helped him remove the tunic. It was painstakingly slow, and he had to keep blowing out breaths, his midsection sending streaks of pain up and down his torso.

If not for reeling from the aching, he would have enjoyed her proximity and the act of removing his clothing.

"I think I need to...sit," Ewan stuttered, barely able to get his breath.

"Ah!" he exclaimed when Catriona lifted his left arm and pulled the tunic off. "Ye should have stayed in bed and not put on a tunic. What exactly are ye trying to prove?"

Now he felt like a lad being lectured by his mother. Things could not get any worse. If it continued, she'd never be attracted to him as a man. Ewan glared up at her. "I need the healer to make me a poultice, as well as some of that vile tonic to take away the pain."

"What ye need is..." Catriona stopped talking when he fell sideways onto the bed. "Are ye about to pass out?"

He opened his eyes and gave her a droll look. "I'm trying to lie down."

"Oh," she frowned down at him. "I am not sure how to help."

"I hate to ask," Ewan began, "but can ye remove my boots?"

Catriona made quick time of removing his boots and then, slowly, they managed to slide him up until his head was on the pillow.

At this point, he blew out breaths, fighting the urge to moan out loud.

"Ewan," Catriona said in a low voice.

"Aye."

"I am going to have to take the bandage off and inspect the wound. It will hurt."

With only the bandage around his midsection, he already felt naked in front of her. When she barely acted as if it were a strange occurrence, he dared to speak.

"Ye helped treat the many wounded after the Clan Mackenzie attack, did ye not?"

"I did," she replied, cutting away the bandage. "I will not bother the healer. I can clean yer wound and make a tonic for ye."

She looked him over. "Other than having someone tie ye to the bed, that is all that can be done for ye to heal properly. If ye insist on getting up and about tomorrow, the same result will occur."

Properly chastised and barely able to breathe through the waves of pain, Ewan did not reply. Instead, he concentrated on the ceiling, counting planks of wood.

"Here, drink this." Catriona lifted his head and helped him drink a murky liquid. It was not as vile as the one he'd had before but, within moments, the pain began to lessen.

From under half-closed eyes, he watched as a maid brought hot water. Together, the women cut strips of cloth. Then after the maid mixed a poultice, Catriona spread it over his midsection.

"It's only one cut. Why do ye put so much on there?" Ewan asked.

Catriona looked up at him. "There is a lot of bruising. There are internal wounds, by the purpling of yer stomach. The poultice pulled it to the surface."

"Th-that must be why I feel near death," he said and then groaned when they helped him to sit so that Catriona could slather poultice on his back and finally wrap up his midsection.

Her amber brown eyes met his for a scant moment. "Ye are not going to die."

"Thank ye," he managed as the tonic began to lull him to sleep. "I am grateful."

"Promise me ye will remain here tomorrow," she said, meeting his gaze and holding it "Promise."

"Only if ye promise to come see me," he replied and attempted to smile. Whether he was successful or not wasn't clear as he could not control his expressions.

"I will come and ensure ye are alive," Catriona replied. He wasn't sure, but he thought she caressed his face. A warm touch to the left jaw soothed him. Whether it was Catriona or effects of the tonic, he wasn't sure.

She was coming back the next day. For that, he'd remain there. Somehow, he would have to come up with a way to convince her to remain for longer than a few moments.

Perhaps he could talk her into traveling north with him when he left. She and his cousin Ruari's wife were childhood friends. Surely the enticement of seeing Esme Ross would be a good way to do it.

The problem was that Catriona had not left the keep in over a year. The recent trip to the village had been an isolated incident and he'd been told by her companion that she'd instantly gone to her bedchamber upon returning and remained there.

If less than a few hours out affected her so, two days of travel would no doubt be intolerable. And yet, he would try.

Ewan would have preferred to remain there with his men at Fraser Keep, but having been asked to leave by the laird meant he was no longer welcome.

Somehow, he had to find a way to not leave Catriona behind. He wanted to spend more time with her, to get to know her better and help her in her recovery from the vicious attack at the hands of the Mackenzie guards.

What pained him the most about leaving was that he would not be able to hunt the man with the red birthmark. As long as that man lived, neither he nor Catriona were safe. It could be that local villagers were not safe either.

Ewan struggled to remain awake as he toiled inwardly on how to accomplish the two very important tasks.

WHEN THE FIRST rays of sunshine woke him the next morning, Ewan turned onto his side and was instantly reminded of why he'd remained on his back all night. He groaned in pain and rolled to his back.

A male servant entered with a tray of food. "Miss Catriona sent me to help ye break yer fast."

"Where is she?" he asked before considering it really was not a proper question to ask.

"In the great room," the servant replied and neared the bed. "I will help ye to sit."

Once the task was completed, Ewan felt rather awkward being fed in bed. Yet the thought that Catriona was to come and visit made him remain there. He blew out a breath and looked toward the window. What he'd rather be doing at the moment was to be on his horse, tracking down the man with the birthmark.

"Ye look unhappy." Broden entered the room, his gaze moving to Ewan's midsection. "Ye're bleeding."

Ewan blew out an annoyed breath. "I am not sure why it is taking so long to heal."

"It's a deep cut. Ye were cut through."

"What are ye doing today?" Ewan asked, not wishing to consider his injury. "Is anyone going after the man who attacked me?"

Broden met his gaze. "If ye were on Mackenzie lands, he did what he was supposed to do and keep ye from them."

"I do not believe I was. Besides, he was responsible for the attack on the farmer."

"There is little doubt in my mind," Broden said. "But that is not what I come to speak to ye about this morn."

"What do ye wish to talk about?" Ewan asked, looking to the man who seemed to dislike him for no apparent reason.

Broden's jaw tightened. "Stay away from Catriona. Leave her be."

The abrupt request made Ewan's eyebrows rise. "What right do ye have to ask that?" The question was stupid as the man had known her their entire lives. And yet, something about the way Broden studied him made Ewan wonder if perhaps something had been said by Catriona.

"The Catriona that ye know is vastly different from the one I've known since childhood. She is fragile. I do not think she can withstand another incident."

Ewan straightened, ignoring the pain. "I would never dare touch her or attempt anything like what ye are insinuating. There is no need for any warnings."

It occurred to Ewan that Broden was there for more than just intervening for a friend. The man was romantically interested in Catriona. By the way he acted, it was possible that Broden was jealous of the attention Ewan had been receiving from Catriona.

He didn't blame Broden. However, the fact that the man had feelings for Catriona did not give him the right to threaten.

"Despite what she's been through, Catriona is a strong woman, much more capable than ye give her credit for." Ewan returned to his meal, but at the other man's silence, he looked back up.

Broden's eyes narrowed and he blew out an annoyed breath. "Ye cannot claim to know her better than I do."

The guard walked out before Ewan could say anything else.

They must have passed in the corridor because it was only a moment later that Catriona entered. "What happened between ye and Broden? He seemed angry just now."

Ewan shrugged.

Catriona neared and looked to his midsection. "Although it is worrisome to see blood, the fact that it is light in color is a good sign. The healer is here and will come momentarily."

"The sooner I am healed the better," Ewan replied. "I have been asked to leave."

Her expression of consternation gave Ewan hope. "What do ye mean? Surely ye are not able to ride for long in yer current state."

"I cannot linger here much longer. Laird Fraser asked that I leave as soon as the healer allows it."

"What is the reason?"

Her question made Ewan scramble for a reply. He could tell her the truth, of course, but she was not ready for any revelation of the sort. "It could be that on my trek back from patrol, I was on Mackenzie lands and fought one of their guards. If I had killed him, the tentative truce between the clans would have crumbled."

"Ye were attacked."

"If I was on their lands, he had every right to defend his clan's territory."

Her eyes narrowed. "I know there is more to the story. Ye should tell me."

His lips curved. "I should. But I will not. Ye do not need to worry yerself with all of this."

"I am not as delicate as everyone thinks. I am overcoming my fears…"

"It is natural for someone who's been through such a trial to be affected. Keithen himself admitted that he often dreams of what happened to him."

Catriona walked to the edge of the bed. "And so ye are leaving?"

He couldn't look at her, scared that she'd see how much he didn't wish to. That he'd give anything to remain near her. It was stupid, of course. She had much more in common with Broden than she'd ever have with him.

"I am."

She shook her head slowly. "Where are ye going?"

"I will travel north back to Clan Ross."

"I see," Catriona replied, her gaze lifting to him.

His heart hammered. "Ye should consider coming with me and the men I will be traveling with. It would give ye an opportunity to visit my cousin's wife. Ye and she are very close, are ye not?"

Catriona bit her bottom lip. Just as she opened her mouth to say something, the healer entered.

The man went directly to the bed, which made Catriona move aside. "I will need clean bandages and some hot water. Can ye see about it?" He slid a look to Catriona.

Although they were not of the elite class, it was still not customary for a single woman to be in a man's bedchamber. However, in the case of healers and caring for the sick, it was overlooked.

By the healer's disapproving expression, he was not of the mind to overlook the fact that Catriona had been in there alone.

Surprising him, Catriona went to the doorway and called to a maid, giving instructions to bring the necessary items. Then to make matters worse, she rounded the bed and came to the other side.

Her gaze lifted to the healer in challenge. "I understand that the bleeding is expected. Do ye plan to stitch it closed? I had the maid boil some herbs so that the wound can be cleaned out."

The healer nodded in approval. "I have heard that many in the southern regions are using different herbal mixtures boiled in water for medicinal purposes. I plan to travel soon to learn more about it."

As Catriona and the healer continued the discussion, tonic was poured down his throat, his wound was washed and stitched together. By the time they wrapped his midsection, Ewan was in pain and very sleepy.

The healer and the maid walked out, and Catriona lowered to a chair that she'd pulled close to Ewan's bed.

"Ye do not have to stay here," Ewan said, annoyed at how hard it was becoming to keep his eyes open. "I will probably sleep until last meal."

Catriona's lips curved. "I doubt that it will be that long."

"I do not wish to take any more of whatever that was. It's not only vile, but also the room is swaying."

Instead of responding, she leaned back in the chair, seeming comfortable. The fact she remained in the room with him was astonishing. Just a few months earlier, she'd barely speak to anyone. She'd spent months locked in her bedchamber, unable to leave and now the same woman sat in a chair alone with him.

"How was yer visit to the village?" Ewan asked, forcing himself to remain awake.

Catriona gave a barely visible shrug. "I enjoyed seeing my parents and sister. She has five children."

"Five," he repeated.

"Yes," Catriona replied. "Four boys and an infant daughter."

"Do ye wish to have children one day?" The moment he asked the question, Ewan realized what a mistake it was. The unspoken, but very real reality of Catriona's tragedy surfaced, bubbling over the edge like a pot of boiling water.

Catriona jumped to her feet. "I should go and allow ye to rest." Her wide eyes met his. "I will send someone later to ensure ye do not need anything.

She would not return, nor speak to him again unless he said or did something then. Unfortunately, nothing came to mind.

Ewan tried to get up, but his recently cleansed and stitched side injury protested, and he groaned.

Rushing to him, Catriona pushed him down on the bed. The action made her arm fold under her weight until she fell flat against Ewan's chest.

Her reaction was the opposite of what Ewan expected. Instead of withdrawing or jerking away, she froze like a small animal attempting to gauge which way of escape proved lifesaving.

"Ye have some very sharp elbows," Ewan said to break the awkward silence.

"I-I…" Catriona broke off and shuddered.

Ever so slowly, Ewan took her by the shoulders and helped her to straighten. It wasn't until she sat in the chair next to the bed that she finally let out a long breath.

"'Tis best I go." She got to her feet and stopped, seeming to consider if she could indeed walk.

"Be with care," Ewan replied and yawned. "Please consider traveling north."

CHAPTER FOUR

T HE WALLS OF the corridor closed in and Catriona stretched her arms out to ensure the walls were not moving. Despite the familiarity of the great room, the path to the stairwell was not clear and she stopped just past the entry.

A few people mingled about, most seeming content to sit and talk and did not seek time with the laird.

Laird Fraser, along with Keithen and the new constable, sat at the head of the room, listening to a pair of farmers. Whatever the men's issue was would be dealt with. One problem solved only to be replaced by another person or people presenting a new one.

"May I speak to ye?" Catriona started and turned at the sound of Broden's voice.

Keeping her gaze forward so that he would not notice her lack of focus, Catriona nodded. "Yes, of course."

Thankfully, with the large warrior at her side, the path across the room past people she barely knew was easy. Broden was tall, muscular and broad-shouldered. His brown hair often lightened significantly during the summer months. Despite having known him all her life, Catriona still noticed how handsome he'd become in the last couple of years.

There was a deep cleft on the center of his chin, his lashes were thick and long, and Broden had perfectly straight teeth. Even though many a maiden sought his companionship, there was little gossip about him.

Despite all the battles he'd fought and the many times he'd gone north to work as guard at the guard post, Broden remained quite unchanged. He was loyal, caring and one of the few men who admitted enjoying cooking.

"Ye can walk with me to my table," Catriona replied, following him to a table away from others. It was her preferred place to eat at last meal because it was away from the others. Broden motioned for her to sit and he lowered across from her. His gaze met hers for a moment longer than normal.

Chills traveled down her spine. Was he about to impart bad news? Was he to leave as well?

"It is best that ye stay away from Ewan Ross. There are things ye do not know, reasons why the laird has asked that he leave."

For a moment, relief fell over her, but it was replaced with ire. "I know why he was asked to leave. He told me about the man who attacked him."

"That is not the only reason why ye should keep yer distance. It is obvious the man has feelings for ye. He is about to leave, and the situation may bring him to make untoward advances to ye. I know ye are not prepared for it."

In truth, she'd given everyone reason to see her as vulnerable. Before the incident, she'd been independent, quick to speak her mind and not keen on anyone telling her what she should or should not do. That part of her was resurfacing and it made her want to laugh.

"I am intelligent enough to know if a man is interested in me or not. I assure ye that Ewan Ross is not."

Broden's face hardened. She reached for his hand and squeezed it. The action, in and of itself, surprised her as much as him. "Thank ye for being a good friend and for yer protectiveness. I must move forward and am becoming stronger every day."

"I am yer friend, but do not wish to be…"

"Are ye threatening to end our friendship?" Catriona teased, but kept a stern expression.

"No. What I wish to tell ye is that…" Broden stopped mid-sentence, his gaze moving from her and up to someone who approached them. "Lady Fraser." He stood, to allow Lady Fraser his seat. Then looking back to Catriona, he gave her a quick nod and stalked away.

"What was that all about?" Lady Fraser asked, looking to where Broden went to join a pair of guards who'd entered the room.

"He was being a big brother," Catriona replied. "Warning me against this or that."

The laird's wife's lips curved. "I believe Broden wishes for more than just a brotherly relationship with ye."

Catriona's breath caught and her throat went dry. "I hope not. I do not wish to hurt him in any way. I have never felt more than one would feel as a good friend to Broden."

When Lady Fraser sighed, Catriona gave her a questioning look. "What is it?"

"Ye have yer eyes on someone else. I have a feeling I know who it is."

"Are ye going to tell me to stay away from Ewan Ross? That is what Broden asked me to do."

"I see. So then he is who ye have feelings for?" Lady Fraser seemed to find the news to be good, because she grinned and held her hands up to her chest. "How delightful that ye are in love."

Love. The word sunk like a pit in her stomach. "I did not say love."

"Of course not, darling. But we know how strongly ye feel once ye set yer mind to it."

A hot flush crept up her face at the reminder of the many years

she'd pined for Keithen. Since she had been very young she'd convinced herself that she was in love with him and had not wasted a
moment to ensure he well knew it. It wasn't until the last couple years
that she'd come to realize it was a fanciful thing of youth and what
she'd considered to be love was truly more of a deep caring.

"Ewan Ross is going to leave soon and once he does, I will never
see him again. Therefore, it is best I do not allow for my feelings to
grow deep."

"Oh, yes, my husband told me. It was a rash decision, in my opinion, to ask that he leave. Sometimes men are so temperamental. They
make a decision when they are angry and then are too proud to admit
mistakes."

Catriona leaned forward. "Do ye think the laird will reconsider?"
She looked to where Laird Fraser continued listening to claimants.

"I doubt it," Lady Fraser replied. "Ewan Ross is not a member of
this clan, so there is no allegiance to him."

"What of the warriors he brought with him? If he leaves, they may
follow suit."

Lady Fraser shook her head. "They came on orders from Laird
Ross. Leaving would be disobedience."

Ava Fraser, Keithen's wife, and Flora, Catriona's companion, hurried over. Each held a basket filled with cloth. Flora pulled a tapestry
from the basket and spread it over the table. "This is the perfect
surface for each of us to work on a different section at once," Ava
announced.

The project gave Catriona time to consider the two conversations
she'd just had. That Broden was interested in more than friendship
made her anxious. The last thing she wanted was to hurt her friend.

"Flora?" she started to ask her companion something, but then
noticed the woman had stopped sewing, needle poised, her gaze
focused across the room. She watched Broden as he stood alone now
by the front exit. Arms crossed over his chest, he looked imposing,

which was done on purpose. Hopefully, most would reconsider before they became disorderly and needed to be dragged from the room.

Not knowing that someone was watching, he reached up and combed his fingers through his unruly mop of hair. The action was quite sensual.

"He is so handsome," Flora said under her breath.

"Who?" both Ava and Lady Fraser asked. Then they followed Flora's line of vision.

Flora blushed. "I shouldn't have admitted that out loud."

"Oh, yes, he is," Lady Fraser replied with a knowing smile. "If I were single and ten years younger, I would comb his hair."

The women all giggled, making the laird and others in the room turn to them.

Lady Fraser held up both hands. "We shall be silent."

AS THE DAY progressed, Catriona couldn't stop thinking about Ewan's suggestion that she travel north to Clan Ross. It had been months since she'd seen Esme, and she did miss her terribly. At the same time, the thought of traveling so far and the risks involved scared her.

As much as she'd tried to convince herself that she was ready to live a normal life, a part of her was still held captive by fear and trepidation.

Some of the mundane tasks she'd set for herself kept her well away from the men who lived in the keep. She loved helping with the tasks of gardening and seeing to the care of the chickens but hadn't done it until recently. And even at that, it was seldom. Now as she made her way past the kitchen to the door that led to the garden, Catriona's steps faltered.

"The garden is surprisingly plentiful for so early in the spring," Eileen, the cook, said as she entered through the door. In her arms, she held a basket filled with vegetables.

Catriona inspected the items. "I was about to go see what needed to be done there."

True to her gruff form, Eileen nodded. "Well, ye know there is always plenty that can be done and never enough hands to do it. Off ye go." She toddled away.

"That certainly put me in my place," Catriona muttered under her breath. Her lips curved as she stepped outside. Just as the cook had warned, there were too many weeds sprouting around the plants. One corner was overgrown so much that the vines crept over the short wall.

Arms on her hips, Catriona frowned and looked around for the old man who'd been the gardener for years. He would certainly get a tongue lashing.

"Who are ye looking for?" A young kitchen lad hurried by with a pail of water in each hand.

"Vincent. Where is he?"

The lad shrugged. "He left several weeks back. He got sick and lives in the village now."

"And no one took his place?" Catriona asked, only to realize the boy had already gone inside.

She shook her head and opened the gate. Once inside the garden, she felt protected. Unless someone came to that particular entrance, no one could really see her in there when she was bent over working.

It was a long time later that Flora appeared and upon seeing Catriona, her eyebrows rose in surprise. "Ye really are out here. I didn't believe it, so had to come see for myself."

"No one has taken the time to weed," Catriona replied but grinned up at her friend. "Can ye believe it?"

"A new gardener should be hired. Vincent has only been gone for a short while and it is overgrown." Flora studied the area Catriona had been working on. "It looks good," she said, pointing to where Catriona stood. "Ye accomplished it all alone?"

"Yes." Catriona looked over her shoulder at the rest of the garden.

"I will speak to Lady Fraser. I will ensure the garden is properly restored. Once the task is done, she can hire someone to take over as gardener."

Flora studied her for a long moment. "Something is different about ye."

"I have decided to take steps to not be so fearful." Catriona looked to her dirty hands. "Like this."

"It makes me glad. Even if it means ye will no longer need me."

"Lady Fraser has grown fond of ye. She will keep ye here in some capacity," Catriona said and then dusted the dirt from her hands on an apron she'd tied around her waist. "I best get washed up. It will be last meal soon."

Flora continued to study her. "What brought about this change?"

"When I visited my family in the village, I realized how much I had missed. My sister gave birth to a bairn. I never saw her with child. Her other four young ones have grown up and look so different, I had a hard time putting names to faces."

"The wee ones change a great deal in the first years of life, and they grow so much," Flora said and took a long breath. She looked to the courtyard. "My son will not remember his father and no matter how much I wish he remain a babe, he is growing quickly."

Catriona sniffed. "I am so sorry, Flora. I forget sometimes that ye lost yer husband."

Once Catriona got water from a rain barrel and washed up, they went inside and walked down the corridor toward the great room. Flora went into the kitchen and Catriona kept walking.

The same maid who'd been offering herself to Ewan headed in the direction of his bedchamber. Catriona walked slowly and, upon passing by, noticed that his door was cracked open. The murmur of a conversation was too low for her to make out what was being said.

A part of her urged that she go see what was happening, while her more logical part insisted she not make a fool out of herself.

Catriona gritted her teeth and continued on to the great room.

The healer walked toward her, a young lad hurrying beside him with the heavy medical box. "Ah, Miss Catriona," the man said. "I may require yer assistance."

"What happened?" She turned toward Ewan's room.

"Come along." The healer continued walking in the direction she'd just come. However, he continued on past Ewan's room and into another chamber.

The door was open and, through it, the smell of blood spilled out along with moans. A warrior was on a table. Other than a cloth thrown over his midsection, the man was bereft of clothing.

Quickly, Catriona understood why. He had horrible wounds from his face down to his legs.

"What happened?" she asked the nearest man. "Who did this to him?"

The man's worried gaze moved from the injured man to her and then back to the table. "He was attacked by wild boars. We were on patrol, he dismounted and, just a moment later, the beasts came out from behind trees."

"He's been gored and bitten. He's lucky to not be dead. Boars are vengeful creatures," the healer said, motioning to Catriona. "See about the injuries to his legs. I will see what I can do about this big one here." The healer pointed to the man's right side.

As she began working, the smell of blood that permeated seemed to grow stronger. Catriona took one of the cloths and tied it around her nose and mouth. The injured man began to shake uncontrollably, and Catriona's heart went out to him.

Despite his injuries, he kept asking for his wife and was assured someone was going to fetch her.

He met Catriona's gaze. "D-do not allow h-her t-to see me like this." His eyes rolled back, and he lost consciousness.

The healer pinned her with a pointed look. "After ye wash his leg, bind it tightly."

For the next hour, several people worked on the man. He was riddled with bites and scratches, some deep, others not as bad. Although groggy from a tonic the healer had made him drink, he was sitting up in bed when a young woman barged into the room, tears streaming down her cheeks.

"Come with me," the healer said as everyone walked out the room. "Ye looked look like ye are about to pass out. Ye should get some rest."

Catriona shook her head. "I am fine." The last thing she wished to do was remain near the smell of blood, so she hurried away. Just as she passed Ewan's bedchamber, the maid once again walked toward it.

"Where are ye going?"

The maid turned, her eyes growing wide. "Eileen asked that I find out if Mr. Ross requires a meal brought to him."

"I have to see him, so I will ask."

The maid's gaze lowered to her dress and Catriona realized she had blood all over it.

"I will speak to Eileen in a moment." She effectively dismissed the maid and went to Ewan's bedchamber. She had no right to the feelings erupting, but Catriona couldn't pull back the annoyance. After rapping twice, Ewan opened the door.

He was dressed, and very pale.

"Ye dressed yerself and now are paying for it." Catriona walked in past him. "Perhaps ye have no wish to get better."

"I plan to attend last meal," he replied in a flat tone. "I cannot very well attend bereft of clothes."

Catriona turned to him. "Ye could have asked Ann, or whatever her name is to help ye."

"Who?" he asked, nearing.

"The maid who is constantly checking on ye." Catriona took a step back, suddenly aware of how much larger he was than her.

Ewan shrugged. "I do not know who ye speak of in particular. Oh, ye mean Annie."

Doing her best to give him a droll look, Catriona looked up to him. "She could have helped ye."

"I would prefer the only woman to see me without a tunic on be only ye."

Catriona's breath caught. "Do not toy with me."

"I would not tease ye in such a manner." Ewan reached up and tucked a stray hair behind her ear. The entire time, Catriona dared not move. Too afraid of her reaction to his touch, she held her breath.

It came out hard when she could no longer hold it. "Ye should not think about me in any other way than just a friend."

"Whose blood is that?"

"What? Oh," she said, realizing again how stained her dress was. "A man was attacked by boars. I assisted the healer. The man will recover. His wife is with him now."

"Ye should sit," she said, changing the subject. "Eileen wants to know if ye wish for yer meal to be brought to yer bedchamber. I will inform her that ye will be eating in the great room."

His gaze locked to hers. "Ye know what I wish for right now?"

Catriona shook her head. "No."

When he leaned forward, Catriona closed her eyes, but dread sent her senses reeling and she opened them just as his lips touched hers. It was a soft kiss, the kind of kiss a woman dreams of. Lingering and with just the right amount of pressure.

When he pulled back she stared up at him. "Ewan, I…"

He placed his hand on her shoulder and studied her with a strained expression. "I am sorry. I should never have done that. Are ye upset?"

It was as if warm heated water was poured over her and Catriona reached for Ewan. "Ye make me feel safe. When I am near ye, all my fears disappear. I feel relieved, actually."

"That is not exactly what I wish for a lass to say after I kiss her…"

Catriona lifted to her tiptoes and pressed a kiss to his mouth. "Thank ye."

The look of astonishment on his face made Catriona smile. "I best go and change before last meal. Do ye need help getting to the great room?"

Ewan shook his head. "I am allowed to go then?" His lips curved. "I will be fine."

Still not believing what she'd done, Catriona hurried out and through the great room to a corridor on the opposite side of the keep. Just then, a man walked out from behind the stairwell and they practically bumped. He held out his hands to steady her and Catriona jerked away.

Shaking from head to toe, she ran to her bedroom and slammed the door closed. The trembling became so hard, she could hear her teeth chattering.

It was no use. No matter how hard she tried to convince herself otherwise, any kind of normal relationship with Ewan was impossible.

There was a knock on the door. "Catriona," Flora called out. "It's me."

Flora walked in to find her sitting on a chair, arms around her waist and head bent.

"I'm fine, just startled," Catriona said before Flora could ask.

Knowing better than to touch her, Flora sat on the bed. "The man ye ran into is Laird Chisholm, here to see Laird Fraser."

"Oh, no! I hope I didn't offend him," Catriona exclaimed, but still refused to look at Flora. "I hate this."

"Ye did not. He asked that someone ensure ye were not hurt."

Catriona let out a breath and opened her eyes. "I will eat here. Would ye mind bringing my meal here whenever ye finish yer own meal?"

How she hated the pitying look on her friend's face. Catriona couldn't think of what to say at the moment. So, she stood and went to the window. The sun had disappeared behind the horizon, but rays of varying colors of amber, yellow and orange painted the sky. It was beautiful, and yet the only thing Catriona could think was that, at the moment, she was to be a spectator and not a participant when it came to life.

"I will fetch our meal and eat here with ye."

When Flora left, Catriona remained at the window determined to see every color until darkness fell.

CHAPTER FIVE

I T HAD BEEN two weeks since his attack and Ewan felt well enough to ride. Needing to test his endurance, he'd mounted and rode his steed short distances without much discomfort. Upon returning to the stables, his men had already gathered and waited for his instructions.

Until the threat from the Mackenzie was over, the Ross had agreed to keep fifty warriors at Fraser Keep to protect the keep in case of attack for the foreseeable future.

"I hope everyone is well rested," Ewan said, earning snickers as many of the men had stayed up late the night before drinking around a bonfire.

Ewan waited for the men to quiet. "In three days, I will return to Ross lands. The rest of ye have another sennight before yer time is up. There are some things to discuss…"

He stopped talking when he spotted Keithen walking toward them. "Perhaps he has something to say on this matter," Ewan finished.

Keithen Fraser walked to them, his gaze taking everyone in before settling on Ewan. "How many are leaving with ye?"

"We have not actually come to that question," Ewan replied. "Re-placements will have to be sent back."

Unsure what his cousin's reaction would be, Ewan considered that not too much time was left between the exchange of guardsmen. He turned to face the men. "Who wishes to return to Dun Airgid?" he asked, referring to Ross Keep. He continued, "Remember that once we arrive, others will be sent to replace ye."

Less than half the men lifted their hands. Many of the single men had already made it known that they planned to remain there for as long as needed. The warriors were settled in new and spacious rooms. The guards' quarters back at Dun Airgid paled in comparison.

"Very well," Keithen called out. "On behalf of Laird Fraser, we thank ye for yer assistance. Please come to the great hall for tonight's last meal."

The men dispersed and Keithen turned to Ewan. "When do ye leave?"

"In three days. Is there anything I should take to yer sister?"

The man shook his head. "No, but I do have something to tell ye."

Ewan frowned. Whatever it was, he hoped it wasn't going to annoy him.

"My mother is requesting to travel with ye. She wishes to visit with Esme and see her grandchildren."

The news was unexpected. Ewan wasn't prepared to escort the laird's wife. "I am traveling with fifteen men. Will ye send more?"

"Aye, an additional twenty-five Fraser men will go with ye. They will escort Mother back, when she returns."

Ewan nodded. "I am going to the village today. I need to gauge my ability to ride."

"I must tell ye something else," Keithen added, meeting his gaze. "Despite whatever reason ye had for killing Laird Mackenzie, we owe ye a great deal."

"I wish I could finish what I had planned," Ewan said.

Keithen's face hardened. "That one is mine. I am biding my time, but it will happen. Catriona's and my mother's capture will not go unpunished."

"I will leave it to ye then," Ewan told Keithen. It gave him peace to know that the marred man would hopefully meet his demise soon.

"I do have one question." Keithen met his gaze. "Is there any reason why ye would choose to remain here other than yer vendetta?"

Ewan wasn't sure what brought on the question. Keithen Fraser was a man of few words. The man often kept his thoughts shuttered. "No, in actuality, there is nothing that keeps me here. I have grown close to some of yer clanspeople, but it is time for me to go."

The man gave him a knowing look. "Ye should consider taking someone with ye to the village. Whoever is attacking may be lurking."

After speaking to Keithen, the fast-approaching time of his departure prompted Ewan to go in search of Catriona. In the mornings, she usually worked in the garden, so he headed in that direction.

As expected, she was kneeling, digging into the soft dirt. When he opened the gate, she looked up. Upon seeing him, her expression softened.

Ewan lowered to one knee next to her. "Have ye been avoiding me? We haven't spoken in several days."

Her shoulders lifted and lowered. "I thought it best to keep my distance. Ye are leaving and becoming close will make yer departure all the more upsetting."

"Why do ye not come with me?" Ewan pinned her with a questioning look. "I will keep ye protected. Nothing will happen. We will be traveling with forty guardsmen."

Catriona stood and he followed suit. "I wish I could, Ewan. I wish for so many things. Just the idea of getting to know ye better is almost enough to push me to do something like that."

"Ye can. Just take a single step and I will help ye the rest of the way."

A battle inside as to whether to push her to make a decision or not ensued. Ewan decided it was now or never. "I am leaving in three days. Can we discuss this more later? I am going to the village. Can I seek ye when I return?"

After a few beats, she nodded. "Very well."

He went back to the stables to find his steed, feeling somewhat better after Catriona agreed to speak to him later.

"He's saddled," one of the two Ross guards who were going with him to the village called out. Ewan went to Ban, his silver horse. Hoisting up to the saddle was uncomfortable and he had to blow out several breaths waiting for the tightness of his midsection to settle.

Another of the men studied him. "Are ye sure ye are able to ride for several days?"

"Aye, I'm well enough. Tis time to leave."

Riding hard, it was about a two-day trek to Ross lands. But now that they were escorting Lady Fraser and, hopefully, Catriona, the trip could probably take at least two nights and three days. Ewan hoped he wouldn't be feverish upon arriving at Dun Airgid if riding became too hard for him.

They rode to the village and he ensured to keep in tune with what his body did. Halfway there, he relaxed as the small amount of pain from mounting abated.

Upon arriving, all three dismounted at the village square. The men instantly went to find a woman who sold beautiful ribbons and other hair baubles. They purchased enough for their own wives and for a few other men that had asked they bring things back for theirs. Ewan studied the display, hands behind his back.

"This would be a beautiful gift for yer lady." A young lass who helped the lady held up a green ribbon to Ewan. "Ye can give her this to match," the lass prodded, lifting a pretty comb in a slightly lighter shade.

"I will take them." He gave the girl the coins necessary and then walked away before she talked him into more purchases.

"A wee sewing basket for notions?" An old woman held up an

intricately weaved creation. The basket was the size of the palm of his hand. Once again, he pulled out his coin pouch and purchased it.

The men came up to where he stood and upon seeing the small basket, also purchased some. "When our wives see that yer lady has that, they will be upset we didn't get one," one of the men complained.

"We should go," Ewan prodded, and they hurried past another two stalls holding out shawls and other creations. At seeing a beautiful green shawl, Ewan hesitated. It would match the ribbons he'd purchased for Catriona. He rushed over, grabbed the shawl, threw coins at the merchant and joined the other men who looked past him to the shawls.

"Are women always this costly?" he asked once they'd settled into chairs at the tavern.

Each man tried to figure out a way to keep the purchases on their laps. It was comical and Ewan was glad he'd only purchased for one woman.

"They are not costly," one of the men replied. "They do so much with little recompense. To me, bringing home a gift for my wife after she's been home alone with the bairns for months is very small compared to what I get in return."

The words warmed Ewan's heart. He'd never considered marriage, if he were to be honest with himself. Usually, the thought of settling with one woman made him shudder. Since meeting Catriona, he'd begun to feel differently.

Just holding the things that he knew would belong to her filled him with a sense of fulfillment that made little sense. The tavern owner's wife brought their meals and, taking pity on the other men, placed a basket on the floor between them. "Ye can put the things in there before ye get everything dirty."

The men thanked her and did as she told them to.

The meal was flavorful. It was nice to go away from the keep and spend time with other men who he'd worked with daily.

"How does yer side feel?" one of the men asked.

Ewan took inventory of his body and realized that although he was in pain, it wasn't bad enough to put off departure. "No pain," he lied. "We will depart as planned. Tis time."

⟫⟫✖⟪⟪

WHEN EWAN WALKED through the great room to where Catriona's bedchamber was, there were very few people milling about. Last meal had been eaten and the tables cleaned. A pair of lads swept up the room and two men he didn't recognize sat at a table talking.

No one paid him any heed when he walked past.

Upon approaching the door, he felt silly holding the shawl and other gifts. What if she resented him doing it? He planned to frame it as a farewell gift. If she decided not to travel to Ross lands, they'd never see each other again. There was no reason for him to ever return to Fraser lands. He doubted she would gain the fortitude to travel to where he would be.

He knocked softly and held his breath, unsure whether or not Catriona would open the door.

Finally, the door opened and she peered up at him. She blinked at recognizing him and pulled him into the room, leaving the door ajar.

"Ye should not be here. Did anyone see ye come?" She leaned to the side and looked around him to the door. "People will talk."

"Is there someone ye wish to hide me from?" he teased.

Catriona sniffed. "I do not wish for Lady Fraser to be cross with me for allowing ye such liberties." She lifted an eyebrow. "This is not funny. Why are ye smiling?"

"Because I am glad to see ye."

Her gaze moved to his hand. "Do ye need mending done before ye leave?"

The comment made it sound like she'd already decided not to go, and his heart sank. Ewan managed to keep a light expression. "No. I bought ye a little something from the village."

"What?" Her eyes rounded. "Ye bought me a gift?"

"Four gifts actually," Ewan said and quickly added. "Ye took care of me when I was injured. Ye ensured my tunics were mended and even made me additional ones. I owe ye a great deal." He held out the items.

Catriona looked like she was about to cry. "I only did what was right."

"No one else offered," Ewan stated. "Here take them."

She took the shawl first and held it up, her lips curving. "It's beautiful."

"I think the color will match yer eyes."

Next, she admired the ribbons and comb. "Thank ye. Everything is lovely, but ye did not have to do it. I did for ye what I felt was right." Her eyes lifted to his. They were shiny with unshed tears. "I wish I was stronger."

Ewan moved closer. "What would ye do if ye were stronger?"

Her head fell. "I would go with ye. I would try to…" She stopped midsentence. "It matters not."

"It does," Ewan said, lifting her face to him. "Catriona, come with me. But if ye do not, I will be waiting for ye. Ye will be ready one day. And when that day comes, send word and I will come for ye."

Her eyes rounded. "I could never ask that of ye. It may never come to be that things change."

"Ye have changed so much since I have been here."

It was true. When he'd arrived, she wouldn't leave her bedchamber. No one, including Keithen, was allowed inside. The only people who saw Catriona for many months were Lady Fraser, Flora and Esme.

"Ye left yer room, ye go outside, and ye even went to the village."

Ewan smiled down at her. "And ye kissed me."

A soft pink colored her cheeks and her lips twitched. "I did, didn't I?"

He took a leap of faith and pulled the beautiful woman against his chest. At first, she stiffened. But then she gradually relaxed and let out a long breath.

When her arms circled his waist, Ewan eyes burned. It was something he'd wished for. "Yer hug is a wonderful gift."

Catriona laid her head against his chest. "I wish I could give ye more."

"Come with me. I promise to keep ye protected. I swear on my life."

When she looked up at him, he smiled at her. Unable to keep from it, he lowered his mouth to hers. The kiss was tentative at first, lips against lips, barely touching. But upon her response, he deepened the kiss and then gently trailed his tongue against her mouth.

Catriona moaned and wrapped her arms around his neck, parting her lips to allow him access. For so long, he'd dreamed of having her against him, kissing her until they both lost the ability to breathe. The reality of it was so much better.

The softness of her curves molded perfectly against his harder body. She was slight, but strong. As much as he wanted to run his hands down her body and touch every inch, Ewan resisted. Instead, he kept his arms around her.

It was Catriona that broke the kiss and took a step back. Her chest lifting and lowering, lips swollen and face flushed, she met his gaze. "That was like nothing I'd ever experienced before. Ewan, ye are a good man. So good to me."

"Promise ye will think about what I ask." Ewan reluctantly turned to the doorway. "I will await yer response. I leave the morn of the third day."

When he turned to look at her, she smiled.

"I promise to think on it. Do not expect that I will be strong enough, however."

Despite the best kiss of his life, Ewan's feet felt heavy as he walked away to seek his bed.

CHAPTER SIX

T HE NEXT MORNING, Catriona hurried from her bedchamber to find Lady Fraser. If she were to go to Ross lands, she first had to discuss it with someone. At the moment, she didn't feel comfortable speaking to Ava, Keithen's wife, about it.

Although they got along at some level, her presence was a constant reminder of Clan Mackenzie. Although Ava had no fault in what had happened to Catriona, Ava's father had been the one to send her away to the dungeon.

Ava Fraser was a good wife to Keithen. They were in love, and he was happily married, which made her glad. At the same time, Catriona often wished he'd married someone else.

At the end of the corridor, Broden stood, his expression ominous. "I have been waiting to speak to ye," he said without preamble. "I heard Ewan Ross brought ye gifts from the village. What gives him a right to do that?"

"He is grateful that I nursed him back to health," Catriona responded while scanning the great room for Lady Fraser. She looked back up at him. "Why are ye so bothered by it?"

"When I return from Ross lands, I wish to court ye."

Noting the softening of his expression and what the words meant sinking in, Catriona took several steps backward. Her breathing hitched. "No. I cannot allow it."

"I am in need of a wife. Ye need protection…" Broden began.

"Ye should consider someone else. I am not the woman for ye." Catriona rounded him and hurried up the stairs to find Lady Fraser. That Broden was traveling to Ross lands complicated things a bit. Catriona almost chuckled at the thought that men found a reclusive woman who feared men worthy to court.

It was like Esme always said, men were strange creatures.

She couldn't wait to see her friend. The thought of spending hours discussing life made her decision to travel seem more possible. Of course, she would take whatever Lady Fraser said into advisement before making a final decision.

Lady Fraser was surprised when she opened the door to find Catriona standing in the doorway. "Come in. Is something wrong?" The woman moved back, pulling the door further open.

A maid was there combing the laird's wife's hair. The young woman smiled at Catriona, but remained silent.

"I wish to discuss something with ye before I make a decision," Catriona began. "It is somewhat personal." She looked to the maid.

Lady Fraser turned to the maid and took the brush from her hand. "Thank ye, Uma. Miss Catriona will assist me with my hair. Ye may go."

Catriona began to brush the woman's hair. "Would ye like a braid?"

"Oh, yes," Lady Fraser exclaimed. "Ye always make the most beautiful styles." She met Catriona's eyes in the looking glass. "What is going on?"

It was hard to come up with how to formulate the words, and Catriona stumbled. "I-I suppose I have concerns. Ye are about to leave…" She took a breath. "Ye're going to visit Esme. I wish I could go with ye…to see her. However, I am very afraid."

Lady Fraser turned to face her, the braid falling from Catriona's hands. "Esme would be so happy to see ye. How splendid if ye were to go there for a season, or even two."

"I am terrified," Catriona repeated. "If something happens halfway there, it could affect the rest of the trip." In her mind, she saw herself curled up in a ball on the floor of the carriage, refusing to leave for any reason. Lady Fraser would certainly have a horrible journey if she could not withstand the long trip.

"I understand," Lady Fraser replied and turned away to allow Catriona to continue. "As of right now, I am traveling with my companion, Gilda, and no one else. There is plenty of room for ye."

The woman didn't seem to take into consideration that, for over a year, Catriona's only travel had been to the village. And although the trip itself had not affected her horribly, it was but a day later that a visiting laird had sent her to spend days in her bedchamber.

"Do ye think I am prepared for it?" Catriona finally asked and held her breath.

The kind woman's eyes met hers. "It is your decision alone, sweet girl. I can tell ye that I've seen how much stronger ye have been as of late. Bits of yer personality have begun to shine through. Not to mention, every man we travel with is familiar to ye."

"I have not met many of the Ross men. They do not eat in the great room and are rarely about. I am not afraid of them. At least, I do not think I am."

Lady Fraser smiled when Catriona finished with the hairstyle, turning her heat side-to-side to inspect it. "What exactly are ye fearful of then?"

"What if we are approached by them? The Mackenzies? What if I manage to make the trip without incident and then finding myself in a strange place sends me to panic again?"

The room was silent as Lady Fraser stood and went to her balcony. Catriona followed her to look out over the courtyard, past the gates and toward the village.

"It is a huge world out there," Lady Fraser said in a low tone. "So much of which we will never see in our lifetime. I often wonder what is happening in this moment over there." Lady Fraser pointed into the distance. "Is someone hurt, someone grieving? Are people celebrating, making love or fighting? Are families forming and relationships beginning?"

Catriona looked from one side of the lands to the other, her gaze following paths toward the creek and to the forest. "It is a beautiful view from here."

"It is," Lady Fraser agreed. "Whatever ye decide, Catriona, I will support ye. However, will ye be angry with yerself if ye decide to remain here and allow yer fear to keep ye from seeing Esme?"

Catriona closed her eyes. "Fear grips so very hard. I want to push it away. I fight to do it every day. However, it never goes far."

"I do not think it is really all fear," Lady Fraser said and placed a hand over hers. "Partly yes, but the other portion is that ye are fretful over a certain man."

Despite the situation, Catriona chuckled. "Why would ye say that?"

"I have eyes," Lady Fraser replied. "One would have to be blind not to know that Ewan Ross is infatuated with ye. The man makes every excuse to see ye."

Before Catriona could reply, Lady Fraser continued. "And I do not think ye are indifferent to him. He is very handsome, indeed."

"Handsome or not, I do not believe any kind of relationship is possible for me."

"Now or ever?" Lady Fraser asked. "If yer heart is allowing the notion of caring for Ewan, then I believe ye will be ready to the possibilities soon."

"What of my parents? They would miss me. I have already neglected them for so long."

Lady Fraser weaved her arm through Catriona's and guided her to the door. "Let us seek to break our fast and then we must send a messenger to invite yer family to come for a visit. I am sure yer mother will be glad to hear ye plan to travel and spend time with Esme."

"I have not decided as yet." Catriona gave the woman a confounded look. "I must consider it more."

"Ye are going. No matter what excuses ye try to make, ye know it is true."

⋙⋘

CATRIONA LOOKED ON as Flora helped to pack her clothing. The woman, giddy with excitement, acted as if it were she that was about to go on the trip. "I have heard that Ross Keep is magnificent. Their courtyard is many times the size of ours and the house itself it said to be grand."

"I wish ye could come with me," Catriona told her, meaning it.

"I have the bairn and my mother to look after," Flora replied with a sigh. "If not, I would beg to come along."

The trunk was soon filled, and she looked around the room only to find that all her belongings had been packed. "I certainly do not own very much. Other than clothing, I have just a few items. I must have left most of my things at my parents' house."

"Yer mother brought a few things," Flora said. "It is true, ye do not have very much, which means ye will not feel out of place once settled at Ross Keep."

"It is called Dun Airgid, Silver Fortress," Catriona said. "It sounds like a fantasy, does it not?"

"It does," Flora replied breathlessly. "Ye must write me and describe every single detail."

Catriona smiled at her friend. "I will. What will ye be doing once I am gone?"

"Lady Ava has asked that I help with household management. With Lady Fraser gone, it will all fall into her hands," Flora replied with pride. "I am looking forward to it. My son and mother are coming to live here again."

"Thank ye for all ye have done for me. Without ye, I am not sure I would have survived this ordeal." Catriona sniffed and hugged Flora. "I can never thank ye enough."

Flora took a shaky breath. "I will miss ye."

"I hope to return in a season or two. Ye will be busy with yer new duties and barely miss me by then, I am sure."

Just then, a maid came to the doorway. "Miss Catriona, yer family is here."

>>>«<<

CATRIONA'S MOTHER STARED at her as if she'd grown a third eye in the center of her forehead. "Ye are traveling away from Fraser lands? No one in our family has ever left Fraser lands."

"That is not true," her father interjected. "I have. I went across the river once."

"To the other Fraser lands," her mother noted, to which her father frowned and sighed.

Her sister was too busy running after the older boys to pay much attention. Catriona smiled at noting the toddlers had attached themselves to Flora's skirts along with her own boy. When she moved, three little ones walked alongside her as she attempted to help her sister.

Just then, Ewan walked by. "Come," Ewan said as he motioned to the boys and they immediately stopped in their tracks to stare up at the large warrior, their mouths falling open. "I need help," Ewan told them. "If ye have time."

The boys nodded and ran to keep up with Ewan's long strides out the front door.

"Where do ye think he's taking them," Audra asked, not seeming at all worried.

Catriona looked to the doorway. "Probably to the stables."

"Good! They need to be put to work and tired out."

"We will stay the night," her mother announced, looking around the great room, no doubt to stake a place to sleep.

"Ye and father can sleep in my bedchamber. I will find Audra and the bairns a room and I will sleep in Lady Fraser's sitting room. There is plenty of room there."

Plans made, Catriona felt good and looked forward to a day with her mother and sister.

"Would ye like to see my gardening?" She stood.

"Let me fetch the wee ones," Audra said, but Flora waved her away.

"Go, they seem content with me."

Audra sighed with relief at only having to carry the sleeping youngest.

Then Flora motioned to a blanket by the hearth. "Put the wee one down. I will watch over the bairn."

The garden was flourishing. Plants of varying heights grew in neat rows and not a weed was in sight. Catriona beamed with pride when her mother stared at the large plot. "Ye did this yerself?"

"I did. Only a lad helps me every now and then."

"Are you sad to leave it?" Audra asked, reaching down to touch a flowering plant.

She'd not considered it, but already knew who would take it over. "I will, but hopefully, I can help Esme with one up there at Ross Keep."

In the distance, she noticed Ewan and her nephews standing around his huge steed. He'd given each boy a brush and they enthusiastically brushed the animal.

"I do not believe I've ever seen a man so handsome," Audra said, following her line of sight. "Who is he?"

"Ewan Ross. He is returning to Ross lands with the same party I am traveling with."

"Is he married?" her mother asked, staring at Ewan.

"Why do ye ask?" Catriona couldn't help but chuckle. "Ye are married."

Her mother laughed. "Just curious. He is very attractive. Large...muscular..."

"Mother!" both she and Audra exclaimed.

Ewan looked over at them and immediately they pretended not to notice, but Catriona was sure he knew they were speaking about him.

"My goodness," Audra said. "I envy my boys right now."

"Ye are married, too," Catriona scolded, but couldn't help stealing another glance toward Ewan.

She had to admit that he was certainly very handsome. His blond hair gleamed in the sun and his tunic fit him well, leaving little to the imagination of his muscular form. The breeches he wore molded perfectly to his well-formed legs. Catriona cleared her throat, forcing herself to look to the garden.

Her sister and mother walked through the garden admiring the different plants.

A few moments later, Flora walked out along with the toddlers. Claiming the children needed fresh air, Flora blew out a breath.

"The babe?" Audra asked, eyeing the toddlers who hurried into the garden and grabbing one as it toddled by. "Stay with me."

"Still asleep. A maid is looking over her."

"They are lovable," Catriona said. Then she asked Flora, "But perhaps three is a bit much?"

Flora laughed. "A bit, yes." Her gaze moved over to where Ewan stood with the older boys, who were now sitting on the corral looking at the horses. "Does he know ye have decided to go?"

"I am not required to inform him," Catriona replied. "A part of me is still unsure. I am petrified of something happening. I hate these feelings."

"Ye will be just fine. I assure it," Flora said with a firm nod. "And so it shall be."

Despite her trepidation, Catriona smiled. "I pray it is so."

Moments later, Ewan walked toward the house with the boys, who raced into the keep. Audra whirled around and dashed after them. Her mother and the toddlers remained inside the garden. They sat on a bench as she spoke to them in soft tones. The children were obviously becoming sleepy.

"I will see about preparing a chamber for them to sleep," Catriona told her mother who nodded. She looked to Ewan. "Any idea where I can find an empty bedchamber?"

"There's one in the same corridor as mine," he replied. "Come, I will show ye." They walked in together.

"The boys enjoyed spending time with ye." Catriona glanced up just as Broden headed toward them. Not paying him any mind, she continued speaking. "I wish Audra's husband would take more time with them. He does work long hours, so I understand…"

"Where are ye going?" Broden asked, interrupting. "I doubt Ross needs any more tending."

The last thing she wished for was any kind of scene with her parents visiting. "I am looking for an empty chamber for my sister and her bairns to sleep," Catriona said, making to keep an even tone.

"Is it necessary that he go with ye?"

Ewan looked from Broden to her and back. "If ye would prefer to find the chamber and help set it up, I am more than willing to return to packing."

He walked away and Catriona turned to Broden.

"Where is the empty bedchamber?"

"I do not know. I live at the guards' quarters."

Catriona glared up at him. "The bairns are falling asleep. They need a place to sleep."

"I didn't mean to…"

"There will never be anything between ye and me," Catriona hissed. "Nor between me and anyone else. Please leave me be." She hurried off, hoping to catch Ewan.

CHAPTER SEVEN

T HE ARROW HIT the target's center. Ewan let out a breath and released a second one. This one was not as accurate.

Despite his injury, returning to archery made him feel whole again. The tension, release of breath, and loosing an arrow was like an extension of himself. Ewan placed another arrow, went through the motions and upon releasing it, he caught sight of Ava Fraser.

The woman watched him from the side of the building. Her gaze moved from him to the target.

He'd leave the next day, so it was best to speak to her once and for all.

At Ewan approaching, she stood her ground. The woman was not easy to intimidate, he knew it first-hand. So many questions whirled in his mind. But the main question was one only Ava Fraser could answer.

"Do ye ever miss?" she asked in a flat tone. "Even with yer injury, yer accuracy is without compare."

"I have missed before, usually when I'm distracted." Ewan looked to the target. "As ye can see."

When she lifted her gaze to his again, he realized why Keithen did not stand a chance in not falling for the beauty. Her golden-brown eyes were slanted up at the outside corners, her lips were full and, although she rarely smiled, they turned up at the corners, just a bit.

"Why did ye come to me?" she asked, motioning to him. "Is there something ye wish to tell me?"

Obviously, she suspected it was he who'd killed her father. Ewan decided it was time to confirm it. "I shot yer father. I assume ye suspected."

"I did." She looked straight ahead. "He was cruel and never kind. However, he was my father and I felt his death."

"Will ye dress as the masked person again and try to kill me to avenge his death?"

She whirled to look at him with an expression of astonishment. "What do ye speak of?"

"The masked person who saved Keithen from attack in the forest. I think it is ye."

Ava blew out a breath and waved her hand dismissing his words. "Ye are wrong. Ye are leaving then?"

"I am."

"Good. I hold ye no ill will Ewan Ross. That said, I hope to never have to see ye again."

"There is still one person who deserves to die. And it is not me," Ewan told her.

She studied him for a long moment. "Who?"

"The guard with the red birthmark on his face. If ye are so bent on vengeance, then perhaps avenge what was done by yer clan to Catriona."

Her eyes narrowed. "I helped her. It was I who demanded she be released upon learning she'd been sent to the guards." Ava took a step closer to him. "Believe me when I say that they have been made to pay. Many died at the last attack by the Ross and Fraser Clans. Then the other attack by lesser clans finished off the rest of them. The current clan is no longer as powerful."

"And yet, they continue to cause trouble," Ewan replied with a sneer. "And he lives still."

"How do ye know this?"

Obviously Keithen had not informed her for whatever reason. He, on the other hand, had no reason to keep the information to himself. "He is the one who left me for dead."

Ava's eyes widened.

Ewan met her gaze. "Or perhaps, ye would rather thank him than kill him?"

When she remained silent, Ewan went back to the marker and pulled an arrow out of his quiver. Out of the corners of his eyes, he saw that Ava continued to stand in the same spot. She didn't watch him now but, instead, looked past the back wall of the compound towards Mackenzie lands.

⤜⤛⤛

DURING FIRST MEAL on the day of travel, Laird Fraser insisted the Ross guardsmen who were to depart eat in the great hall. Every table was filled as the Fraser guards who were to travel also ate inside.

With the great hall filled to capacity, Ewan imagined Catriona would not eat there. It would be too much for her. He kept an eye across the room to where her bedchamber was on the off chance she'd emerge. The table in the corner where the women sat was currently filled with guards.

"I wish to thank the men of Clan Ross for coming to our assistance," the laird exclaimed, holding up a tankard. "Ye have ensured that the people of Clan Fraser feel safe and, for that, I am forever indebted to Laird Ross."

The men banged their tankards on the table in reply, everyone looking around the room to each other.

"Ewan Ross," Laird Fraser called out his name and Ewan stood and walked to the front of the room.

The laird placed a hand on his shoulder. "I thank ye for commanding yer men and honoring yer laird." The man met his gaze directly. "Ye are a great leader and warrior who fights well, and we are grateful for yer being here."

It was the first time Ewan had ever felt so proud. He swallowed at the thick knot in his throat. "It was my honor to serve ye, Laird."

The laird motioned to a guard who brought a leather bundle. "This is for ye," Laird Fraser said, unwrapping the folds to divulge a beautiful broadsword. The handle was intricately etched with a vine and thistle. "Thank ye."

When Ewan reached for the gift, his hand shook just enough to be embarrassing. "I will carry it with pride," he replied. Then he spoke softer. "If ye ever need me, I will come to do whatever ye may require."

"I know ye will," Laird Fraser replied and patted his shoulder. "Godspeed. Take care of my wife and the lass, Catriona."

At the laird saying "Catriona", the room seemed to close in. Had he heard the man right? The laird motioned to the table where he'd been sitting.

"A special feast will be served for all," the laird announced and the people in attendance cheered.

Broden, who sat at the same table as him, stood up when Ewan lowered to his seat and went to another table. At the moment, he could care less. Catriona was traveling to Ross Keep and he decided it was because of him.

THE NEXT MORNING, there was a frenzy of activity after first meal. The laird's carriage was prepared along with a packed cart that would carry whatever Lady Ross needed for the trip. A wagon was already loaded with items needed for the two nights they'd be spending on the road, as well as foodstuffs for preparation.

Ewan maintained a distance as he had his own items to prepare. He now had more tunics and other things that he'd not had on his way there, which presented a problem. Already, the bags that he'd thrown over the horse were full.

After consideration, he yanked older tunics that he'd hoped to keep for sword practice out of the bags and replaced them with neatly rolled newer ones.

He went to another guard who seemed to be finished packing. "Do ye have room for these?"

The guard shook his head. "No, I had to leave items behind."

Just then, he noticed Catriona standing by the wagon where items were still being loaded. He went to her, feeling silly with his old tunics.

"Do ye have room anywhere for these?" He looked into her wide eyes. Clearly, she was nervous but doing her best to stay busy.

"Put those there," she told a lad who emerged from the kitchen with a basket filled with flat bread covered in a white cloth. "In the corner."

She then grabbed the tunics from Ewan, not looking at him. "If there is anything else ye need a place for, I may have a bit of room under the bench in carriage." She hurried to the door of the carriage and set his tunics on the bench. She wrapped them with a shawl and then smiled at him. "A pillow for my head."

Ewan wished he'd brought the newer tunics. "I do not have anything else. Thank ye."

This time, she lifted her gaze to him. "Of course, I wouldn't wish ye to leave anything behind that matters to ye."

Searching her face, he was glad that some of the nervousness seemed to dissipate.

"Miss Catriona," someone called from the wagon and she hurried away.

He helped carry a few more things from the kitchen and soon it was time for the party to begin the trek to Ross lands.

Ewan mounted and called for his men to line up outside the gates. In lines of ten men each, he gave instructions for how they'd move forward.

Ten Frasers and ten Ross warriors would ride in front of the party. A group of six, including Ewan, would flank the carriage. Broden and a mixed team of warriors and archers would bring up the rear.

Once positions were assigned, everyone realigned, and they were ready.

Ewan rode back into the courtyard to see Lady Fraser and the laird bidding their farewells.

The couple hugged openly, followed by Ava and Keithen who bid both Lady Fraser and Catriona their farewells.

The women were then assisted into the carriage by the coachman's assistant, who would ride on the back of the wagon.

Finally, after the lead guards called out, the coachman urged the horses forward, and the carriage went through the gates.

Ewan wasn't sure why, but he turned back to the entrance. Standing in the doorway, next to Keithen, Ava watched him intently.

There was much that had been left unsaid between them. He wondered if she learned the reason behind his actions, would she understand. Probably not. It was her father, after all, that he'd killed.

Whether the man was evil or not, he represented a place in her heart. Ewan lifted an arm in farewell. Laird Fraser, Keithen and Flora, who wiped at her eyes, all returned the gesture.

Ava did not.

CATRIONA SAT BACK in the carriage. As nervous as she'd been when packing and getting everything settled, now that they were moving, calmness overtook her.

"I do detest the traveling portion of travel," Lady Fraser said, peering out to the passing landscape. "We can barely see anything with the horses in the way."

Following the woman's line of vision, Catriona had to agree. To her right was a black horse, to the left, Ewan's silver stallion. "They could move a bit forward and allow us to see better."

Lady Fraser chuckled. "True." She then settled back and closed her eyes. "I will sleep for a bit and then work on the embroidery I brought with me."

For a long while, Catriona kept watch. Although she was sure the men who escorted them had a better vantage point, she still wanted to ensure to catch sight of some kind of threat.

Ewan leaned down and caught her looking. He motioned for her to sleep by putting both hands to the side of his head and leaning to the right.

A quirk to her lips, she rolled her eyes and he smiled. A warmth seeped through her and she was sure her cheeks had turned bright pink. Catriona looked away and pulled the curtains closed so she and Lady Fraser could rest.

When they came to a stop, Catriona was grateful. She and Lady Fraser, escorted by two Fraser guards, went away from the others to relieve themselves. It was a bit uncomfortable to do so with the guards so close, but Catriona understood the need to keep the laird's wife safe.

Upon returning to the carriage, many of the men were walking about, stretching their backs and legs. Ewan remained astride his horse. He and a group of men, including Broden, were grouped and talking.

When she and Lady Fraser returned to the carriage, Broden and another man came to them.

It was Broden who spoke. "Lady Fraser, we will ride until sunset to ensure we are away from Mackenzie lands before setting up camp."

At the mention of being on Mackenzie lands, a tremble traveled up

Catriona's spine. Immediately, she was on high alert, searching the area for any movement or sound.

Broden must have realized his mistake because he moved closer to her. "We are not on their lands..."

"We should go," Catriona managed to say past the chattering of her teeth. She stumbled sideways and Broden reached for her. Immediately, she slapped his hands away and began walking backward.

"Catriona." Ewan's voice sounded behind her. "Was yer pillow comfortable?"

She turned to look at him, sure that her eyes were wide. "What?" The tunics, of course. She'd enjoyed using them. The thought that they belonged to him seemed to help her nerves.

"Oh...yes. It was." Studying him, she recalled it was his first time riding for so long since the injury. "How do ye feel?"

His wide shoulders lifted and lowered. "A bit sore," he answered, walking her to the carriage door. "I will be ready to rest when we reach the place we will camp." His gaze met hers. "Mayhap ye can join me in walking about then. I will need to stretch out my back and legs."

The woods that surrounded them seemed to close in. She looked to Ewan, meeting his gaze, and everything settled within her. "Very well. I may need it myself."

He opened the door to the carriage, and she turned to Broden who watched them.

Broden took a careful step toward her. "I apologize for not thinking before speaking."

"It is not yer fault," Catriona said. "Thank ye."

She waited for Lady Fraser to be assisted in and then allowed Ewan to take her elbow and assist her to do the same.

Once settled on the bench, she let out a long sigh. "It was not as bad as it could have been."

Lady Fraser nodded. "It is fortunate that Ewan is here. He seems to know exactly what to do or say to ye."

Catriona considered what Lady Fraser was saying. "I suppose ye are correct. He does have a way of calming me."

"Can I guess it is because ye have feelings for him?"

It was useless to deny it to herself or anyone. "I do care for him. It is not fair."

"What do ye mean?"

"To him or to me," Catriona said, her breath catching. "It is doubtful that I could ever allow a man to touch me in an intimate manner."

"Bah!" Lady Fraser exclaimed. "I will venture to guess that ye have kissed him. Am I wrong in that ye have been held by him?"

At once, her face became so heated that she covered her cheeks with both hands.

"I am right!" Lady Fraser shouted. "I knew it."

"Ye should lower yer voice," Catriona said at noting men on both sides of the carriage were leaning down to peer at them.

Lady Fraser waved them away with a wide grin. "If ye have already allowed the handsome man those liberties, it will not be hard to let yerself go. Live, sweet girl. The years fly by and before ye know it, ye will be old and crying for the wonderful things ye allowed to pass by."

Considering the woman's words, Catriona sat back and closed her eyes. With her right hand, she reached for the bundle of tunics and pulled them against her leg. She did care for Ewan a great deal and wished for nothing more than to be in his presence constantly. The reason she was traveling, despite her horrible fear, was him.

When she opened her eyes, the sun was setting. As darkness fell, dread rose. All her self-talk about not being afraid left to be replaced with doubts and a terrifying foreboding. What had she done?

Too soon, they came to a second stop. Broden came to the door and instructed them to remain in the carriage until everything was set up for them.

Lady Fraser sighed. "It is much too dark to see what I'm doing," she complained. "Where did I put...?"

Moments later, the interior of the carriage was lighted by a candlestick Lady Fraser held. "There, that's better. Now, we will only need something to sleep on. Once the tent is set, we can undress and get our travel dresses aired out."

Lady Fraser's companion, an older woman named Gilda, had opted to ride with her husband, who drove the wagon with the foodstuffs. Now she neared and grinned at them. "I am sure ye are ready to walk about and then sleep."

Catriona looked out into the dark forest. "I am not sure I can sleep out there. I should probably stay in the carriage." The lower the sun fell, the darker the forest became.

"Nonsense," Lady Fraser said. "No one will be here with the carriage. The horses will be unhitched and given a place to rest. We will be a few yards away."

Outside, a tent had been erected, a fire started, and people milled about. Not too much later, a second bonfire came to life, illuminating the area so that it was easy to see.

"I suppose it does look safe enough," Catriona said, not moving.

Lady Fraser rapped on the door to tell whoever was outside she wished to go out. "Our tent is in the center. We will be thoroughly protected."

Catriona was pleasantly surprised that upon exiting the carriage, the surroundings did not intimidate her. Instead, it was as Lady Fraser said. It felt safe.

CHAPTER EIGHT

"How do ye feel?" Ewan had come to fetch her, asking if she'd like to walk a bit. He'd invited both her and Lady Fraser, but the older woman refused saying she'd rather remain in the tent and walk in it.

"The tent is much too small for her to get any proper walking done," Catriona said as they walked a short distance to a nearby creek.

"I do not believe she plans to walk in there," Ewan replied. "Lady Fraser will probably go see about her companion and oversee preparations for the meal."

Catriona stopped and turned to Ewan. "I should go help her."

"Ye can, after we walk a bit," Ewan prompted. He gave her a sad look and she finally relented.

"Very well, but only for a bit." The shadows grew larger and she shivered. "I could never travel alone. It is so dark out here."

"Not so much when the moon is full," Ewan said, pointing up at the half-moon. "Even now, there is enough light to see." He guided her in a circle around the camp, ensuring they remained close enough that Catriona could see the fires.

She had so many questions and yet, in his presence, her thoughts evaded. All she could think about was what Lady Fraser had stated.

That it was possible she'd allow herself to love and be loved by Ewan.

"Ye're quiet this night," Ewan said. "How was the first day of travel?"

"Better than I expected. I have never traveled so far. I cannot believe it. To be so far from home."

Ewan bent and picked up a small stick and threw it. "I suppose it can feel strange. From my home on the Isle of Uist to Ross lands, it took me ten days." He picked up a second stick and threw it. "I was taking my time, not sure of what my reception would be."

"Why did ye leave Uist?"

His face hardened for a moment, but then he relaxed. "I am fourth-born son. A future of farming or guarding my father's keep was all that I could hope for."

"So ye left hoping for more?" Catriona sensed there was more to the story. "Is that not what ye do now? Guard?"

"Aye, a bit, on a much larger scale. I have a group of men under my command. I have the power to make decisions that impact important things. Not just what pig to slaughter for the next meal."

Catriona remained silent for a moment, not sure whether to ask another question about his decision. She looked up at him. "One day, perhaps ye will tell me why ye took it upon yerself to carry out revenge against the men who attacked me. I hope that ye explain it to me, because I do not understand."

"I have told ye. Because it had to be done. For too long and too often, men have mistreated women. There is no reason for it to happen. I do not stand for it."

Catriona was shocked at his anger. "It is true. I know others who've been mistreated, beaten and taken by force. I doubt it will ever change."

"It should not be allowed."

When she placed her hand on his arm, Ewan stopped walking and turned to her, questions in his gaze.

"I often wonder if yer vengeance has anything to do with me." Catriona kept her voice calm. "It worries me that ye could have died because of it."

His lips curved, the smile unconvincing. "Ye should not worry so much. My reasons are nothing that ye should concern yerself with. All is fine. We should go and see about the meal."

Despite wanting to continue talking, Catriona was very hungry. She allowed him to guide her to sit with Lady Fraser. They'd brought several stools for them to sit to eat. The food was flavorful and throughout the meal, Lady Fraser kept those that sat nearby entertained with a story of her uncle's travels across the sea to a wild isle.

Every so often, Catriona would look to where Ewan sat eating with several of the Ross guardsmen.

He seemed at ease with the men. He listened to whatever the other men said, his head falling back with laughter. Whatever had caused him to leave Uist and not wish to return had to have been something horrible. Perhaps it was the same reason he'd killed the men who'd held her prisoner. Or perhaps, she was overthinking the entire situation.

By the time they went into the tent and removed their dresses, both she and Lady Fraser could barely keep their eyes open.

Catriona lowered to her cot and unbraided her hair. Using the comb Ewan had given her, she pulled it through her stands and then once again braided the long strands. With care, she placed the comb into her satchel and lay back onto the cot.

Lady Fraser looked over to Catriona. "I am so proud of ye. Ye did well." The woman blew out the candle in the lantern and the interior went dark.

The bonfire outside gave sufficient light that she could see just enough. "Thank ye for allowing me to travel with ye," Catriona replied.

Someone outside called to another and Catriona started. The men seemed to have a problem keeping quiet.

"They speak loudly to keep beasts and the like away," Lady Fraser said. "When they are walking, they will throw rocks or sticks for the same reason."

Catriona recalled what Ewan had done during their walk. "Men can be quite smart."

"Some of them, yes."

Catriona giggled.

THE NEXT DAY was a repeat of the first, except somewhat more tiring. Catriona shifted in her seat, wishing for the next stop to happen so she could stand upright.

"It seems we should be stopping soon," she complained, peering out the window.

"Ye can ask Ewan or Broden. They will stop for ye," Lady Fraser said, looking up from her embroidery. "What has ye so restless?"

Catriona didn't want to admit that the foreboding sense from the day before was growing stronger. She bit her bottom lip and shook her head. "Nothing. I am just very nervous. It is almost as if I sense danger."

"Stop!" Lady Fraser called out and, moments later, the entire party came to a full stop.

"What is it?" It was Broden who came to the door.

Lady Fraser motioned him closer. "Please ask Gilda to come at once."

The woman came to the door and glanced first at Lady Fraser and then to Catriona. Lady Fraser motioned for Broden to help her inside.

"What is wrong?" Gilda climbed in and then cupped Lady Fraser's face in her palms. "Do ye feel unwell, Lady Fraser?"

"No." Lady Fraser pushed the woman's hands away. "Miss Catriona has a sense of foreboding. Since ye know more about this sort of thing, I thought to ask ye. Do ye feel the same?"

"I am not a seer," Lady Fraser. "What I tell ye is what I feel."

When Lady Fraser didn't reply, the woman looked to Catriona and held out a hand. When Catriona took it, Gilda let out a long sigh.

"I think what ye fear is not out there." She motioned to the carriage door with her head. "Ye hold it inside and it is not good. There is nothing to fear on this trip. All will be well."

For some unexplainable reason, Catriona's mind settled at the woman's words.

They left the carriage, taking advantage of the unplanned stop to walk about. After relieving themselves, Catriona and Lady Fraser returned to the carriage.

Ewan walked up to them. "Is all well?"

Turning to Catriona, Lady Fraser replied, "Catriona is a bit nervous. I thought it best that she get some fresh air."

Holding out his arm, Ewan looked to her. "Care to walk about a bit?"

It felt odd to slip her hand into the crook of his arm. They walked slowly and she had to admit that stretching her legs and taking in the fresh air helped as much as Gilda's words.

Swaying slightly side to side, Ewan's steps were not as steady as the day before.

"Are ye feeling unwell?" she asked. "Ye should be resting and not walking about with me. I will be fine. Just all of this, knowing how close we are to the Mackenzie lands...it is unsettling."

"I can imagine," Ewan replied. "Ye are protected. Nothing will happen. The Mackenzies are busy with other matters. They've made many enemies and their latest tactics to turn smaller clans against one another failed."

Catriona consider it. "I do not understand the need of some for so much power. Yes, they should control their land and should protect it, but why kill and cause harm to so many to gain more?"

"I suppose it is the nature of some," Ewan replied and slowed.

Pride was something men held dear. It was obvious that Ewan did not feel well and, yet, he did his best to hide it. "I think ye are in pain," Catriona told him.

"A bit sore, but nothing unbearable. A night's rest will help," Ewan told her, his gaze colliding with hers. "This slow walk is actually helping."

A short while later, Ewan covered her hand. "Ye were very unsettled earlier. Did something happen?"

"The mention of Mackenzie lands as well as nerves, feelings of foreboding." She looked to the side where men were mounting again. "I thought I saw some new faces."

"I should have informed ye and Lady Ross that a small party of guards heading to Ross Keep have joined us. Forgive me."

"It is not yer fault that I am easily affected."

He shook his head. "I promised to keep ye safe."

"And ye are," Catriona insisted. A part of her was still in disbelief that she'd allowed herself to be taken away from all she knew and everything familiar. Now, so far from her village and home, it was surreal. As if adrift in a large body of water, unable to see the shoreline, she fought for a foothold. When Ewan pulled her against him, every feeling of disorientation evaporated.

"How do ye do that?" she asked, pulling away, afraid they'd be seen. "Why does yer touch settle me so? I do not understand."

"Come." He took her elbow and guided her to sit on a fallen tree. "There is something I must tell ye."

Her heart began to beat faster. Was he about to declare his love? If so, would she be able to let him go?

"Ye have asked me a question several times and I have not responded. It is time ye know the reason why I left Uist."

CHAPTER NINE

T HE EXPECTANT LOOK in Catriona's eyes made Ewan reconsider what he was about to tell her. Was it a good time? No, he'd not been thinking. It was stupid to do it while out on the road.

"I'm sorry," he began. "I do not think I can speak of it right now. I thought I could." He blew out a long breath. "I will tell ye, just not now."

When he lowered to sit next to her, she laid her head on his shoulder. "Did ye have a love in Uist?"

The unexpected question caught him off guard but, at the same time, he was grateful that Catriona had not insisted he divulge his secret. "I did at one time."

"Why did ye not stay and marry her?"

The memory of what happened remained vivid. "There were circumstances," he replied cryptically.

Catriona looked up at him, and he kissed the tip of her nose.

"So ye were heartbroken then?"

"Aye, I was."

He then gave her a quizzical look. "What about ye? Ye are a young beautiful lass. I bet ye turned down many who attempted to court ye, because ye found them lacking."

"Oh, no," Catriona exclaimed. "I was so busy thinking that I was in love with Keithen that I barely gave notice to anyone else. I am glad for him and Ava, and now for the realization it was merely an infatuation of youth."

Catriona studied him. "Do ye think ye will ever return to Uist?"

As calming as it was to be away from Uist, he did miss his home at times. "I do miss my mother and my siblings. We are very close."

"Am I to assume then that they had nothing to do with ye leaving?"

His lips curved at her attempts to find out the truth. Ewan shook his head. "I left because I needed to. I wish for more than fishing and the simple life on Uist."

They were quiet for a long while. Ewan fought the urge to kiss her, to hold her close and demand she stay with him that night. However, it was impossible and once they arrived at Ross Keep, time alone with her would be hard to come by.

"Catriona. Can I court ye for marriage?"

As he expected, she straightened with an expression of dismay. "I-I..."

"Do not answer me right now. Consider it. I know ye will require time and I will be patient. I have come to care for ye a great deal."

"Ye deserve someone who will be a good wife to ye..."

"And ye plan to be a bad wife to someone?" Ewan jested.

She didn't smile. "I am not sure what to say."

"Ye have said yerself that I ease yer fears. When we kiss, ye do not pull away." He took her hand and lifted it to his lips. "I want to be yer husband, Catriona."

When she turned away, Ewan wondered if he'd made a mistake. Time was not on his side. He had to take every opportunity that he could alone with her before arriving at Ross Keep. If he didn't tell her how he felt, then he'd forever wonder. It was best she turn his offer down and tell him that to be together was impossible then to never truly know.

Tears began to fall, sliding down her pretty face as she met his gaze. Ewan reached for her, but she put her hands up, effectively stopping him. Pain radiated from her and his heart sank. Catriona would not even consider anything between them.

She let out a shaky sigh. "I care for ye, Ewan, I truly do. A part of me wishes to accept immediately. Inside, I am not sure that I would ever be truly a good and proper wife to ye. There is so much to consider."

Watching her walk away without stopping her was one of the hardest things he'd ever done.

"We will camp here," a guard announced when Ewan walked back.

A campfire was started and, soon enough, warmth emanated to keep everyone comfortable.

Catriona joined Lady Fraser, their heads together as they talked. He wondered if the woman was on his side and would help his cause. Or perhaps Lady Fraser agreed with Catriona. She would never marry anyone.

"Ye do not heed my warning to stay away from Catriona. Instead of helping her heal, what ye are doing is making things worse." Broden's words contained barely concealed fury. "Return to yer people and leave mine alone."

Ewan swung to face the man. "So ye can go after her? Do not try to hide behind a façade of nobility. What ye wish is for me to be out of the way. Leave a clear path for ye."

"And if I did," Broden said slowly. "I have time to wait for her to be ready. We have known each other since we were young. There is trust between us."

It was no use to speak to the man. They both wanted the same thing. As far as Ewan knew, he and Catriona had deeper feelings than she had with Broden. Admittedly, she did seem comfortable when around the warrior, but he'd not seen any kind of emotional response from her.

"I will continue my quest and ask Catriona to be my wife. There is nothing ye or anyone can do to stop me." Ewan walked away. His words stronger than what he actually felt in that moment.

⇒⇒⇒≪≪≪

THE NEXT MORNING, they continued toward Ross Keep. Thankfully, they would be arriving before sundown.

Ewan rode on one side of the carriage and Broden traded with someone else to ride on the other side. They ignored each other for most of the day, which suited Ewan just fine.

When Lady Fraser asked them to stop, the party did so that the women could refresh and stretch. They walked together to a trickle of a creek and washed their faces and arms. It was obvious an attempt to look presentable for their arrival at Ross Keep.

While that was happening, Lady Fraser's companion cleaned out the carriage, sweeping the floor and fluffing the pillows.

Watching the woman made Ewan consider that although she was a village girl, Catriona was treated like part of the laird's family. She was accustomed to a much better life than he, or Broden for that matter, could provide for her.

His life at Ross Keep was as part of the archer ranks. He would live at the guards' house with very little privacy. The married men who worked for the laird often had houses in the village for their families, who they visited several times a week. For the most part, the wives had to deal with everyday life on their own. Cooking, cleaning and caring for any bairns.

When Catriona walked back toward the carriage, she looked to be in good spirits. She actually looked up to him and smiled. His chest expanded when he met her gaze and her cheeks turned pink. There was definitely something between them and he would do everything in his power to ensure she would come to understand how much he cared about her.

Since they were to board on Broden's side, the warrior assisted the women back into the carriage. He leaned to Catriona's ear and whispered something that made her giggle. Ewan narrowed his eyes at Broden, but the warrior ignored him, taking longer than necessary to help Catriona up.

Finally, they moved forward to the final leg of the trip. The closer they got to Ross Keep, the more Ewan considered what his next step would have to be.

There was always the possibility of returning to Uist. There, Catriona would live in his family's large keep. They had a full staff that waited on the family. The thought of returning to his father's realm didn't sit well with him.

Although not as grand as Malcolm's home, his family's keep was impressive and large enough for them to live there comfortably.

"There it is, Dun Airgid," someone said, pointing to the huge keep on a hillside. *Silver Fortress*. The name suited it perfectly.

Obviously, the scouts had announced their imminent arrival because the gates were open, and several family members stood at the home's entrance to welcome them.

Lady Fraser was who the honors were for, but it was nice when his cousins waved at him in greeting.

After entering the courtyard, Ewan guided the carriage driver to the center so that they could allow for the rest of the escort to flank in. The guards waited on horseback until someone assisted the women out of the carriage.

As per tradition, Ewan hurried to the door and opened it. He peered into a wide-eyed Catriona and a smiling Lady Fraser.

"It is best that ye assist Catriona. Take her quickly inside to a small space," Lady Fraser instructed.

Once Ewan assisted Lady Fraser down, the woman waved him away. Just then, Broden approached. "I will see that Catriona goes inside…"

"See about assisting me," Lady Fraser interrupted. "Ye are my head guard and will act as my escort."

A subdued Broden nodded. "Yes, of course. I apologize Lady Fraser." He took Lady Fraser's arm and, together, they walked to where Malcolm, Tristan and Esme Ross waited.

Ruari Ross, his cousin, came over and greeted him. Ruari then began to instruct the guards as to where to take the horses and such.

Catriona sat in the carriage not moving. Her wide eyes were looking from one side of the carriage to the other.

"Come, I will ensure ye are safe," Ewan said and held out his hand. "Take my hand."

After a moment, she reached out and he pulled her gently forward. Once she descended the stairs, although obviously nervous, she was curious enough to look about.

"It is huge," she whispered.

"Indeed, it is."

"Oh, my, what a happy surprise," Esme Ross said, while hugging her mother and looking to Catriona.

She released her mother and rushed to Catriona and the women hugged tightly. Catriona's bright eyes met his and she mouthed "thank you".

Lady Fraser and Esme flanked Catriona's sides and, together, they walked into the keep. Lady Fraser motioned for Ewan to follow close by. Although he was glad to remain nearby, he hoped Catriona would not need to be calmed.

Once inside, Esme motioned to a corridor. "Ye will be staying at my and Ruari's home. But for the next couple of days, we will be here."

As they walked past a doorway, Esme motioned to it. "That is where Ruari and I sleep." They stopped and went into a room right next to it. "And ye will stay here."

"Oh, look at the view." Catriona hurried to the window that overlooked the side of a steep mountain.

Esme turned to Ewan. "Thank ye so much for convincing her to come. I am beyond grateful." The woman threw herself against Ewan, hugging him tightly. "Ye have no idea how happy I am at this moment."

He nodded and looked to Catriona who watched them with an unreadable expression. Upon their gazes meeting, she attempted at a smile, her lips barely inching up.

"Yes, thank ye, Ewan. I am glad to be here."

"Of course." He left the room feeling there was so much left unsaid. And yet, there was no reason for him to remain inside.

"Ewan." Esme followed him out. "I wish to speak to ye later." After the cryptic statement, Esme rushed back to the room where he guessed the women would spend hours talking and catching up.

"WELCOME HOME," TRISTAN Ross said when Ewan entered the great room. His huge cousin gave him a curious look. "What did ye do?"

Ewan shrugged. "Do ye want a list?"

"Malcolm will need to know if there are repairs to be made to Laird Fraser."

"We can speak later. But I am confident that, instead, they owe me gratitude," Ewan replied.

In the great room, the men who'd traveled were already being fed and would soon learn which duties they were to take over.

Lady Fraser was already seated and chatted animatedly with the Ross wives, seeming to enjoy being the center of attention.

Feeling a bit out of sorts, Ewan followed Tristan to the head table and greeted Malcolm. His cousin motioned for him to sit at the high board. "Is there anything we need to discuss immediately?"

The table was far enough away from the others that their conversation could not be overheard. Given the many discussions at the moment, they could speak in normal tones without worry.

"So ye have been told I was asked to leave then?" Ewan said.

"Aye, the warrior, Broden McRainy, was told by Laird Fraser to inform me."

Ewan looked to where Broden sat with other Fraser guards. "And he did not give ye a list of my offenses?"

"He started to, but I told him ye would tell me."

Letting out a breath, he looked to his right and left. Flanked by his cousins, each one of them a strong warrior, Ewan felt his family's support. And yet, he wasn't sure how Malcolm would react to what he did.

"I killed the older Laird Mackenzie. I killed three Mackenzie guards and I was caught on Mackenzie lands when trying to hunt down another."

His eyebrows high, Tristan looked at him. "Anything else?"

The youngest Ross brother, Kieran, met his gaze. "And I considered ye to be the least frightening of us."

Malcolm blew out a breath. "So, it was ye that started the battle between the Frasers and the Mackenzies?"

"No," Ewan replied. "That had started before I arrived."

Malcolm gave him a flat look. "The second battle."

Ruari chuckled. "He started a clan war."

"Aye, I killed the first Mackenzie. I believe yer wife killed the son," Ewan replied in an equally flat voice.

Everyone went silent for a long moment. Ruari shrugged. "Esme was saving her brother." In truth, she'd saved Keithen Fraser when he was hung by the Mackenzie. Her precise arrow had saved him from imminent death.

"Why did ye kill the guards?" Malcolm asked in a low voice.

At this question, Ewan hesitated. Why had he? Was it truly over a woman he'd barely known at the time?

"They deserved it. They kidnapped and attacked Lady Fraser and Catriona…"

"That has nothing to do with ye or our clan," Malcolm interrupted. "If anything, it would fall on a Fraser to take such action. Avenge what happened."

"Keithen Fraser did," Ruari commented. "I believe during one of those ventures is when he was captured."

Laird Malcolm Ross was intimidating and stern, however, he was a fair leader who put his people first before anything. In that moment, Ewan wasn't sure how to reply in a way that would be understandable.

"I have my reasons," he said, knowing it was a weak excuse.

"The woman? Catriona?" Kieran asked in a flat tone. "That is a stupid reason."

"Says the married man," Ewan retorted. "Do not judge me without knowing my motives."

A guard approached. "Laird, did ye wish to speak to the room?"

"Yes," Malcolm replied and stood. Immediately, the room went silent.

His cousin addressed the room, welcoming Lady Fraser and her guards. He informed them there would be much to do in the next day as a large contingent of warriors departed in response to a threat.

The Fraser guards were asked to remain at the keep until Lady Fraser decided to leave. They could assist with guard duties.

It was not much longer before everyone sought their beds and Ewan wandered to his old room. Thankfully, it remained unused. So he carried his bags in and set them on the floor.

Someone had freshened the linens and aired it out, for which he was thankful.

After washing up with water from a basin, he pulled a clean tunic over his head and went to the narrow bed.

He wondered what Catriona was doing at the moment. Was she having a restless night being in a new, unfamiliar place?

After tossing one way and then the other, he got up and yanked on breeches and walked out barefoot.

In the great room, there were only a few people sleeping on the floor in front of the fireplace. He guessed it was guards who'd come from the village and would be leaving the next day.

He'd have to ask Malcolm about it. If his services were required, he would not hesitate to go.

Upon reaching Catriona's room, he knocked softly and whispered. "Catriona, it is me, Ewan."

The door opened immediately, and she collapsed against him. "Thank ye for coming."

CHAPTER TEN

C ATRIONA HAD BEEN praying fervently that Ewan would come to her. Despite spending time with Esme and sharing last meal with her friend, upon Esme leaving, she became frantic.

It wasn't so much being nervous or scared. Quite the opposite, she wanted company, needed someone familiar to be with.

"I know it is too much to ask, but will ye stay here with me tonight?" she asked Ewan. "I am in need of company."

The request was unfair, she was well aware. To ask a man to spend the night without offering anything was not what a normal male expected.

"Come," he said and walked with her to the bed. He lifted the blankets. "In ye go."

Once she slid between them, he covered her and kissed her forehead. "Of course, I will stay with ye. Just ensure to wake me at dawn so I can slip away. I do not think it will be looked upon well to know ye allowed me here."

Catriona wasn't sure what to think. Why was he acting so cavalier about it? She was about to ensure he knew she would not offer herself when he climbed on the bed, lay atop the blankets and put both hands under his head. "This bed is much more comfortable than mine."

Never had she been so sure of a good man until that moment. When she snuggled against his side, he immediately wrapped one arm around her shoulders and kissed her temple.

"Do ye like living here more than yer own home?" Catriona asked.

His shoulder shifted in a shrug. "My cousins have welcomed me here. It is like a second home. My own home in Uist is as large, but I do believe this one to be a bit grander. This family was raised by parents who loved each other. That makes a difference."

As she knew him to be reluctant to speak of his father, she asked of his mother instead. "What is yer mother like?"

Ewan chuckled softly. "She is a champion. She managed to keep me and my brothers in line and never once raised her voice. It was her low tone and sharp gaze that made us quiver."

"I remember those looks. My own mother has accomplished them rather well."

Nudging her with his shoulder, Ewan got her attention. "Ye will feel comfortable here, Catriona. Not only will I and my cousins ensure ye are protected, but the women here, their wives, are a close-knit group who will have ye too busy to worry about anything."

"I hope so."

"Sleep," he whispered.

Despite the awkwardness of sharing her bed with Ewan, very soon after, Catriona could barely keep her eyes open.

The sound of Ewan's soft breathing, and the rise and fall of his chest were the perfect lullaby. His chest was broad and strong, his muscular arm heavy and yet comforting on her shoulder. In a way, she didn't wish the night to end. Would she be so bold as to ask that he sleep there with her nightly?

It was horrible to do it, because she wasn't sure that it was possible to promise him anything. With the bedding between them, she didn't feel any kind of threat. However much she wanted his skin against hers, Catriona wasn't sure what her reaction would be.

The memory of every moment at Mackenzie Keep remained vivid. Simple things would bring back a stark reminder and it was as if she were there once again. Being held down, hit, bitten and taken by a bunch of savage animals.

She let out a deep sigh, forcing the memory away. It was easy to feel protected when lying next to Ewan's larger body. He exuded strength and security.

CATRIONA WOKE WITH a start and took a sharp intake of breath until remembering that she'd asked Ewan to sleep in her room.

He remained on his back. He faced away from her and was fast asleep. His soft snores made her smile. For some reason, during the night she'd pulled a blanket off and put it over him.

Perhaps he wasn't the only one who felt protective of the other. Outside was still dark but, in the distance, a rooster crowed alerting dawn would break soon.

For a few moments, she soaked in the moment. Once she woke Ewan, he'd have to leave, and she wasn't sure they'd have a moment alone for the entire day.

Outside the security of the room were new things. Different people, who'd she'd yet to meet and had to, otherwise it would be rude. Then there were the surroundings to explore. Esme had promised to take her to the adjoining house where she and Ruari lived with a smaller staff and only a handful of guards.

Once she left Ross Keep, she'd not see Ewan because he'd remain there.

There had to be something she could do. If she agreed to allow their courtship, it meant she'd have to be open to a physical relationship. No matter what Ewan said, a marriage could not last without the physical aspect of it.

It was time that she spoke to Esme. Hopefully, together, they could come up with a plan.

Esme kissed Ewan's jaw. "It is almost dawn."

When he murmured something undecipherable, she kissed his cheek. "Wake up, Ewan."

His eyes popped open and he looked around confused. At seeing her, it was obvious he recalled the night before. "I'd hoped to wake up before ye did," he complained.

Instead of getting up, he wrapped his arms around her and yawned loudly. "Did ye sleep well?"

"I did," Catriona replied and yawned in return. "I hope ye were not too uncomfortable."

He pressed a kiss to her temple. "From how soundly I slept, I would say it was a good night's rest." Stretching, he looked at her. "It's best I go."

"Thank ye," Catriona said, not wanting him to go. "Ye are kind."

Ewan rolled over her and held his body up with his elbows and knees so not to place any weight on her. The serious expression on his face hovered just above hers. "My staying here has nothing to do with kindness. I want to be close to ye because I wish ye to be my wife one day."

"I owe ye a reply. I promise to as soon as I can," Catriona replied.

When his mouth covered hers, automatically, her eyes fluttered closed and she grabbed his shoulders.

Just as she tried to pull him closer, he broke the kiss and gave her a crooked grin. He got up and stood over the bed. "Go back to sleep. Mayhap dream of ravishing me."

Catriona remained still, looking straight up. What would have happened if he would have collapsed over her? She'd actually wanted more, needed more.

She couldn't wait for Esme to come and fetch her for first meal. There was so much to talk about.

"Ye did what?" Esme's wide eyes met hers. The curve of her lips made Catriona feel like less of a wanton. "He is quite strong-willed. I do not know of many men who would sleep with a woman and not demand she give herself to him."

Catriona frowned. "I know. Should I feel badly?"

"Of course not," Esme replied emphatically. "However, do not think it can happen often without him losing control. Men are very physical creatures."

Lady Elspeth Ross came to the door. With her were two other women. Catriona was quickly introduced to the other Ross brothers' wives. Tristan's wife, Merida, a McLeod, and Kieran's wife, Gisela. Each of the three women were vastly different in features, but all quite striking.

Much like their handsome husbands, Esme had informed her.

Elspeth hugged Catriona. "Lady Fraser informed us of yer reluctance to go about freely and we came to ensure ye know we understand."

"If ye are brave enough, we planned a separate first meal in the room next to the kitchen," Merida said with a wide smile. "I myself prefer to eat there."

Catriona instantly like each of them. "That would be perfect. I will strive not to remain a recluse. I promise."

Together, the group walked past the great room and down a side corridor. Catriona caught sight of Ewan and several warriors going out toward the courtyard. Obviously, they'd all eaten earlier.

Catriona slid a look to Esme, whose lips curved. She'd seen Ewan as well.

"Stop it," Catriona whispered.

"Did ye know that there are cats that share yer bed and promptly leave at dawn to go hunt mice?" Esme said in a singsong voice.

Gisela's dark eyes twinkled with glee. "Aye, and they have little remorse for it."

"That is why we must lock the door and keep them in, if we wish for more than a simple purr when they awaken," Elspeth added.

Obviously the women were well aware of what Esme had alluded to. Hopefully, they'd all think it was her own husband she spoke of.

"Who is this cat we speak of?" Merida asked Catriona in a soft voice. "Is he handsome?"

Catriona covered her face and the other women chuckled. "I have no idea what ye are all speaking about."

For the first time in her life, she was in a group of women who were paired off and it felt as if she, too, had a man in her life. Despite the anxiety nibbling at the edges, Catriona allowed herself a time of lightness and enjoyed the moment.

"Tell me who is he," Elspeth demanded.

Merida, who seemed the quietest of the group, patted Catriona's hand. "Ye do not have to. When ye are ready, we will be glad to know."

"I have an idea who it is," Gisela said. "A certain gentleman seems overly interested in knowing when Ruari and Esme are going back to their house."

Esme huffed and rolled her eyes. "Ye will eventually find out. He is not the best at hiding his admiration for Catriona."

"I cannot stand the curiosity," Elspeth cried out dramatically.

When they entered the small dining room, the cook hurried over to them. Her warm gaze went to Catriona. "I am Moira. If there is anything ye need, no matter the time, ye come and ask."

Lady Fraser appeared at the doorway. "I had to hunt for ye," she complained, but immediately sat next to her daughter, Esme. "I like the idea of eating separately."

"I apologize," Elspeth replied. "I did send a maid to fetch ye."

"Ye did, but she came much too early. I had yet to begin to comb my hair." Lady Fraser didn't seem bothered at all. "I must say, this home amazes me. It is so beautiful."

Elspeth met the woman's gaze. "Thank ye. It is indeed lovely."

"Ye must remain here with me while I visit," Lady Fraser told Esme. "It is only for a season. It would be preferable to yer smaller home. This one has a proper staff."

It was obvious by the look between Esme and Elspeth that she'd warned Lady Ross about her mother's inclination for indulgence.

"We did invite ye to visit us. Whether Esme remains or not, ye are more than welcome to remain here," Elspeth told Lady Fraser.

Lady Fraser gasped. "It is so very kind of ye. I must, however, go wherever my daughter goes. It is her I wish to spend the most time with." She glanced at Catriona. "Catriona, as well. It is imperative that they spend time together."

"Very well, Mother, I will remain here for a bit longer. Eventually, ye and Catriona will come to my home. It may not be as grand as this, but it is very comfortable, and I have enough of a staff that ye will find it adequate for yer every need."

Of course, what Lady Fraser was interested in were the constant activities, the feasts and any celebrations at the larger keep, since she and Laird Fraser only attended smaller gatherings. The entire trip there, she'd spoken of little else but hopes for several large celebrations.

As if reading her mind, Elspeth spoke. "Tonight, we have invited several neighboring families to attend a welcome celebration in yer honor, Lady Fraser."

The woman looked about to swoon with delight and Catriona slid a knowing look to Esme, who then gazed upon her mother indulgently.

After first meal, Esme gave Catriona a tour of the home. By the time they returned to the great room, Catriona was completely lost. "I do not think I will ever learn my way around here."

"Everyone gets turned about at first," Esme said with a chuckle. "I would get so angry when trying to find my way to the great room for meals."

Esme looked around. "I will introduce ye to Laird Ross and his brother," Esme said, not giving Catriona an opportunity to reply before pulling her toward the high board.

When she looked up and met the icy stare, she almost turned around and ran. However, Esme held her arm. "Laird Ross, this is Catriona, who is like a sister to me."

The man was as handsome as he was frightening. After a nudge from the man to his right, he seemed to soften. "Welcome to Dun Airgid. I hope ye will enjoy yer visit."

Catriona bent her head forward in greeting.

"Catriona, this is Tristan Ross, the laird's brother, and Merida's husband," Esme explained.

Like his cousins, Tristan also had hazel eyes. His, however, seemed lighter. The man nodded in greeting. "Welcome, Miss Catriona." Unlike his brother, Tristan Ross set her mind at ease enough to speak.

"Th-thank ye," Catriona stuttered, looking to Esme, hoping for an escape.

"Ewan has gone to meet with the guards. He shall return by last meal," Tristan informed her.

To her utter dismay, she felt a wave of heat fall over her face. "Oh." It was the only sound she could make. Thankfully, Esme rescued her.

"I'm sure he will seek Catriona upon his return," Esme replied, tugging her arm. "Let us go see where the women are."

"How do they know?" Catriona hissed as soon as they were out of earshot.

Esme gave her a droll look. "Ewan must have said something to them."

"I should speak to Broden," Catriona said. "He has been making attempts to court me."

Her friend stop mid-stride. "I was not aware Broden was interested in ye. I wonder if it is more about feeling possessive over ye."

"Either way, I feel that I should speak to him."

"I will send for him later," Esme said. "Ye need to get yer breath and rest a bit first."

THEY WENT INTO a large sitting room where Elspeth and several women sat about sewing. Elspeth waved them in. "Ye have to tell me about yer home. I do not believe I've ever been to yer village."

After a while, Catriona was shocked to find out the beautiful Lady Ross had grown up a simple village girl. She'd agreed with Catriona that her husband was quite frightening when first meeting him.

"He is a strong leader who grew up a warrior and witnessed death many times. As much as I try, I cannot imagine what it is like."

Merida looked to Catriona. "Ye haven't met the youngest, Kieran, yet. If ye think Malcolm is unsettling, then ye will find Kieran absolutely terrifying."

The women chuckled, except for Catriona, who could not imagine anyone scarier than Malcolm Ross.

DRESSED FOR LAST meal, Catriona was still astonished at her lack of nervousness. It could be that the change in location helped. She hoped that when it was time to sleep, her fears would remain at bay.

Since no one had offered to stop by for her, she decided to make her way there. Leaving her bedchamber, she went to the end of the corridor, turned right down a second one. She'd memorized the way. Right, left and then left.

However, upon reaching the end of the corridor, she found herself not in the great room, but in a different one. This one was smaller, with several sitting areas. Over a fireplace, there was a portrait of a couple. The man resembled Malcolm, but it was not him. The woman was seated, her hands folded, her gaze straight ahead.

She wondered what the room was used for. Perhaps small gatherings. She turned just as a man entered the space.

In all her life, she'd never seen a more astonishingly angelic being. He looked to her with interest before motioning to the doorway. "Ye must be lost."

There was no warmth in his tone, nor animosity, however something about him gave her pause. It was as if restrained ferocity floated just beneath his skin. His movements, although graceful, seemed measured.

When his gaze met hers, her lips parted at the heavily lashed, lovely and yet icy gaze.

He seemed to understand her hesitation. "I am Kieran Ross. The laird's younger brother. Ye can follow me. I was sent to find ye for last meal."

Catriona was thankful he did not come near and wondered if he'd been forewarned of her fears.

"Why did they send ye?"

One wide shoulder lifted. "Ewan is held back and will be late. He wished to ensure ye were not bothered by a warrior named Browen...or the like."

"Broden. Ewan sent ye?" Obviously, men were not aware of Kieran's intimidating presence.

"Aye."

"Very well. Shall we go?" Catriona took a breath and went to where he stood. If Ewan trusted Kieran, she would as well.

"I do not believe I am afraid of ye. However, I must admit to a compelling need to keep looking at ye. Ye must find it bothersome."

Kieran tilted his head to one side and looked down at her. "Sometimes. I do not notice it much."

At his words, Catriona relaxed. Everyone had burdens, even the beautiful man who now walked beside her.

Once in the great room, Catriona went to sit at a table with Esme. The meal was bountiful, musicians entertained, and tankards were kept full.

Meanwhile, Lady Fraser, who sat at the high board next to Elspeth, beamed, her face bright with excitement. Catriona had to smile at seeing the woman's happiness. It was a full circle that night, a contrast to the worst time in both of their lives.

Esme squeezed her hand. "Ye seemed changed. More like yerself."

"I am hopeful," Catriona replied. "For the first time in a long time, I want to be happy."

After everyone ate, several people danced, while most sat and watched. It was the first time in a long time that Catriona had attended a large gathering. She remained at the table ensuring to keep her back to the wall, but able to watch those dancing.

"How do ye feel?" Broden lowered next to her, his gaze moving from her to the dance floor.

"I am well," Catriona replied. She was well aware that Broden wished for more from her than just friendship. It was interesting that for the many years she'd been so infatuated with Keithen Fraser, she'd not taken time to notice other men. Now, however, she could not think of anyone else except Ewan.

"Ye should find a lass and dance," Catriona suggested. "Several kept an eye on ye when ye walked across the room."

"I would dance with ye," he said.

"Broden," Catriona began. "Ye and I cannot be more than friends. Please understand."

He leaned closer so she could hear him. "Ye cannot consider Ewan Ross. He has no home to call his own. He is but a drifter. Have ye asked why he left Uist?"

Catriona wasn't sure what to say. She had asked, several times, but he'd yet to tell her the real reason.

"He left behind a wife and a bairn," Broden said, his voice flat.

"Ewan Ross is a married man."

Her entire being constricted. It was as if a strong fist gripped her body and squeezed. Her breath caught and every ounce of her fought to inhale, but it was impossible.

At her gasp, Broden touched her arm. Esme hurried around the table and took her by the shoulders.

"Breathe Cat, please breathe."

She tried. Gasped, but no air entered her body. It was as if her throat had closed, not allowing anything to pass.

Desperation struck and she clawed at Esme's clothing mouthing "Help me".

Ruari Ross pushed Esme aside, placed his hand flat on Catriona's stomach and pushed hard. A loud whoof of air escaped and she was finally able to take full, desperate breaths.

"What did ye do?" Esme screamed at Broden. "What did ye say to her?"

"Something she had to know," Broden replied, giving her a concerned look. "I apologize."

Catriona pushed away from him and looked past Esme and Ruari. Thankfully, no one seemed to take much notice of what had happened. Just then, past the tables, Ewan and several warriors entered. His bow was still strapped to his back, his dark hair wild from the wind. He looked every bit a fierce archer.

"I need to go to my room," Catriona told Esme, grabbing her hand. "I do not wish to speak to anyone right now."

CHAPTER ELEVEN

THE GREAT ROOM was overfilled with revelers and Ewan was motioned over to the archers' table, where he sat and reached for a tankard. Someone asked for food and servants hurried off to get it.

Searching the room, he didn't see Catriona. If she'd been there, he assumed there would be too many people for her to remain. Once he finished his meal, he would find a way to seek her out. Hopefully, she would ask that he stay with her another night.

"We leave the day after tomorrow to the north post," Naill, the head archer, told him. "Ye will come as well."

It was not a request, but an order. He'd thought plans were already in place for who would go. "For how long?"

"There are threats from the Sutherlands. We must ensure they are kept at bay and understand we will not stand for intrusion on our land," another archer replied.

So, they were not sure how long it would be. If he were to go for longer than a season, it could be that Catriona would be gone by the time he returned.

He had little choice but to ask Catriona for her reply. He had to let her know he was going off to battle with no idea when he'd return.

The meal seemed to drag on. Finally, he saw an opening when

Laird Ross motioned for the music to stop. The festivities were to end.

Ewan stood and made his way to the high board to catch Tristan Ross' attention. The warrior looked to him and stood. Although Ewan was taller than most, Tristan still towered over him. In actuality, Tristan towered over everyone, except for Ruari, who was about the same stature.

"Did Naill tell ye we leave the day after tomorrow?" Tristan asked without preamble. "At least the weather will be warmer than last time."

Ewan nodded. "Aye, he just did. How long do ye think we will be gone?"

His cousin shrugged. "Hopefully no longer than a pair of months."

There was a strong possibility that Catriona would be gone before he returned.

"I must see about something," he said and then placed a hand on his cousin's shoulder. "I will be prepared to ride with ye."

He hurried away and down a corridor to Catriona's bedchamber. Praying she'd be alone, he knocked on the door.

There was no answer, even after the second and third time. Perhaps she'd gone to the ladies' sitting room. It was late and he doubted she would be anywhere other than perhaps Esme's bedchamber.

When he turned away, a sound inside the room caught his attention. Catriona was in the room. Why did she not open the door?

He tried the handle and the door opened. Catriona stood by the window looking out. Even when he called her name, she did not turn.

"Is something wrong?" Ewan asked, walking to her. He stopped when she turned and held out both hands, palms facing him.

Hitching her chin, she met his gaze. "I have much to thank ye for. It is because of ye that I can leave the confines of a room and was brave enough to come here. Ye have made me realize that I am stronger than what those bastards did to me."

Something about her tone sent warnings through him. Whatever had caused her to become so different, he needed to know.

"Ye are strong."

"I am stronger, but not who I once was." She let out a long breath. "I have made a decision that ye must be informed about."

Ewan searched her eyes for whatever she was about to say. Instead of the normal warmth and softness, all he could see was pain.

"Tell me what happened, Catriona."

She swallowed, managing to remain stoic. "I have decided not to marry ye. If I do get married, it will be to Broden."

The room swayed and he reached out with both hands to steady himself. Of course, he'd heard her wrong. It was glaringly obvious that Catriona didn't care for Broden as more than a friend, a brother.

"What did ye say?"

"I cannot marry ye, Ewan. I wish to remain with my clan, my family. It is preferable that when he asks, I marry Broden. He and I are from the same clan. He will keep me safe."

Betrayal was not a stranger to him. In that instant, Catriona betrayed him, perhaps not in actions, but in closing her heart to him.

In that moment, it was as if ice enveloped him. It was not the first time someone he loved had turned against him. Didn't consider him valuable enough to choose.

There was nothing to say. He would not beg, nor would he allow the woman who stood in front of him the satisfaction to see him break down.

He nodded, meeting her gaze evenly. "I wish ye well then."

Somehow, he managed to walk to his bedchamber without breaking stride and then barely past his doorway, Ewan fell to his knees, tears that he'd somehow held back bursting like rivers down his cheeks.

Pain tore through him and he let go, falling sideways onto the floor. More than anything, he wanted to release a primal yell, to scream out how he felt, but someone would overhear, and he didn't want any witnesses to his foolishness. How audacious of him to think someone would love him and remain true.

How utterly, utterly stupid of him.

>>><<<

THE RIDE TO the northernmost portion of Ross lands was long. Ewan knew the group he traveled with purposely rode slowly. A party of two hundred warriors and fifty archers were a sight to behold. Surely the Sutherland would not have a problem getting the message that they were more than ready for battle.

The sounds reached them and then a large contingent of Sutherlands appeared.

Warring was never something Ewan relished and, yet, it had a beauty to it. The calculated movements were like a dance between two armies. The sounds the horses made because they sensed the tension of their riders. The climactic moment when both parties rushed at each other with primal yells that broke the silence of the surroundings like thunder from the skies.

From then on, it was not at all pretty. In fact, it was quite the opposite. It became garish and horrible. Men's battle cries turned to screams of pain. Horses fell sideways, their thick red blood staining the ground.

He kept Ban back. The stallion was anxious to run. But like the rest of the archers, Ewan was to remain behind the flanks of men with swords and battle axes.

Naill held the archer line tight, just behind the warriors and called for them to stop and fan out on a well-planned slight incline. From there, they could fire arrows at will, hoping to hit enemy warriors. While half the archers shot arrows at the men fighting, he and the other half focused on the enemy's archer line.

Ewan narrowed his eyes and pulled back. In his bow were three arrows that would fell a man, immediately killing him.

He released the arrows and, seconds later, his victim collapsed forward and onto the ground from atop a horse.

Just then, Naill toppled from his horse. No one tried to help him. This was not the time to care after casualties, but to continue in their fight.

Warnings were cried out by the Sutherland warriors as a second wave of Ross warriors arrived. The men from the northern guard post had received notice and rode toward them, hungry for a taste of battle after long days of watch.

It was not much longer before those left of Clan Sutherland called retreat and did their best to gather their wounded before escaping.

The causalities were plenty on both sides, although most of the dead were Sutherland men.

Ewan and the rest of the archers kept vigil while the men below sought out the injured. It was hours later that they set up camp just a short distance away.

"We will stay and ensure they do not return," Naill said while being tended to by a healer.

"It is doubtful they will," Tristan said, waiting for someone to see about a cut on his leg. "They have to travel much further, and their numbers are not as plentiful."

Clan Sutherland's lands bordered the Ross' northern border. Looking to grow his territory, the Sutherland did not care about the loss of men. It made little sense to be at war with all the surrounding clans, but the man's greed was out of control and it seemed no one in his clan did anything to stop him.

That night while the men ate, Tristan shouted out orders for who would remain on watch at which times.

Ewan volunteered to take the first shift as he doubted he would be able to sleep. Whenever he closed his eyes, all he could see was

Catriona's face. Her stoic expression as she'd broken his heart. It was as if she'd not known him at all.

He walked to a tree and looked up at the night sky. It was a clear night, the sky filled with stars. For a while, he traced patterns, noting some he'd seen many times before. Although he had no idea if they had names, it was comforting to see the familiar formations.

Tristan approached and looked up to the sky. "See anything interesting?"

"I like looking at the stars," Ewan replied. "How is Naill?"

"He's asleep. The healer managed to get him to drink something that would make him rest."

The man was married with two children, which made it important for him to return home alive. It was an unspoken truth, often warriors did their best to ensure the married ones made it home.

"What happened between ye and Catriona?" Tristan asked. "Merida told me ye asked her to marry ye."

It had not occurred to her that his cousins were informed of everything through their wives. He'd been glad to see that the women got along well with Catriona fitting right in. Now it would be a stark reminder of her absence once she returned to Fraser lands.

"She decided to marry someone else."

Tristan frowned. "Who?"

"Someone from Clan Fraser."

"I am sorry," Tristan replied and placed a hand on his shoulder. "I am also surprised. From what Merida told me, ye and Catriona have become very close."

Once again, he looked up to the sky. "Once she leaves, I hope I never see her again."

Tristan nodded. "Do ye plan to remain with us then?"

In that moment, he made a decision. "Yes. There is nothing for me in Uist and here I can make a life working for Malcolm."

"I am glad to hear it," Tristan said. "I best walk about and see about the others.

For a long time, Ewan considered his life moving forward. He'd do his best to serve the laird and fight with all his might against aggressors. After staying in the keep for a while, he'd work on building a house for himself. Perhaps he'd ask Malcolm for a piece of land to call his own.

He began formulating what to do when a moan caught his attention. One of the injured was in pain. Deciding to see if there was something he could do for the man, he went to him.

"Water, please," the injured man asked. He was feverish and so Ewan went to get water and cloths to wash his face.

It took some time, but the man finally fell into a fitful sleep.

"He will not be returning to the northern post," a guard said, looking down on the sleeping man. "I'll have to ask for a replacement."

"I will do it," Ewan said without thinking. "I can take his place."

"Ye are an archer. We need a warrior." The man looked him up and down. "Although, ye're built like a warrior."

"I am both a warrior and an archer."

"Yer archery skills are legendary," the man said, holding out his hand. "I am Glenn Ross."

Ewan studied him. "We are related then?"

"Distant. I am from the northern and smaller Ross Clan."

Ewan noticed that Glenn's likeness was distinct to the northern Ross Clan. Most of them had a lighter complexion and coloring of hair. Glenn was blond, but instead of blue eyes, he had the distinct hazel that most Ross' were born with.

"I will inform Tristan of my decision," Ewan said. "If ye will have me."

Glenn nodded with a curious expression. "Did ye not only recently return from Fraser lands? I do not know that Tristan will agree for ye to come to the post so soon."

"He will," Ewan replied, knowing that Tristan would agree it to be a good idea to stay away until Catriona left. It would only lead to problems if he returned to both Broden and her still at the keep.

The cold wind blew, and he yanked the tartan over his shoulders.

He hated the cold.

Two weeks passed at the camp. The injured had been taken back to their families to recover, the dead to be buried. Other than Sutherland men returning and asking permission to retrieve their dead, no other challenges were issued.

Ewan paced the length of the camp, restless even after brushing down his horse and helping others with their mounts. The worst thing about being away from the keep was idle time. There were many hours of not much to do other than sit in wait.

They did not partake in sword play as they had to keep a keen ear to ensure no one approached. For the most part, they rode in a large circle, guarded the forest on the northern front, ate and slept.

One night, finally the call to withdraw was given. Those that were to return to Ross Keep would do so in the early morning. Those returning to the northern post, would leave a day later, ensuring there was no one in wait for them to leave and attempt to trespass.

Ewan rested well that night knowing he had a plan for the next several months. He would take on leadership responsibilities with a team of archers. Formulating plans for helping the men become better marksmen, he looked forward to the days ahead.

And yet a picture of Catriona came to mind. Her beautiful amber brown eyes meeting his, the soft smile on her lips when he'd woken lying next to her. The softness of her lips against his.

Nothing had prepared him for what she'd said. That she'd rather marry someone else. Why had she changed so drastically?

An owl's sad hoot drew him away from thoughts of a love that would never be, and he silently thanked the bird. From now on, he would divert his thoughts. Catriona nor any woman would take any priority in his mind. If he ever was to be with another woman, it would be one that he cared little about.

The morning the contingent headed north, Ewan couldn't help but wonder what would happen when Tristan returned to Ross Keep. Tristan had promise to send a message to let Ewan know once Catriona left, and it would be safe for him to return.

Until then, he was satisfied that his not returning would send a clear message.

CHAPTER TWELVE

WHEN CATRIONA OPENED her bedroom door, Merida walked in. As of late, her expression of worry remained. The quiet woman studied Catriona. "I came to see if ye would pray with me for Tristan and Ewan's safe return."

"Of course." Catriona had yet to tell anyone about what she'd learned from Broden. It seemed strange to her that although he was married, none of them had yet to inform her. Perhaps they saw nothing wrong with Ewan leaving behind a family with no care for what happened to them.

She joined Merida on the floor and prayed. Despite how angry she was at Ewan, Catriona did not wish for anything bad to happen to him. Even though archers were less likely to be killed in battle than warriors, they still faced danger.

Several injured archers had returned weeks earlier just after the first battle. They'd not heard whether or not they'd battled again.

Once they finished praying, Catriona opened her eyes to see that Esme had entered the room. Her friend looked first to Merida and then to Catriona.

"The men return."

Catriona's stomach flipped, forcing her to take a sharp breath.

With a happy cry, Merida flew from the room, not waiting to see if they followed. Catriona went to the window but unable to see, she gave up.

"Let us go up to Elspeth's bedchamber. From there, we can get a clear view of the courtyard and gates."

Together, they went up the stairs to a bedchamber. The door was open and inside were Gisela and Elspeth. Both turned and waved them forward to a small balcony. Sure enough, from there, they had a clear view of the contingent of horsemen riding through the front gates and into the courtyard.

The laird, his brother and others were not visible as they probably stood by the front entrance.

Her heart thumping, Catriona searched the lines of men for Ewan. It was hard to tell one from another, but she was convinced that she could find him because his horse stood out.

The women commented on certain men, naming them and pointing. Catriona finally could not take it any longer. "Does anyone see Ewan?"

There was silence as they searched together for the familiar handsome face.

After a long while, it was Esme who spoke. "I do not think he is here."

"He may be standing at the front door. Perhaps he dismounted before we thought to look," Gisela added.

"I agree," Elspeth said. "I am sure he is somewhere, and we cannot spy him."

Catriona nodded. "Yes. Of course." She kept scanning the faces the entire time as the men were spoken to by the laird and then began to disperse. Those that lived outside the keep rode away, while those who lived in the guards' quarters dismounted and guided their horses to one of two huge stables where lads would take over care for the animals.

"We best prepare for last meal," Elspeth, said. "I should go and see if Malcolm requires anything."

As the women dispersed, Esme came up beside Catriona. "We should go and see if any help is required in the kitchen."

It was comical, since Esme was the worst cook. However, it was obvious her friend was trying to distract her.

Catriona looked to Esme. "If he is about, I do not plan to speak to him. Do not try to come up with a way to leave me alone with him."

Esme gave her a pointed look. "Ye should speak to him. Ask him about what Broden said."

"He's already lied by not telling me. Every time I asked about his reasons, not once did he reply. There cannot be anything between us. He has a family to care for."

"I find it strange that no one here has mentioned it."

"Yer own husband said he knew nothing about Ewan having a wife. How is it possible?" Catriona said.

"Ewan lived in Uist. It is quite a long distance away," Esme explained. "What the family here knows about his life is only what he has told them. Besides, how would Broden even know?"

"True."

Esme took her hand. "If ye wish to know the truth, ask him directly. It is what ye should have done from the beginning. At least that way ye could be sure."

"I should. Ye are right. It is best to know, although I have already made up my mind," Catriona replied.

Together, they went down the stairs and past the great room. Everyone remained outside so the space was empty. Just as they turned down the corridor to the kitchen, Tristan entered with Merida under his arm.

"We are grabbing our bairn and heading to our home. I will come back to see ye tomorrow," Merida said with a bright smile.

Unlike her, Tristan's expression turned hard at seeing Catriona. He remained silent, only nodding in their direction.

"Tristan," Esme said, much to Catriona's dismay. "Where is Ewan?"

The huge warrior met Catriona's gaze for a moment. It was obvious he was not happy with her. "He replaced an injured archer at the northern post. He will not be returning for many months."

At the news, Catriona wasn't sure how to respond. A heavy sadness fell over her as she realized she would never see Ewan again.

Esme said something, she didn't hear. Tristan replied and both looked to her.

"Ye are pale," Merida said. "Ye should sit."

"I am fine, thank ye," Catriona replied. "I should go to the kitchen. There is much to do."

Tears threatened and Catriona blinked to keep from embarrassing herself. She hurried into the large kitchen. Thankfully, everyone was too busy preparing the large meal so that they took no notice of her.

The head cook, Moira, motioned her to come closer. "Help or get out of the way," she said, pushing a long-handled spoon into her hand. "Stir and do not let it stick."

Before long, Catriona donned an apron and was stirring the sweet pudding like her life depended on it.

Every so often, Moira stopped by, dipped her finger into the pot and tasted it. Each time, she declared, "It's almost done," before hurrying away.

By the time the first trays were being taken by a group of serving maids, Catriona sat at the long kitchen table placing loaves of bread and blocks of cheese onto large platters.

Unlike Clan Fraser, where small groups were entertained perhaps every fortnight, Ross Keep seemed to entertain nonstop.

"Who is this feast for?" Catriona asked Moira, who waved the next group of tray-carrying maids off.

Moira gave her a puzzled look. "For the men returning from battle, of course."

"Yes, of course," Catriona replied, attempting to force a smile. "How silly of me to ask."

The activity continued for hours until Catriona could barely stand upright. How Moira and her helpers could continue on, seeming not to tire, was a testament to their tenacity.

"I will go rest now," Catriona announced to the kitchen at large. One maid waved her off with a bright smile.

"Thank ye for helping."

Once in her room, she lowered to a chair. Ewan had volunteered to stay away. It was a relief not to have to bump into him daily. At the same time, it was hurtful that he was not at all the man she'd believed him to be. A married man with a bairn should be home, helping to raise the child, not gallivanting about the country in battles and courting women.

How could she have misread him so much?

THE NEXT MORNING, her eyes felt as if someone had thrown sand in them. She'd barely slept a wink, vacillating between worrying for Ewan and being angry at him.

Finally, she decided there was little to be done about it. For one thing, Lady Fraser and the guard contingent, including Broden, had left. Secondly, she had nowhere to go, and therefore had to forge ahead until the opportunity to return to Fraser lands presented itself.

Upon entering the great room, once again, she was amazed at the amount of people present. If ever there was a place for her to face her fears, it was Dun Airgid. Catriona weaved through tables until reaching the one where Esme and her husband, Ruari, sat. With them was an older couple and a woman. They motioned for her to sit and Esme introduced her to the others.

The meal was simple, but plentiful. Soon, Catriona faced what would be another day.

"Esme," she said when her friend lingered at the table after the other left. "What exactly should I occupy myself with? At Fraser Keep, I mended for the guards. Do ye think there is a need for it here?"

"There is much need for many things here," Esme replied, blowing out a breath. "There are many men that require help with such things and also the making of tunics. We also weave blankets."

Catriona could not help but laugh. "Ye, weaving. I do not believe it." Her friend had always been averse to household duties. Esme had always preferred instead to practice archery or other such things.

"Aye, I have taken on some things. I learned to weave a basket," Esme said, motioning to a lopsided pitiful attempt in the center of the table.

After a moment of studying it, Catriona gave up on trying to come up with a compliment. "I see marriage can change even the wildlings."

"I am still part wildling, I'll have ye know," Esme rebutted with a saucy grin.

Catriona pushed away from the table. "Come show me where I can get clothing to mend and let us begin with the handsome men."

Esme's eyes rounded. "Cat. Ye are back."

"What are ye speaking about?" Catriona shook her head at the same time she realized that for the first time in a long time, she'd not sat with her back to a wall and she'd just asked to go where the guards were. "I suppose I am."

Her friend slid her arm through hers. "We will watch the men's early sword practice for a bit. There are a few that are worthy of study."

"What of the mending?" Catriona protested.

"I will send a lad to fetch the clothing."

DAYS TURNED INTO weeks, and the weeks into months. Catriona remained at Dun Airgid, unable to leave Esme again. Despite missing her parents and Fraser lands, she was becoming accustomed to life at Dun Airgid. With its huge walls and enormous army, it was, in her opinion, the safest region in Scotland.

The women of Ross Keep were all her friends now. Often, they embarked on adventures that ranged from picking flowers to archery contests. More often than not, the husbands would accompany them. But thankfully, because the men rotated in and out of the northern post, there was always a woman for Catriona to pair off with.

This day, it was only the women that went berry picking. Guards stood a distance away, not at all disguising their boredom as the women plucked ripe fruit and dropped it into baskets that hung from their arms.

Esme plopped one into her mouth. "These will make delicious tarts," she proclaimed. "If I can keep from eating them."

"Yer stomach will ache if ye eat too many," Elspeth warned as she rocked side to side, a bairn strapped to her chest. "Believe me, I know."

They continued until their baskets were becoming heavy. Finally, Merida announced that she was too tired to continue.

A blanket was spread on the newly grown green grass and they sat to rest. A servant brought them bread, cheese and wineskins.

The sun was warm on her back and Catriona took a deep breath of the fresh spring air.

"It is a beautiful day. I could spend more like this out here."

"I agree," Esme replied.

One of the guards who watched over them came close. "My lady, there is a party moving past."

They watched as the other guard rode just a bit farther and kept vigil.

"Someone probably comes to visit. They bring a contingent of men," Elspeth said with a groan. "I forget who is supposed to visit now."

"It may be my parents," Merida said, standing and straining. "If they do not come today, it will be in the next two."

As the women continued to keep vigil, Catriona sipped on wine and nibbled at bits of cheese. No one was coming to see about her.

"It is my parents," Merida said with a bright smile.

"Hmmm," Elspeth replied. "We will wait for them to pass by and then make our way back to the keep."

The carriage and escort were a distance away. From what Catriona spied, Merida's parents, the McLeods, traveled with about thirty or forty guards.

"Ah, some of the Ross men return as well," someone said. The comment made Catriona's breath hitch. She looked to the traveling group but, from the distance, she could not make out who was who.

However, a horse got her attention. Its peculiar prance and beautiful coloring was different than the others. The silver animal shook its large head, the mane waving like shiny streamers in the wind.

Ewan Ross was back.

CHAPTER THIRTEEN

"YOUR FATHER IS dead."

The words floated in the air until finally landing over him and Ewan breathed them in. They weren't exactly a blow, but more like a powerful gust of wind that filled his lungs.

His mind went elsewhere, not hearing whatever else was said in the room.

"Ye should leave," Una, his wife, once again sent him from her bedchamber. She lay upon the bed and had pulled the bedding over herself, covering her nudity from him. It was not the first time he'd practically had to force her to make love to him. And like many other times, she'd laid under him like a corpse. This time, however, he could not bring himself to take her unwilling body.

"Will ye not even look me in the eyes?" Ewan shouted. "Ye have been with another. Ye smell of him."

Una crossed her arms, her gaze slowly lifting to his. "Our marriage was an agreement between our fathers. There is no need to pretend it is more than that. I refuse to. Ye are gone for weeks. Am I to remain true to a man I barely know?"

"Ye have not even tried…"

Una got up from the bed and yanked on a robe. When Ewan reached for her, she whirled away. "I do not wish to be yer wife." This time, her voice was low, sullen. "Please go."

"I have told ye many times that I love ye, Una. I will do whatever it takes to ensure ye are happy."

"Then leave now. Go to wherever it was ye went for so many weeks."

"If I go, I will never return."

Her eyes narrowed in challenge. "If only that were true."

He stormed to the front of the great room to stand in front of his father. The man looked up at him with a frown. Despite how much he tried, as of late, it was as if his father resented each breath Ewan took.

"I demand my marriage be dissolved." Ewan stalked across the room. "As soon as possible."

"Dissolve the marriage?" His father glowered. "I will not allow it. There are many marriages between two people who do not care for one another. Find a mistress. Distract yerself with other pursuits."

Ewan leaned forward, not wishing to air his problems before those present in the great hall. "I do not wish to continue to be tied to a woman who detests me. What would make ye happy, that she try to kill me?"

"Again?" Darach, his older half-brother, added with a hard stare to their father. "I am not convinced it was not she who made my brother so ill in the spring. It was poisoning, the healer attested."

"It must be done, Father," Duncan, his brother, insisted.

Ewan looked directly at his father, his jaw tight. "I wish her gone from here."

By the lowering of his shoulders, it was apparent his father was about to relent. "Very well. I will allow the dissolution of the marriage, but Una must remain here. We cannot insult her clan by returning the lass."

He and his brothers exchanged confused looks but remained silent.

It was strange that his father, a man who should take his and his brothers' side over someone of another clan, would not in this case. However, Ewan cared little about it. If anyone would know about a marriage of convenience, it was his parents.

They rarely shared more than a meal together and, even then, did not speak to one another. Of course, there was a strong reason for it. His mother hated his father.

He went to his mother's sitting room, finding her sitting with her companion. The women shared some secret because they laughed and then quieted upon seeing him. He couldn't help but smile, loving that his mother was in so much better spirits. For a long time, she'd been sullen and withdrawn. Slowly, she'd emerged from the shadows and was almost the woman he remembered from boyhood.

"Come sit, darling." Lady Ross patted the seat next to her. "What brings ye to visit me so late?"

Her companion stood and went to sit on the opposite side of the room. It mattered not if she overheard as Ewan suspected whatever anyone said to his mother would always be repeated to the woman, as Lady Ross shared everything with her.

"I asked Father to dissolve my marriage to Una. He finally agreed."

Lady Ross frowned. "I am glad. Ye should have never married her. But there are consequences...will she be sent back to her clan? It will be an insult."

"Father said she must remain."

His mother looked to her companion. "In what capacity?" his mother asked, searching his face. "I suppose she can remarry. However, it will be most strange that she continues to live here."

Ewan nodded. "I agree and do not wish for her to remain. However, I am willing to accept anything as long as she is no longer my wife."

"I am sorry to interfere," his mother's companion said. "Dear, yer wife is with child. Did she not tell ye?" She looked to his mother. "I am sorry, but he must be told."

His mother nodded and sighed. "I planned to wait and see if she would inform ye first."

"Who is the father?"

"That, I cannot tell ye," Lady Ross replied. By her expression, it was obvious she had suspicions.

"Ewan, do sit." Malcolm pressed a glass of whisky into his hand. "I am sorry."

"For?" He looked about the room as his cousins exchanged looks of confusion. "Ah, yes, my father," he finished. "I am sorry as well."

"Ye will go to Uist, will ye not?" someone, perhaps Tristan, asked.

His mother, would she be glad? Ewan could not picture her to be sad. His father was not a good husband to her. He had turned out to be worse than anyone could have imagined.

For a long moment, he considered not telling his cousins the truth. Then he decided it wouldn't matter one way or the other.

"I am not sure if I will go or not. There really isn't much need. Being that I am the fourth born of five brothers, I am sure they will have matters well in hand."

He looked around the room and realized how different it had been for Malcolm, Tristan and Kieran when they'd lost their father. All three of them had mourned the late laird and been heartbroken over his death. The only one in the room that perhaps understood him was Ruari. He'd never truly known his father.

"My father was not the great man like yer late father," Ewan began. "I wish it was different, but it was often left for the council to handle all of the clan affairs. My father was a cruel man who cared little for the people. He devoted his time to things I would rather not speak of.

Malcolm looked to his brothers. "What of yer mother? Does she not require ye there? It would be an insult to the clan if ye do not attend yer father's funeral."

It was true.

"Ye are right. I am thinking only of myself. In this matter, it is important that I be there for my family. They are not the reason I do not wish to return."

"A moment," Malcolm said, motioning for everyone to leave. The solemn young laird waited for his brothers and Ruari to leave.

"What is it?" Ewan asked, pouring a second glass.

"Naill and Kieran will travel with ye to represent the clan. Is there anyone else ye would like to go?"

"No, thank ye. I will rest one day and then we head to Uist. It will be best to ride hard, so no wagons will be required."

Malcolm nodded. "I agree."

Ewan considered what kind of a return would be best. For him to return the same, without anything to call his own or perhaps different? Truthfully, nothing had really changed about him. He remained a younger part of a family without a wife, land or any titles.

"I would like to return a landowner."

"I am not sure I understand," Malcolm said.

Ewan nodded. "I wish to purchase land from ye, so that I can have something before returning to my family. I left without anything. I gave up my land, my life, as it was. In all this time, I have not acquired anything. No wife, bairns or land."

"Ye have done many things, Cousin. Ye have saved lives and fought for our clan bravely." Malcolm exhaled. "I understand yer need to have something tangible. As a reward for yer service to me, I grant ye the land east of Ruari's. There is a creek that runs south that divides the two. Ye can take the eastern portion as far as the Macdonnell lands. It is not very large, but it does include two villages."

His heart thudded with disbelief. "That is much too generous. I cannot accept such a large gift."

"It is what ye deserve. No member of my family should have nothing to their name. Upon returning to Uist, ye return a laird in yer own right."

Laird.

He took a deep drink of whisky and coughed. "Thank ye." He stood and hugged his cousin. "I will make ye proud. I swear it on my…"

"Yer name is good enough," Malcolm said with a wide smile. "The villagers there will be glad for a laird who lives closer and can give them the attention they need."

Ewan could not believe what had just happened. "What about

Tristan and Kieran? Will they not resent that ye give me this?"

"Neither can leave Dun Airgid as their responsibilities are here. Not to mention, if any of us separate our wives, they would serve us our balls on a platter."

Ewan nodded, understanding.

"It will be announced at last meal. Ensure ye are present."

"I would not miss it."

Walking to his bedchamber, Ewan considered what would be required of him. First of all, and perhaps most importantly, he would begin the search for a wife so that he could start the lineage for his new lairdship. Of course, it would not be a love match, but one of convenience. He would choose a meek young lass. One that would obey him without question and one he would never love.

That very day, he would begin his search. He'd make inquiries to Lady Ross and the other wives. Surely one of them would have the perfect candidate for him.

The opportunity presented itself rather quickly as he walked from Malcolm's study to his bedchamber.

"Welcome home, Ewan." Lady Ross and Kieran's wife, Gisela, walked toward him.

Both waited in silence as he bowed and greeted them. "I am glad to be here although I fear it is only for a day, as I must go to Uist the day after tomorrow."

"I am so very sorry," Lady Ross said. "I am sure yer father will be missed."

He didn't wish to correct her, so instead he bowed his head. "Thank ye."

"I must inquire," Ewan began. "Upon my return from Uist, I will be building my own home and will require a wife soon thereafter."

After exchanging looks, the women remained silent.

"I have to make sure that my last marriage was indeed dissolved, which I am sure it is. If I can place on ye the burden of finding a woman for me to marry, I would appreciate yer assistance, Lady Ross."

"Ye wish to marry so quickly?" Lady Ross asked. "Why?"

"I prefer a meek lass. One with little opinion. Looks do not matter to me. If ye would kindly think on it."

Once again, he gave a slight bow and walked away, ignoring their astonished looks.

Before last meal, he needed to sleep. The ride from the northern borders had been hard. After encountering a group of men along the way, they'd been forced to slow. He'd considered going faster, leaving the group and arriving back at Dun Airgid before the others, but then decided against it.

It wasn't that he'd hoped Catriona remained or that she'd gone. What he didn't want to face was knowing either way. Over time, he'd gone from hurt to anger and, finally, to accepting that it was best for him not to ever allow his heart free rein again.

Whether the woman remained or had gone, at this point, mattered little. He was prepared to see Catriona again and he was equally ready not to ever do so.

Now he had to not only face the current situation, but also to return to Uist where he would once again have to be ready to see Una.

Thankfully, no one except him knew the reason why he'd left Uist. And if he had his way, no one ever would.

Ewan flopped onto his bed, not bothering to remove his boots. Upon closing his eyes, the memory of the last time he'd seen his father immediately appeared.

"Go to Una, Son. Tell her the marriage will be dissolved. Ask that she consider returning to her own clan," his mother advised. "If she refuses, then set some ground rules. If she is to take a lover, it must be discreetly."

"What of the child?" He paced in front of the fireplace. "Everyone will think it is mine."

"There is naught we can do about it," Lady Ross said with a sigh. "The

only thing I can suggest is that ye go away. Create a life away from here."

"Yer son will be seen as a bad father who deserts his own child," her mother's companion interjected. "Perhaps what should be done is for her to be sent away. If we find out who the father is, he can be bribed to take her."

Moments later, Ewan returned to his wife's chambers, not at all looking forward to the argument that would no doubt ensue.

Familiar noises made him stop from knocking. Grunting and moaning came from behind the door. Immediately, his hand went to his broadsword. Before drawing it, Ewan considered this was a good thing. He was about to find out who his wife's lover was. He would barge in and demand the man take her away or face death.

The swishing of his sword slipping out of its holdings somehow permeated through the thundering blood rushing past his ears.

Stepping through the doorway, he allowed his eyes to become accustomed to the dimness. The couple was so enthralled that they did not notice his presence until he was beside the bed.

It was then the male turned and met his gaze.

For a moment, Ewan was sure he'd made a mistake, walked into the wrong bedchamber. But Una's gasp brought him to realize he had not.

His father pushed away from her slowly, withdrawing from her body in a way to ensure Ewan saw it clearly. All the while, Una remained frozen, her legs spread.

"I thought ye said he would not return tonight," his father said to Una, who other than to swallow visibly had yet to move. "I suppose it is best for it to be known. I tire of hiding," the laird said in a bored voice.

When Ewan's fist crushed his father's nose, the sounds of bones crunching seemed to hang in the air. It was not a fair fight. Ewan was over a head taller than the laird and outweighed him, all muscle.

The second punch to the midsection slammed his father into a table that toppled over, spilling the contents and breaking the furnishing with loud crashes and cracks.

Ewan punched him a third and fourth time, each hit harder.

When the older man fell to the floor, Ewan fell upon him like a wild beast, pummeling and pounding him until strong arms dragged him away.

And still he continued fighting, landing punches to both his brothers and a guard who'd come when hearing Una scream.

The door was slammed shut to keep others out, but not before some of the servants, who'd also rushed there, saw what was happening.

"Stop, Ewan!" Darach shouted, shoving Ewan against the opposite wall while Duncan lowered to the floor next to their father.

"To the dungeon," his father sputtered. "Lock him in the dungeon for daring to strike me."

Neither brother replied. Instead, Darach motioned to the guard to help him carry the bloody man out of the room. "Take him to his bedchamber then find the healer."

"The dungeon!" their father screamed. "Ewan! Ye are dead to me!"

The room became eerily silent. Ewan shoved Darach aside and went to the bed, his face twisted in fury. "Ye are a whore. Ye are my father's whore."

Una, who'd yanked blankets up to cover herself, seemed not to hear him. Instead, she looked straight ahead to the door.

When Ewan turned, his mother stood there, her gaze riveted on Una.

Knocks woke Ewan and he called whoever it was to enter. Two servants carried in a wooden tub and another two, each with pair of buckets filled with water.

A woman walked in last with a fifth bucket, this one steaming.

"I can assist with yer bathing if ye'd like, sir," she said with a light smile.

Once the water was poured into the tub, he sent all the servants away but the woman.

"YE LOOK REFRESHED," Ruari said, looking Ewan up and down. "I have been told the news of yer lairdship. I am glad for ye." They hugged, his cousin patting his back a bit hard. "Do not let it mean ye think yerself better than us commoners."

Ewan laughed. "Only when it comes to the last bits left at the bottom of a bottle. Then I will demand that what is left is mine."

They walked into the great room and Malcolm motioned for him to join those at the high board.

As was customary, the McLeod and his wife were seated on Malcolm's left, first the visiting laird, then Lady McLeod and, lastly, Lady Ross.

As per usual at Dun Airgid, conversation and music filled the air. Food a plenty was brought out and Ewan's mouth watered. Of all the things he'd missed the most since leaving, it was the food. The cook there had no compare.

Movement caught his attention. Three women entered the room. One was Gisela, Kieran's wife, the second was Merida. Upon noticing the third, he waited for the familiar pang to fill him. Instead, he managed to taper it down.

Catriona was still there.

She and the women commanded the room's attention as they walked in and forward to the high board where he sat.

It was interesting that despite the passing of time, he could sense that she knew he was there. Purposely, she kept her head turned just enough so that he could not make eye contact. When it was impossible for her not to acknowledge Malcolm as was customary, she managed to only look to the laird.

He kept his gaze on her until she slid a glance toward him. When she did, he did not break eye contact. Instead, he pinned her with a dismissive arched brow before looking away, effectively dismissing her.

If possible, Catriona was more beautiful than before. She seemed to have blossomed there in the new environment. Despite everything, he hoped for her full recovery and a future like that of most women.

So far, he'd not seen Broden about. Surely he and Catriona had to be married by now. He'd been gone half a year and, in that time, many things must have occurred.

The room went silent as Malcolm Ross stood to his full height.

The young laird scanned the room, his direct gaze landing on several people.

"Our sincerest welcome to Laird and Lady McLeod, who grace us with their presence." The people present murmured their welcomes.

Malcolm waited for the room to quiet and spoke again. "It is with great pride that I present to ye a new laird. My cousin, Ewan, will be laird over the region that borders Clan Macdonell lands. I present Laird Ewan Gerard Ross, Laird of Tuath Avon."

"North River." His new keep was named after the direction of it from Ross Keep.

Ewan stood and held up his tankard. If he was to be laird, it was time for a change of how he acted. From now on, the easy-going man who sought comradery with every man he came in contact with was gone.

"I am grateful to my cousin for this honor. He has agreed to allow fifty warriors to go with me. Upon my return from Uist, I will begin construction of Tuath Avon."

The room erupted with applause and shouts from the guardsmen. Ewan had never felt so much pride. Thankfully, before any emotions crept up, Malcolm once again spoke.

"Those of ye that wish to go with the new laird, come to me with yer requests."

As per usual, the feast was beyond reproach. Every platter over-spilled with flavorful herb-encrusted meats, organs in broth and plump bright colored vegetables.

A band of traveling bards entered through the doors and began walking between tables, singing and strumming on string instruments.

Ewan lifted his tankard along with his cousins, each of them toasting to his good fortune and wishing him well. None showed any sign of ill-will, which boded well. He'd wondered about Kieran, the third born, who would have benefitted from his own lairdship.

"Did ye not consider asking for the land?" Ewan asked his cousin whose brows joined as he considered how to reply.

"My brothers and I each have huge responsibilities here. Tristan is in charge of making sure that our army is always trained and ready to defend our lands and keep. I not only help Naill lead the hundreds of archers, but I'm also responsible for seeing to the security of our northern borders. I considered building a keep there, but my wife, Elspeth and Merida threatened to kill me in my sleep." A twitch at the corners of his lips was the closest Kieran ever came to smiling.

Ewan looked to the right where their cousin, Ruari, and other warriors sat. "What about Ruari?"

"He has no desire to be a laird. He is content with horse breeding and such."

There was no one else. As much as he suspected any of the men would have accepted the lairdship and been thankful for it, it was he who was in the best position to accept.

"I will forever be grateful," he finally said. "Your brother has treated me much better than my own in Uist."

"We are all family," Kieran replied and straightened as a young man, escorted by two guards, approached.

"A scout, Laird," one of the guards said.

Malcolm met the young man's gaze. "What is it?"

"Laird and Lady Munro will arrive one day hence."

"Of course," Malcolm replied without inflection. He then motioned the guard closer. "See that he is fed and given a place to sleep. Inform Lady Gisela of who comes to visit."

"Yes, Laird."

"The keep will be quite full," Kieran said with a displeased expression. "Perhaps it is time that I go to the north post for a spell."

"I leave that decision up to ye, Brother," Malcolm replied.

There were so many things that Malcolm had to handle on a daily basis. This just showed how understandable it was to keep his brothers close. The young laird was lucky to have two men he could trust without question.

Once the meal was over, Ewan had no desire to be around people, so he went to the stables to check on Ban, his horse.

Finding the horse was easy, its silver tone visible in the darkness. He'd often been kidded by others that with the horse, he was a riding target. Most of the time, Ban wore a dark covering, mostly at night when traveling near enemy lands.

Despite knowing it was unwise to ride a steed of light coloring, he'd raised the animal since its birth and was attached to it. Ban was a warhorse through and through. Ban rarely showed fear and was eager to rush forth at the first sounds of battle.

"Is there anything ye require?" A lad appeared and looked up at Ewan. "I brushed him down and fed him well."

"No, I come just to be with him for a moment. Go on and find yer bed."

Ewan led Ban out of the stall and began to check the horse's legs. They'd ridden through a patch of thorny bushes and the horse's legs had been cut in several places.

Poultice had been administered and one of the legs was wrapped. Thankfully, the stable master, under Ruari's tutelage, was proficient in tending wounds.

Satisfied that Ban was well taken care of, he led the animal back to its stall, produced a carrot and fed it to the horse.

Music and laughter wafted from the house out to the courtyard and Ewan diverted toward the side gardens. There could be some people milling about there, but at least it would not be as loud. He was not ready to retire to his room, much too excited still at what had transpired. There was so much to consider: the building, selecting men, purchasing of livestock, not to mention hiring staff.

"Oh."

The word brought Ewan out of his musings. He reached for the person he'd bumped into.

"I apologize…" He stopped midsentence at seeing who it was.

Catriona's rounded eyes matched her open mouth. "I-I came for fresh air. I thought ye were inside."

"Obviously, I am not." He turned away.

"Wait."

Ewan didn't fully turn, just his head. "What is it?"

"I am sorry for the loss of yer father."

Instead of a reply, he gave her a curt nod.

"And..."

He let out a breath and waited for her to continue, not bothering to face her.

"Ye will make an excellent laird."

He turned. Stalking toward her, like an animal of prey, he expected the only way to stop his progress would be her asking. Instead, she met his gaze, tilting her face up, her lips parting.

When his mouth crashed over hers, Catriona grabbed his tunic, her hands clenching the fabric as if it were the only way she could keep from falling.

In his arms, she felt perfect, soft and yielding, just like he'd remembered every single day since leaving. And exactly what he'd fought hard to forget.

She was not to be his. Ewan took her shoulders and pushed her backward gently.

"This must never happen again."

Catriona's chest heaved, her lips enticingly swollen by his kiss. "We were friends once."

"Were we? Enjoy the fresh air." Ewan walked away, needing space between them. Upon his return, he would have to hurry the building of his new home so he could move away.

Without looking, he knew she was watching him walk away. For whatever reason, it felt good that he did not give her the satisfaction knowing how much she'd hurt him. Yes, it was immature of him, but self-preservation was much more important than whether or not he hurt Catriona's feelings.

CHAPTER FOURTEEN

Fraser Keep

"FLORA." LADY FRASER stood by the fence waiting for her to respond.

"Lady Fraser." Flora straightened from the row of plantings she'd been tending to and lowered her head. "What can I do for ye?"

The woman was kind and a good mistress of the house. Every day, she would appear at the kitchen to speak with the cook and maids and give instructions for the day's meals. She would visit the laundress to ensure all was well. She also met with the chambermaids and lads regularly to do the same.

After Catriona left, Flora had requested and gotten a position there at the keep, without a clear capacity as yet. Her mother had taken ill as of late and could not remain back at the village caring not only for Flora's son, but the small cottage as well.

Nearing the woman, Flora did her best not to get her hopes up. With Catriona gone, her duties as companion had ended and she did what she could to help around the keep.

"Ye have been working hard," Lady Fraser began. "It has not gone unnoticed how much ye do here."

"I do what I can to be helpful. It falls on me to provide for my mother and son."

The clouds parted, allowing the sun to shine down, warming her back as she waited for whatever Lady Fraser had decided. Flora chose, in that moment, to see it as a good sign.

Lady Fraser motioned for Flora to come out of the garden. "Walk with me."

The request surprised her, but it boded well, perhaps. So, wiping her hands as clean as she could with a cloth, Flora hurried to do as told.

They walked in the unhurried pace that most nobles seemed to prefer. Lady Fraser looked toward where the guards were practicing.

"I need ye to consider something," Lady Fraser began. "Are ye averse to marrying again?"

The question caught Flora by surprise. Marriage was not something she'd thought about much. Sure, every once in a while, a handsome guard caught her eye. Some nights, her body craved a man's touch. But she'd been much too busy to think about marriage.

"I suppose I am not."

Lady Fraser's face brightened. "It would alleviate some of yer burden. Ye are young and pretty. There is no reason for ye to remain alone."

Flora looked to the field where the men continued to practice. "Who do ye have in mind, Lady Fraser?"

The woman followed her line of sight. "Keithen's friend. He needs a wife and I feel that he and ye would be a good match."

"Who?" Flora turned once again to the field.

"Broden McRainy. Ye must know him."

Immediately, the warrior came into focus. He was sparring against another man, his arms and face glistening with perspiration. In the sun, his hair was almost blond, the tresses pulled back into a queue with a leather strap. Flora had noticed him many times, but had never spoken to him.

A few times, he'd come to visit Catriona during the recovery time, and it was only then that Flora had observed him up close. He and Catriona had known each other for most of their lives and had a relationship like that of siblings.

"Why do ye think he needs to marry?" Flora finally asked.

"He has stated it himself. But then he does little to move forward. Before he makes a mistake and marries am unsuitable woman, I have decided to intervene."

"Ye must care deeply for him that ye wish to find him a suitable wife," Flora stated.

Lady Fraser smiled in the warrior's direction. "Aye. He has been close to our family. He was practically raised here at the keep."

"He seems highborn. I am but a mere village girl."

With a quick flick of her wrist, Lady Fraser waved her concerns away. "Firstly, Broden is third...no, fourth born son of a local landowner. He has nothing more than the McRainy last name."

Once again, Flora returned her attention to Broden, seeing him through new eyes. Handsome, courageous and from a family in high esteem to her laird. Marrying him would prove not only advantageous to her in her current situation, but a man would be good for her son.

"If he agrees, I am not against it." Upon speaking the words, it was as if Broden sensed their attention because he turned to them. The piercing gaze went from Lady Fraser to her. Then to her utter dismay, it lowered down from her face, scanning her body as if assessing if she was worthy of his bed.

Lady Fraser cleared her throat. "I will admit to him being a bit of a rake. But I do think once he settles..." She left the rest of the sentence unsaid. "Come, let us see about the day's meals."

As they made their way to the back entrance of the keep, Flora turned to look over her right shoulder toward where the men continued to spar and met Broden's gaze. His eyes narrowed for a moment before he gave a slight nod.

Obviously, he suspected they had been talking about him. A warrior did not survive many battles without sharp senses.

Flora caught up with Lady Fraser. "Have ye spoken to him about this?"

The woman looked up to the sky. "Not yet. I wished to get yer reply first. Like I said, I am sure he will be a good husband to ye."

She didn't have to think about it. Despite the fact that she had not consider remarrying, two years had passed since her husband's death. "I am agreeable to a marriage between me and Broden McRainy."

The cook looked up when they entered. "Lady Fraser, I was about to send a lad to find ye. What do ye think of lamb?"

As the women discussed the meal, Flora went to find her mother and son. The warm sun would be beneficial for them both.

Her mother sat in a chair by the window of the room the three of them shared. Flora would not dare complain as it was quite kind of the laird and his wife to give them a place to live. Better a sturdy roof, warm food and safety, than remaining in the cottage with a leaky roof and having to figure how to procure their meals.

"I came to fetch ye and Hamish. The day outside is beautiful. The sun will be good for ye."

Every day, her mother looked worse. Pale and drawn, she did not look like the same woman from just a month earlier. Flora could barely look at her without crying and, yet, she managed to smile. "Come, Mother, ye can sit while I finish my work in the garden."

"Of course, dear." Her mother stood and wrapped a shawl around her narrow shoulders. Before she could try to lift Hamish, Flora took the toddler's hand.

Together, they walked slowly outside.

Her mother turned her face up to the sky. "I am so glad ye came for us. It is indeed a beautiful day. I will help ye."

"Ye can sit and watch after Hamish. The rascal has become quite adept at escaping."

"I can do both," her mother insisted and, before long, they worked side-by-side. While Flora worried about her mother's energy and how tiring the work would be, she also understood the need to feel useful and to make one's way in repayment for kindness.

"I am not so unwell that ye have to constantly keep watch over me." Her mother gave her a stern look. "It was my stomach. It pained me to eat for days. Until this morn. I feel so much better. Eileen suggested to boil a mixture of boiled herbs. Today, I ate without pain."

The news made Flora smile. "I wish ye would have told me, Mother. Ye must continue to drink it."

"There is already much for ye to worry about without adding my aches and pains to yer list," her mother replied with a soft smile.

"Mother," Flora began. "Ye never married after Father died. Why?"

After a moment, her mother replied, "I had ye and yer sister to look after. Besides, my parents were always there to help and give us what we needed. I didn't feel a need for it." She looked at Flora for a long moment. "Is there someone ye wish to marry?"

"Lady Fraser asked that I consider it. To one of the guardsmen."

"Ah." The corners of the ill woman's lips lifted. "Ye are not averse to it, I presume."

Her mother knew her well because, immediately, her cheeks heated, and she realized that it was true. Broden was handsome and his body was enticing. Not that she'd ever seen him bereft of clothing. But it was easy to imagine upon watching him in only a light tunic and breeches when sparring. The perspiration had caused his clothing to cling to every part of his powerful back, arms and legs.

"If ye are to marry again, I would be very happy for ye."

Her heart swelled with love for the woman who'd stood by her through thick and thin. No matter if she married or not, Flora vowed to never be away from her mother. It was right that she take care of the woman who'd always been there for her.

"I miss Catriona," Flora said. "Since I'm not sure what my duties are since she left, I feel a bit adrift."

"Did Lady Fraser not say?"

Flora shook her head. "Now that I think about it, I should have asked for what my responsibilities would be. She did comment on how my hard work has not gone unnoticed."

"That is good then."

❯❯❯❯❮❮❮❮

AFTER NOTICING LADY Fraser and the widow, Flora, speaking, Broden noted that the women studied him for a long time. Whatever was said, he would find out. Flora had been a companion to Catriona. Perhaps with Catriona gone, Lady Ross was trying to find her a new position. Yes, that had to be it. One of Catriona's duties had been to keep the guard's clothing mended. Perhaps it was to be Flora's job now.

The niggling feeling that something was afoot, however, did not abate. He scanned his surroundings, noting that the guards continued to spar. Those that were done, now stood talking while waiting for their breathing to slow.

Actually, it was good timing if it was mending the women spoke about, as he'd noticed several tears in most of his tunics. The one he currently wore was practically a rag hanging from his shoulders.

"Deep in thought about something?" Keithen approached and looked toward the house. "Hungry?"

"Aye, very much so. It is still a long while until last meal."

Without having to discuss it, both knew that if they went to the kitchen, Eileen, the cook, would grumble but give them something to eat.

"What is to happen to Flora, the widow?" he asked Keithen. "I saw your mother with her earlier. They were watching us."

Keithen's shoulder lifted and lowered. "I do not know. She will be kept on as we cannot very well turn away a widow and child."

"Child?"

"Yes. Her mother and son live here with her. They have rooms in the servants' quarters." Keithen motioned with his head. "Ah, there, ye see? The boy is there with her in the garden now."

The child toddled about the plants, bending every once in a while to touch one and then yank another out of the ground. Flora and another woman, who he presumed was her mother, were deep in conversation and did not notice the devastation the child was causing away from their watchful eyes.

When the boy let out a happy scream, the women turned. Both he and Keithen had to wait to see what the reactions would be.

"Oh, no!" Flora cried out and hurried to the child. The boy let out a happy yell and did his best to get away.

His mother caught up with him and lifted the boy into her arms. She peered at the boy's dirty face and shook her head. "Ye should not pull plants. I know ye see me doing it, but I know which are good ones."

"I put back," the boy pronounced, squirming while still holding plantings in his tiny fists. "Down."

She kissed his brow and placed the little boy on the ground. The child toddled to the area where he'd pulled the plants out and shoved both hands into the ground, doing his best to replace them.

Clear laughter rang out as his mother watched over him. "Very good. I love ye so much."

Broden looked away and continued toward the kitchen. No matter how long he searched his memories, he was sure he'd never had an experience like that with his own mother.

CHAPTER FIFTEEN

CATRIONA LEANED ON the back of the bedchamber door, her chest heaving from a mixture of anger and confusion. Why had Ewan kissed her? Worse yet, why had she responded?

The man was not to be hers and despite being convinced she was strong enough to keep an emotional distance, it had all shattered at the touch of his lips to hers.

With a huff, she paced the length of the room. She thought on the way he'd looked at her. Instead of warmth, there was only coldness in his gaze. It was obvious he no longer felt anything for her. If anything, the kiss was further proof of it.

The only reason he'd kissed her had been to prove how easy it was for him to step away. The kiss had not affected him in the least.

Her hands curled into fists as she turned and paced in the opposite direction. The gall of the man. How was it that he could turn emotions off so easily? Why did she, after months of fortification, crumble at the first touch?

When someone knocked on the door, she stopped walking. "Come in," she said in a weary voice. She took a breath and did her best to appear composed.

"Ye will not guess what happened!" Esme stormed in. "It's the most peculiar thing."

Catriona needed a distraction, so she went to her friend and pulled her to sit. "Tell me what has ye so anxious to share."

"Elspeth and Gisela were in the great room when Ewan happened upon them," Esme began.

Catriona sighed. Not exactly a distraction. However, curiosity got the best of her. "He approached them?"

"I think so. As ye know, he is to be laird of the lands north of here. He walked up to them and casually asked that Elspeth assist him in finding a wife."

"A wife? He already has one."

"His marriage was dissolved prior to him leaving Uist. No one knows the reason. Whatever the cause, Ewan is not married. Broden's information was wrong."

Her heart sank. She'd never given Ewan an opportunity to tell her the truth. After all he'd done for her, she'd doubted him instantly. Instead of approaching him and asking for clarification, she'd turned him away.

"I am not sure what to think."

Esme's eyes bored into hers. "Ye must speak to him. If he is to marry, ye were his first choice."

"I turned him down. Besides," Catriona added, "it is obvious the man detests me now. Ye should see the way he looks at me. Pure disdain."

"He was hurt, and his pride wounded, but I am sure if there were feelings once, they remain still. Ewan is not indifferent to ye."

Considering her lack of skills and general nervousness, Catriona doubted there was any way she could ever pursue a man effectively. "I will not interfere in his quest for a bride. I had the opportunity and lost it. If anything, he deserves a woman who will never doubt him."

Esme frowned, her gaze sliding to the side. "He did ask for something very specific."

"Such as?"

"A meek woman who would not question him."

Despite the pang in her chest, Catriona could not help but laugh. "Ha! He would grow bored in a day. Why would he wish for a woman with no spirit or opinion?"

A thought occurred to her. "Do ye think me meek?"

This time, it was Esme who laughed. "Not even when ye were recovering. Ye have always been headstrong and stubborn."

"True, I can be."

Her friend studied her. "Ye are the best adviser. I was very fortunate to have had ye as my friend to keep me from doing the wrong things. It could be that ye should consider what is happening. What would ye say to yerself, if ye were not ye?"

"Somehow that made sense," Catriona said with a sad smile. "I would tell myself to allow Ewan his freedom. He should marry whoever he wishes, whether a wilted weak woman or otherwise."

"Bah!" Esme exclaimed. "Ye should pursue him. Tell him that it was all a misunderstanding. Perhaps, do not disclose it was Broden who told ye, because it will seem ye took another man's word..."

"That is exactly what I did," Catriona said. "I need time to think. Even if it is to help find a good wife for him. I owe Ewan that much. He should not marry a simpering dull person, but someone who will be a proper laird's wife."

When Esme's brows lowered and her eyes narrowed, Catriona reached for her hand. "Whatever ye are planning, do not do it. Ye are impulsive and never have good ideas when it comes to matters of the heart."

"It could be," Esme started, "that Malcolm is already considering who Ewan should marry. With him being laird, he must make a good match in order to form alliances with the neighboring lairds."

Catriona had not considered that. It was true. If anything, with his new lairdship there was the added benefit to Clan Ross of another strong alliance. Her heart sunk. Of course, it mattered not what Ewan wished for or even her for that matter. Nothing was ever easy when it came to clan life.

"I have mending to do," Catriona said, standing.

Esme studied her. "I would never take ye for someone who would give up on love so easily. My goodness, ye carried on after Keithen for years. And now that ye finally meet the perfect man, ye are giving up so easily?"

"He is to go to Uist. He may return with a wife," Catriona replied. "This trip of his gives me time to consider things. Right now, I am hurt and feel foolish for what I did."

Patience was not Esme's strongest attribute, so Catriona met her friend's gaze. "Esme. Give me the time."

"Oh, very well. But allow me to say this. If ye were to speak to Ewan alone before he leaves, it will give him fodder for thoughts while he travels."

Catriona decided it was best to heed her friend's advice. After all, what could it hurt to apologize to Ewan. If nothing else, he did deserve that much. Whether he no longer cared for her or not, it was the proper thing to do.

IT WAS FOOLISH to do so, of course, but just before dawn, Catriona went to Ewan's bedchamber and knocked softly.

Just as she was about to knock a second time, the door open and a disheveled Ewan stood in the opening. He blinked several times, until recognition was followed by the hardening of his face. "What in God's name do ye want?"

"I wish to speak to ye before ye leave." Catriona did not wait to be invited in, but pushed past him.

Upon turning, she noticed he only wore a long-sleeved tunic and no breeches. Immediately, she looked up from his bare legs. "I must tell ye something. I just ask for a moment of yer time."

Ewan crossed his arms and gave her a bored look, followed by a wide yawn. "I cannot imagine anything ye can say that is worth my loss of sleep. I have a long journey ahead of me."

There was a flicker of something akin to regret for the words he'd spoken, immediately followed by him looking away. "Go on."

There was no need to prolong the moment. It was best to say what she had to say. "I am so very sorry to have doubted ye. I was wrong to not explain to ye my reasoning for turning down yer offer of marriage. Ye were a good friend to me. Ye were there when I needed someone to lean upon. I hope that one day ye will find it in yer heart to forgive me."

He closed the distance between them until she felt the warmth of his large body. "What brings this on, Catriona? That I am laird now? That ye gave up the opportunity to marry a man of standing?"

At the words, she took a step back. "How dare ye?" Fury like she'd not felt in a very long time flickered deep in her gut. Why had he changed so much? Did he actually hate her now?

"I can think of no other reason for this sudden change of heart. Ye had plenty of time to write, to send a message to me. I was in the northern post for many months."

"I didn't know the truth."

"I'd hoped ye would be gone when I returned," Ewan retorted.

It was Catriona that closed the distance this time. "Why? Because ye still have feelings for me? Because yer pride was hurt? Ye knew very well that I would not immediately accept a proposal. I needed time to make the right decision."

"Ye told me ye were to marry Broden."

She'd forgotten about that. It had been an impulsive statement. In actuality, when Broden had announced he was to return to Fraser lands, Catriona had made it clear there would be nothing between them. Her heart was broken. She wanted time to forget Ewan.

"Someone told me ye were married. That is why I said no."

"Who?" His mouth formed a tight line as he waited. He didn't seem to believe a word she said.

Catriona thought for a moment. She didn't want to say it was Broden. That would only make things worse. "A guard. Someone who'd been with ye at Fraser Keep. Ye told him, or a group of them when ye were drinking. I do not know who all overheard."

Turning his head, he looked toward the bed. When he faced her again, all he did was give a slight nod. "Very well, Catriona. I will accept yer apologies. Please go."

"One last thing," she added. "I care for ye a great deal and am hopeful that one day we can be friends again." Catriona placed her hand on his forearm. "Safe travels."

His gaze fell to where her hand was, but he remained still.

Catriona hurried from the room as tears threatened. Ewan would never be her friend again. By his body language and expression, he wished to put everything that had to do with her behind him.

At least she'd taken the opportunity to say what had to be said.

Upon returning to laird over his own lands, she would rarely see him. It was best she resign herself to being Esme's companion. To live the simple life of servitude. It would be easy and best to keep away from thoughts of marriage. At least for the foreseeable future.

People beginning to mill about in the great room made Catriona pause. No one looked in her direction, yet she hoped not to be seen leaving from the direction of guards' bedchambers. She turned way and hurried toward the kitchen.

For some reason, every member of the laird's family seemed to find themselves in the kitchen speaking with the head cook, Moira, who handed out warm porridge, advice and encouragement in equal measures.

It was Kieran Ross who sat alone at the table this morning. Although his presence gave Catriona pause, she was through being afraid of men who had no intention of causing her any harm.

His hazel gaze lifted to her, and he gave a slight nod by way of greeting.

"Just who I wished to speak to," Moira said, motioning for her to sit. "I was just telling my dear boy about a beautiful village that I once visited, just past Fraser lands. But I cannot recall the name of it."

"There are several," Catriona replied, accepting a cup of hot cider. "What stood out about it?"

As Moira described the village, Catriona studied the quiet man. His bond with the cook was interesting. She'd sighted him there in the kitchen in the early mornings more than once. Although he remained quiet, it was obvious that he felt comfortable there.

"Ye must be speaking of Mulling," she finally said.

"Yes, that is it," Moira replied with a wide grin. "There is talk of a magical fae in the nearby woods around it that has kept it safe from attack for centuries."

The warrior gave Moira an indulgent half-smile. "I will keep an eye out when traveling through and if I see one, I will capture it for ye."

"Oh, I wouldn't wish to trap a poor wee creature, but perhaps ye can ask if they can send some to live up here. Keep ye safe up here."

Catriona could not tell if they were serious or not. She waited for the next silence before speaking. "How long do ye think ye'll be gone?"

One of his broad shoulders lifted and lowered. "Perhaps as short as a sennight but, in reality, I would say a fortnight."

"I am sure they will not be long. There is much planned for setting up Ewan as laird," Moira exclaimed with a broad smile. "A celebration and then we will have to start seeking servants for him."

"It seems rushed," Catriona said. "The keep must be built first."

"There is a small home already there," Kieran said. "It will be forti-fied and rooms added. However, it will be ready for Ewan to move there in a short time."

Moira rounded the table and placed a hand on Catriona's shoulder.

"Lady Ross is to speak to ye about it. I suggested that ye could help with setting up the home and hiring the servants. She alluded that ye wished for new responsibilities. Perhaps ye could be the housekeeper there since Laird Ewan is not married."

"I couldn't possibly…" Catriona could not think of a good reason to refuse. She had no other duties at the moment, and it made sense, since she was not married and not tied to remaining there at Ross Keep. "Oh, goodness."

CHAPTER SIXTEEN

D ESPITE THE CHANGE in season, Ewan could not warm up. He
shivered in his makeshift bedroll and considered leaving the
slight warmth of it to add wood to the bonfire.

Finally, unable to take it anymore, he pushed out of his bedroll and
grabbed several pieces of wood that he threw into the fire.

"Ah, yes, thank ye," someone called out.

"One of ye could have done it," Ewan grumbled. But he smiled
knowing he, too, had been waiting and hoping someone else would
add wood.

The heat from the flames was instant. He went back to his bedroll
and pulled it just a bit closer to the fire and then slid between the folds.

In the morning, they would arrive in Uist. They'd make their way
across the water in bìrlinns and be greeted by whoever was sent.
They'd sent a scout ahead to announce their arrival so his family
would not be caught unaware.

When the sun rose, everyone moved quickly, attempting to warm
themselves by moving about as it made little sense to add wood to the
fire at this point.

Kieran came up to Ewan. His cousin looked to him and then away.
"Is there anything ye require me to do upon arriving?"

"Aye, can ye be present when I tell my brothers about my becoming laird? I will require a show of support from Malcolm."

"Of course." Kieran frowned. "Anything else I should know?"

Ewan wondered many times while traveling if Una remained there at the house. Hopefully now that his father was gone, she'd been sent away.

"I hope not to see anyone but family. I presume the burial ceremonies are over. The main purpose of this visit is to see my mother and siblings. There is no reason for me to pay any kind of homage to my father."

Kieran waited, not saying a word, but obviously wishing to know a good reason.

"My father fucked my wife. I caught them together, saw with my own eyes. I almost killed him. My brothers tore me away. I demanded she be sent away."

Ewan took a breath, looking toward the trees. "When my father refused, I left."

When he looked to Kieran, there was no pity in the warrior's gaze. His eyes were flat, as if he heard this type of thing regularly and it ceased to surprise him.

"I will endeavor to avoid that topic of conversation."

Ewan laughed. "Cousin, sometimes ye surprise me. Who would guess the most intimidating of the Ross brothers had a sense of humor?"

After a simple meal, they mounted and rode toward the shore. At the scent of the salty ocean air, Ewan closed his eyes and inhaled deeply. It was the one thing he missed the most, the smell of the ocean. He also missed the sounds of lapping waves upon the shore.

There were three birlinns waiting, each of them manned by four men. Two would be for their horses and one for Naill, Kieran and him.

Ewan immediately recognized several of the men. He called them out by name and was given warm greetings in return. The trip over the water was swift. Ewan looked anxiously over at the larger vessel where Ban was. The horse was used to the water, but it had been some time since he'd been on it. Nonetheless, the silver animal kept its head down, seeming to be asleep.

"My horse looks like it's about to jump over the side," Kieran said, his gaze locked on the animal. "If he does, I will be most cross."

"At who? Me or the animal?"

"Both," Kieran replied.

Thankfully, Kieran's horse remained safe and once they landed on Uist, both men and Naill mounted again.

It wasn't long before Ross Keep came into view. The large keep was surrounded by planting fields which were kept by local villagers.

The wall that surrounded the home was not as tall as the one at Dun Airgid, mainly because they fought most battles at the shores and not at the keep.

However, if it came to it, the gates would be closed and archers posted atop. It was a safe fortress.

Ewan straightened in his saddle. Soon, he'd be faced with familiar faces and he was admittedly happy about it. Just as they neared, three men on horseback headed toward them. Kieran turned to him with a questioning look.

"Darach, Stuart and Gideon. Duncan is missing. He lives away from the keep with our half-brother, Calean. I am sure he will turn up later."

When they got close enough, Ewan called out greetings and his brothers returned the greetings to him, Kieran and Naill.

As a group, they rode through the gates. Introductions would be made once they were indoors.

"How is Mother?" Ewan asked Gideon, the youngest brother.

"She is in good spirits."

In other words, his mother, who had stopped caring for the late laird, was now free of him and his various lovers. It was on the tip of his tongue to ask if Una was gone, but he refrained. There would be time for that later.

The courtyard was well kept, just like he remembered. Everything in its place. The one thing his late father had passed down that was useful was his penchant for orderliness.

They dismounted and gave instructions for the care of the horses before heading into the house.

At the top of the stairs was his mother, her arm weaved through his sister Ella's. Both were beautiful in their own right and beamed upon his approach.

"Welcome home, Son," his mother said before hugging him tightly. "I hope ye have returned for good."

There it was. The one thing he feared: breaking his mother's heart again when she learned he was to never return to live there.

"We have much to discuss," he told her and pressed a kiss to her brow. "I have missed ye, Mother." When Ella pressed against his side, he placed an arm around her. "And ye as well."

Once inside the great room, he waited for everyone to be together and he began introductions.

First he named Kieran, son of their father's first cousin. There were the expected astounded looks by his mother and sister at Kieran's attractive looks. Then he introduced Naill, head archer for Clan Ross. Finally, he motioned to his family and introduced them in order. First Darach, who was to be the new laird, then Stuart, and Gideon. Finally, he introduced his mother and, lastly, Ella.

It was Darach that spoke next. "Our brother, Duncan, and half-brother, Caelan, live away from here in another family estate on the southern end of the isle. We have a large family home there from where we can better keep watch over the large village there."

Kieran nodded in acknowledgement and everyone went to sit around a long table in the great room.

Servants quickly brought food and drink, which Ewan was extremely grateful for. He was quite hungry.

While they ate, his brothers filled him in on what had occurred while he was gone. It seemed that the youngest, Gideon, had won many a competition in the games and Stuart had recently become engaged. Ewan wasn't used to being center of attention. It was nice that his family was glad to see him.

Everyone ate and continued speaking. It was curious that no one brought up his father's death. Even his sister, who'd been utterly devoted to their father, did not bring up his name. Finally, after lingering much too long, Naill was shown to his rooms so he could rest.

Ewan asked to speak to Darach and his mother. Of course, his other siblings insisted on being present and he could not deny them.

They sat in his father's study, which instantly brought back memories he wished to push away. When Darach stood behind the desk that his father had spent many hours at, it was instantly clear that things were to be very different now.

Unlike their father, Darach Ross would be a decisive but fair leader. Darach was first a warrior and second a man who put the needs of his family and people before anything else. Since young, he'd been raised to be laird. Thankfully, he'd been taken under their uncle's wing, since their father showed no interest in training the young boy and later man to rule one day.

Darach was actually Ewan's half-brother. His mother had died birthing him. He was muscular in the right places and lean where it mattered, looking every bit a laird.

"Once we found out ye were coming, I held back on taking my oath until yer arrival," Darach informed him. "It is only right that all of us be together for this."

Ewan nodded and let out a breath. "I am honored to be present. Ye will be a good and fair laird. I have no doubts ye will lead the people well."

By Darach's questioning look, Ewan knew his half-brother suspected he had more to say. "What is it?"

The room was crowded, with the four Ross siblings, Lady Ross and Kieran. Stuart and Gideon had to stand against the wall.

Despite having prepared exactly what to say, in that moment, he hesitated. Just then, there were voices and his brother, Duncan, and half-brother, Caelan, entered. They each greeted Ewan with a hug. Then seeming to sense tension in the air, they took their places and stood by the door and wall.

"I have something to tell everyone," Ewan started. "Malcolm Ross has granted me a large parcel of land as well as a home. Part of my accepting the land is that I will be laird to the people there."

There was a stunned silence. It was rare for someone to be given such a large gift, especially a second cousin.

Darach looked to Kieran. "Why not ye or yer brother? Is it a land that is under threat?"

Kieran nodded. "There are always threats in our region. However, the area that my brother granted to Ewan is fairly peaceful. A laird is much needed there as it is very far from our keep."

"And yet none of ye would take it?" Stuart asked.

This time, Ewan answered. "There are only three brothers, Malcolm is laird, Tristan manages the hundreds of warriors and Naill and Kieran are tasked with not only the army of archers, but also guarding the northeastern borders. One of them must remain near at all times in order to ensure the safety of the laird and the family line."

"Our other cousin, Ruari, lives in a home near the keep and has no desire to go to live farther away from the family as his wife is a Fraser and he has given his oath to go to their defense if needed," Ewan explained.

"And he prefers breeding horses and such," Kieran added.

Once again, there was a long silence. Finally, it was his mother who spoke. "It is a great honor to be mother to not one, but two lairds."

"I will not bow to ye," Duncan said, punching Ewan's shoulder. "Ye will always be my younger brother."

"I am everyone's younger brother, except Gideon, and will continue to be. However," he added with a smirk, "when ye come to my home, ye must address me as Laird."

"I have a hard time imagining that will happen," Stuart quipped, and everyone laughed.

Kieran pushed away from the wall. "If ye do not require that I remain, I must admit to needing sleep." The warrior looked anything but tired. Obviously, he wished to give them privacy as a family.

WHEN KIERAN LEFT, the family began telling Ewan of things that had happened. They kept to light topics until he began to yawn.

"We should let him rest," his mother announced and everyone began to drift from the room.

When the men lingered, Ewan realized they would speak of what happened the night before he'd left.

"Father kept her here for many months. Finally, Mother demanded she be sent away, and she went to live in a house in the village," Stuart said. "She remains there, along with two bairns now."

Knowing the woman was not there made Ewan feel better, however, he still wondered at times if the eldest was his son. According to his calculations, the child could to have been conceived while he was gone. Una had tried to convince him the child had been born early, but the babe was well formed and quite large.

"What about my marriage?" Ewan asked. "Was it dissolved?"

"It was," Darach replied. "Soon after ye left."

He was free. He could marry, raise a family of his own and be laird. In that moment, he wanted to know more about what the position entailed. He looked to Darach. "I hope to spend a few days with ye and learn what I can."

Darach nodded. "I expected that Mother would try to convince ye to remain."

Obviously, there was more Darach wished to say on the topic as he waited for Ewan's response. His family had always been close. In a way, they had to be in order to stand united against the ruthlessness of the patriarch. Their father had done his best to divide the brothers, to bring some to hate the ones who disobeyed him.

It had worked when they were younger, until they grew up and realized how unbalanced the man truly was. Their father's animosity toward Caelan, the son from his mistress, had driven Duncan to move out of the family home.

While, the other brothers often went from one home to the other, depending on what occurred at the keep, Darach had always remained. The eldest knew he'd be laird one day and had done his best to stay there to keep an eye on whatever his father did.

"I miss being here. This will always be my home. I am thankful that ye are at the helm now," Ewan said. He met Darach's gaze for a long time. "I hope ye and the rest of the family will travel to my new home to visit."

Darach nodded. "Of course."

THE BEDCHAMBER WAS dark and a bit cool. Ewan sunk into the bedding and visions swam before him.

His arms wrapped around her body, pulling her under him, needing access to every delectable inch.

She squirmed under him, her lips curving as his hardness pressed against her inner thigh.

"I am hard for ye," he murmured, looking into her beautiful amber brown eyes. "So very hard."

It was then the enticing pink buds caught his attention, and he took to them with unreserved hunger, sucking on one and then the other while her moans of pleasure enveloped him.

The creaminess of her skin delighted his senses, each satiny inch passing beneath his fingertips as he trailed them lazily up her legs until reaching her apex.

Her mound fit perfectly in his palm and he slid a finger between the moist folds. Her moan was like music.

At the same time, her hands were all over his body. She dug her nails into the back of his thighs and bottom.

Lowering her head, she licked lightly over his nipples until he, too, let out a moan.

Finally, he thrust into her body and the grip of her sex around his length brought a gasp that seemed to echo in the darkness.

Again and again, he plunged fully into her, the sound of flesh against flesh floating around him. It would not be long. He'd not last. That was a pity as he hated the thought of their time together coming to an end so soon.

Bright heat pooled between his legs and Ewan's body quaked with the need to release.

"Kiss me." Her soft whisper played in his ears. "Kiss me, Ewan."

His mouth opened wide in a silent scream as every inch of his body grew taut and then he came, his seed spilling, hot and wet.

To his dismay, she disappeared.

Ewan rolled over to his side, his hand still tightly gripping his manhood. It wasn't the first time he'd done it...thought of Catriona while pleasuring himself.

Blowing out a breath and looking around the empty bedchamber, he was glad to have the room alone. Hopefully, he'd not been so loud that Naill, who slept next door, overheard.

He had to marry. He needed a woman. It wouldn't do to continuously dream about a woman he could not have.

Catriona's last words came to mind. She'd come to him and apologized and admitted to caring about him. He'd not meant to be cruel when insinuating that she'd only done so because he was to be laird.

Although it was actually the first hurtful thought that came to mind.

The accusation, as unfair as it was, had served its purpose. Catriona had become angry. Of course, he knew she wasn't the kind to marry for position or title. It was not in her nature. She'd left everyone behind to be with her friend.

He was the one who'd convinced her to travel so far. The new location and home had, in fact, proven to be the best thing for her.

She'd grown stronger, more outgoing. According to Esme, Ruari's wife, Catriona was more like the woman she'd been before the attack.

As much as he wanted to trust her, experience had taught him that love was a dangerous thing. It was the act of exposing oneself to be torn from limb to limb, left for dead without the ability or the energy to defend oneself. Catriona had not touched her heart when turning down his marriage offer. She had sent him away without any regard for his feelings.

The woman he married would be someone unremarkable. Not so much in looks, but someone whose personality and manner would not be attractive to him. He wished for a good wife, a good mother, but not someone he could ever love.

Then again, that could be Catriona, because what he felt for her now was indifference.

CHAPTER SEVENTEEN

C ATRIONA SAT BACK, her mouth open.

In the room, Malcolm and his wife, Elspeth, watched her with interest. Elspeth smiled. "It shouldn't come as a surprise. I know he proposed to ye before."

This time, Ewan was asking for her hand in marriage through the laird and his wife. He wasn't present as he'd told them it would be easier for Catriona to make the decision. She looked to Esme, who seemed to be holding back a smile.

"It is not funny," she finally said to her friend. "Why is he proposing so formally?"

Malcolm cleared his throat. "I believe it is because I had to approve the match. He is to be laird and things are done through negotiation."

"What are the terms?" Esme asked since she was there as Catriona's family's representative.

"Nothing unusual," Malcolm replied. "Marriage within a fortnight, word sent to the Frasers and yer family so they can attend. Live together at Tuath Avon."

Then by the change in the laird's expression, there was to be another term that was not usual.

"What else?" Catriona asked.

"That ye cannot take a lover. Any children must be from him."

"Why would…" she stopped, knowing it had to do with his previous wife. "Anything else?"

"No."

Catriona contemplated the terms. In truth, she could never consider anyone else to marry. And she would never insult Ewan by turning him down a second time. She lifted her chin and met the laird's gaze. "I will marry Ewan Ross."

"If ye will remain here for a few moments, I do believe he wishes to speak to ye." Elspeth smiled warmly at her. "I do love the idea of planning a wedding."

When they walked out, Catriona looked to Esme. "Does this all not seem overly formal to ye?"

"In his defense, ye turning down a proxy would not be as personal, I suppose." Esme looked to the door. "I best go."

For some reason, Catriona wanted to beg her to stay. The Ewan who'd returned from the northern post was not the same man she'd known up until then. He'd changed.

Ever since returning from Uist, she'd not had an opportunity to speak to him. There had been constant travel between there and his new home as they'd done all kinds of preparations to ensure it was habitable.

Catriona herself had gone there to help clean and organize, each time spending three or four days. He'd never been there when she was. It seemed whenever she headed back to Ross Keep, he left to go to his new home. And so, she'd not been around him for many weeks.

Even before seeing him, she felt his presence. Ewan entered the room dressed casually in a loose green tunic and tan breeches. He wore boots and his hair had recently been cut. Still, the dark waves fell almost to his shoulders.

"Catriona," he said, his hazel eyes meeting hers. "I am glad to know ye have accepted my proposal."

She stood. "I was surprised by it. I thought ye did not care for me."

His mouth opened as if he were to say something but thought better of it. "We should set a date."

He'd not made to move near her. In truth, she'd expected an amorous encounter as he'd never shied to approach her before...before he'd gone away. Before she'd turned him down.

Instead, he went around to the other side of the desk.

"As ye will know, the house is almost ready. We only require a few staff members. Moira assures me that she has that matter well in hand."

Unsure of how to handle this new Ewan, Catriona decided to act as if nothing had changed between them and they remained friends. "I will require at least a sennight for my family to be sent for and return. Once we marry, I will be ready to relocate to Tuath Avon."

"About the wedding," Ewan said, his gaze touching on her only for a moment before sliding away to somewhere past her shoulder. "I would hope we can settle for a small affair. No need for more than the family to attend. There will be plenty of festivities once we arrive at our home."

Catriona wasn't sure if he wished to keep things small because of her, or because it was to be his second marriage. Either way, it was something she'd not considered yet. Usually, it was the groom's family who handled the plans and intricacies of a wedding. In their case, neither lived with their immediate family.

"What of your family, Ewan?" Catriona asked. "Will they be in attendance?"

"No. I extended an invitation for them to come once we are settled. I expect Mother, my sister and several of my brothers may come then."

When he didn't offer any other explanation, she decided at the moment it wasn't important enough. There were many questions lingering in the air, she had but to utter them. Yet, there was something about Ewan, a sense that he wished to be anywhere but there, alone with her.

"Why?" Catriona uttered, but then hesitated when his eyes flashed to hers. "Why are ye marrying me?"

Something akin to dread settled in her chest. The tightness of when one expects bad news. She tried to convince herself in the moment of silence that she was being silly. The longer she waited for his reply, the harder it became to breathe.

"I wish to marry ye, because ye will make me the perfect wife. I trust ye to be true, and to not seek to betray me."

It was the strangest of answers. Each word strung together almost haphazardly, not making much sense. But because, in that moment, she too wished to leave, Catriona nodded as if understanding exactly what he'd meant.

><<

THE WEDDING WAS as Ewan had dictated, quite small. The three Ross brothers and their wives, Ruari and his wife, along with Ian McElroy and Naill Hay, both members of the guard, and their families all sat in the chapel to witness the marriage.

From Fraser lands, both Laird and Lady Fraser had traveled, along with Flora. Her parents and sister, minus her brood, had traveled with the Frasers, making her feel special that Laird and Lady Fraser had ensured they traveled in comfort.

All through dressing and allowing the women to fuss over her appearance, Catriona couldn't shake the feeling that something was amiss. Since their engagement, Ewan had not once called upon her to walk in the garden. Nor had he sought her alone for any reason.

For goodness' sake, they'd slept in the same bed while friends. And now as an engaged couple, they'd not even shared a kiss.

According to Esme, he had been overly preoccupied with all the preparations of having to take over new responsibilities. And in truth, he seemed to spend every waking hour with Malcolm, either in the laird's study or with the guards. When not with the laird, he'd been gone to Tuath Avon for days on end.

She let out a breath studying herself in the mirror. The woman who stared back was pale, but not unattractive. Someone had added a pinch of color to her lips and cheeks, which Catriona had to admit was quite flattering. She wore a pale green dress, her favorite color. It had been made for her by a local seamstress who was extremely talented by the way the gown fell so perfectly, enhancing each curve of her body.

The long sleeves fell just past her elbows before falling in a cascade of fabric, hanging beautifully from her arms.

A veil was placed on the crown of her head and allowed to fall down her back. Catriona wasn't sure why they'd gone to such lengths to ensure her hair was pinned just right when the veil would cover their creation.

"It is time," Elspeth, Lady Ross, announced.

The chapel smelled of fresh flowers, all sorts. Usually, one kind was chosen for a wedding. But in her case, it was like a field of wildflowers, bouquets of different colors hanging from the end of each pew.

Her lips curved at seeing the familiar faces turn to her with expectation. Then upon meeting Ewan's frosty gaze, Catriona only felt one strong emotion.

An unwavering urge to flee.

He did not plan to love her, quite the contrary. It was as she'd inwardly known all along. The reason Ewan Ross was marrying her was because he would never love her and, for him, it was exactly what he wished for in a wife. Someone to control, keep in hand and who would bear him children. A perfect partner, but nothing more.

Catriona's footsteps faltered and her father looked to her, a questioning look, but said nothing. They continued forward, her legs heavy now, as if she dragged an anvil from each ankle.

Knowing it would be impossible to keep from either crying or glaring at Ewan, Catriona did not meet his gaze. Instead, she kept her eyes downcast, raising them only when the priest asked that she repeat the vows and, even then, she kept them on the clergyman.

By contrast, Ewan kept his gaze on her face. She could feel it. His voice was clear and without any hesitation as he recited the words.

They were pronounced husband and wife and the kiss was as chaste as one between a brother and sister. Or of strangers mistakenly kissing on the lips when meaning to kiss each other's cheek. A lump caught in her throat until she thought she'd choke from it.

"Breathe," Ewan whispered into her ear. "Relax. It is over."

"On the contrary, my laird," she murmured back, finally meeting his gaze. "The farce has just only just begun."

His eyes widened, but he did not say anything in return. After all, what could he say? Deny the truth that he'd tricked her into marrying him by playing on her guilt over hurting him?

What a fool she was to think he was the same person who'd been so kind to her. Ewan Ross had changed. Perhaps from his time at the northern post or because of his trip back to Uist. Or even, a combination of both. Whatever it was had turned him into a stranger, someone she could not claim to know.

"This is the most beautiful wedding I've ever been to," her mother exclaimed, her face bright and eyes shining with unshed tear. "Ye look so very beautiful. Like an angel."

"A bit pale," her sister interceded, studying her closely. "Is yer bodice too tight?"

"I think it is," Catriona said, happy for an excuse not to cause her sister or mother to worry about her. "Perhaps we can steal away to a private room and ye can loosen it a bit."

Her mother smiled indulgently. "I think ye can withstand it another few moments. It will be suspicious for the bride to disappear so soon after the vows have been spoken."

"Well look at ye," Catriona teased. "So well versed on etiquette."

"I have asked Lady Fraser for counsel," her mother replied with a light blush. "The entire way here, she told me all about the duties ye will be expected to perform. I plan to ensure that ye spend as much time with her while we are here so that ye can be prepared."

Catriona hadn't considered it. In truth, she had little idea of what would be expected of her. Now that she thought about it, both Lady Fraser and Lady Ross barely seemed to have time to themselves as the duties of running a keep were many.

Thankfully, she'd have that. She would have the distraction of running a household to keep her busy and from having to spend time with a husband who she did not respect.

"I would be eternally grateful for that, Mother," Catriona said, meaning it. "I am so very glad ye bring it up, as I'd not given my future duties much thought."

Together, they walked into the great room where Ewan, surrounded by his cousins, seemed to be enjoying themselves with rousing toasts and loud laughter.

"Men are so basic in their actions," Esme said, rolling her eyes. "I can only wonder how they would ever get on without women to guide them in daily necessities."

The other women laughed. Catriona could only stare at her new husband, who seemed to have already forgotten her existence.

"Should he not be sitting here with me?" she whispered to Esme. "Should we not be toasted as a couple?"

Esme's eyes narrowed. "What happened?"

"What do ye mean?" Catriona regretted her questions. Now, Esme would suspect not all was well between her and Ewan.

"Did ye exchange words? Are ye cross with each other? Ye seem perturbed."

"I am a bit," Catriona said with an exaggerated pout. "He should be fawning over me at this moment."

As she'd expected, Esme laughed loudly. "Ross men do not fawn. I would pay dearly to see it."

The laughter made Ewan turn to them. Catriona pretended not to notice, joining Esme with soft chuckles.

"Bending over and kissing our feet would be a good start," Esme said between giggles.

"Bowing as we pass by," Catriona added. As much as she didn't quite feel up to being jovial, the picture of any of the Ross men acting that way was comical.

Finally, the meal was to begin. She and Ewan were seated next to Laird Ross at the high board.

Ewan acted the part of the dutiful new husband, ensuring to place food on her plate and filling her cup with sweet mead. He asked about her well-being and listened as she told him with sarcasm that she was doing so well, it was hard to imagine a happier time in her life.

Hazel eyes met hers and, for a flicker, she thought to have seen the old Ewan, but it could have been her imagination as they was flat when she studied them.

⇻⇺

"YE DO NOT have to submit to me until ye are ready," Ewan said when they finally went to what would be their shared bedchamber until they moved to the new keep.

Catriona brushed the tangles from her hair. Already in her nightshift, she hadn't expected there would be any type of formal bedding ceremony. Everyone was aware of how delicate her situation was and, therefore, any talk of what would happen once they were alone was left unsaid.

Well, except for a few drunken men who'd picked on Ewan.

"I will do my wifely duty by you."

Ewan didn't reply. He went to the wardrobe and began undressing. Once he disrobed, he donned a white oversized tunic with long sleeves and went to the hearth.

She couldn't help but slide a look to his muscular legs as he bent to add wood to the fire in the hearth. The room brightened when the flames grew larger, and also grew warmer.

Unable to delay the inevitable, Catriona stood and went to the bed. A part of her wondered how ready she actually was to be taken by a man. Shivers traveled down her spine.

Would it bring back the nightmares? The visions that would appear out of nowhere, forcing her to relive the horrible episode of her life.

She slipped between the covers, at this point, shaking so hard that she could barely keep her teeth from chattering.

"Come here," Ewan said, joining her and pulling her against his side. "Relax."

Unable to keep from it, she clung to him, her fingers digging into the fabric of the tunic. "Do it, please, quickly."

IT OCCURRED TO Ewan that Catriona had never been made love to. She was, for all intents and purposes, a virgin when it came to intercourse.

At the moment, she shook so hard, it was as if she were naked out in the snow. He held her gently against his body and ran a hand down her arm and the other across her back, soothing the woman.

Despite the fact he did not love her, he did care and would never do anything that would bring any kind of distress.

In a ploy of distraction, he took her mouth with his. Kissing her gently, softly lingering in one place before trailing his lips to the edges of her pouty lips.

He continued the soft kisses until her body finally stopped shaking so violently and now only trembled just enough that he felt it.

That night, he would not take her, nor perhaps the next. Even before the wedding, he'd decided it would be Catriona who would initiate intimacy. Ewan knew enough to realize that because of her traumatic experience, it could be no other way.

"Sleep," he whispered, pressing kisses to the side of her jaw, then trailing his tongue on a path down her neck.

Catriona gasped when he cupped her breast, allowing the pad of his thumb to circle the pert tip.

"Rest," he said, his mouth moving back up from the enticement of her breasts. "I will hold ye all night."

When she let out a long sigh, he realized she was relieved. At the same time, perhaps subconsciously, her hand rubbed his shoulder almost as if she tried to calm him in some manner. It was not meant for him, but a way of her settling, so he accepted it for what it was.

CHAPTER EIGHTEEN

T HE LIST OF duties and responsibilities made Catriona's head spin. The women had gathered in Lady Ross' sitting room. Some embroidering, others mending, a pair with bairns on their laps, everyone discussing the topic of running a keep.

Ladies Fraser and Ross were the most vocal, which was understandable as they were, in fact, doing the work that was required of a laird's wife.

"By far, my most enjoyable task is visiting those in need. Whether in the village or neighboring farms," Lady Ross said with a wistful smile. "I do hate when winter sets in and I cannot venture out."

Lady Fraser nodded. "I agree. Mrs. McKay will attest to the fact that I spend many a day visiting and bringing food to widows and orphans in our village. There is always much need," she said, referring to Catriona's mother.

They'd already given her lists of what to have on hand to give out to travelers and the needy. They'd also provided her with detailed explanations of how to treat those in service at the keep and who to trust and hold in higher regard among them.

A housekeeper, a cook and several maids had already been hired. A companion had not been chosen yet, but Catriona was considering the young woman who'd been caring for her since her arrival. Maisie was sweet and quite proficient at ensuring her needs were met.

"May I ask," Catriona said looking at Elspeth Ross, "will ye protest to me asking Maisie to be my companion?"

Elspeth thought about it for a moment. "I will not. Ye may want to include her brother, one of the stable lads in yer offer. They have no other family."

"I will ask her then," Catriona replied with a smile.

"I am sad not go be going with ye," her mother said. "But the weather will soon turn cold and I must head back with Lady Fraser."

Catriona kissed her mother's cheek. "Audra must see about her children as well. Do not worry, all will be well. Next time ye visit, ye will be coming to my home. I insist ye bring all the bairns so ye both can stay longer."

Lady Fraser and her mother and sister were to leave the following day. Soon after, she and Ewan, along with their companions, would be leaving for Tuath Avon.

It has been over a week since the wedding and, still, she and Ewan had not had relations. If anything, the man's patience was beginning to wear thin on Catriona.

Every night, he kissed her, touched her, caressing her breasts until she wanted to scream. It was heavenly for those short moments and just as passion threatened to overcome them, Ewan stopped. He'd then kiss her on the forehead and tell her to sleep.

"Would ye like to walk in the garden?" Esme asked her. "I need fresh air."

Catriona practically jumped up, glad to be away from the stuffiness of the room. As much as she was delighted to be with the women, she wanted time alone to ask Esme questions.

Seeming to sense they were not invited, no one made to join them.

"What is going on?" Esme asked as soon as their privacy was ensured. "Ye seem totally unchanged at being bedded by yer husband. I expected some sort of...oh, I don't know. Distress perhaps?"

Catriona let out a breath. Her friend knew her better than anyone else. "It is because nothing has occurred between us. Kisses, caresses, but that is all. I do not believe my husband desires me, which I suppose I should be thankful for."

"Has he said anything to ye about it?"

Biting her bottom lip, Catriona thought back to their wedding night. "He said that nothing would occur between us until I was ready."

"And are ye?" Esme asked, studying her with interest. "Do ye think ye are ready?"

"What exactly should I be ready for?"

Esme's lips curved. "Do ye feel heated? A sort of pooling between yer legs?"

Catriona's eyes widened at the exact description, especially the night before when Ewan had kissed her longer than the previous times. "Aye. I do. My body seems to crave more."

"I believe ye are ready."

"What do I do?" Catriona asked.

Pacing before her, Esme looked up to the sky as if for inspiration. "When a man is aroused, he becomes hard. His member, between his legs."

Catriona shuddered at the thought of a man's hardness. She'd experience first-hand what they did with it. It had been painful and humiliating.

"Not like that," Esme said quickly, seeming to understand where her mind went. "It turns hard, but the skin surrounding it is so very silky."

"Is it?" Catriona looked at her friend, interested in knowing more.

"Ye will become moist, making it easier for him to enter ye. The heat will only be sated by his cock, not that it's cool or anything." Esme giggled. "But the movements...oh, the way he will slip in and out of ye, will bring ye to…"

"What?" Catriona asked, entranced now.

"Well," Esme looked around to ensure no one could overhear. "It will bring you to lose all control. Ye will not know whether to scream or laugh at the wonderful culmination it will bring. Then just as ye feel as if ye can take no longer, ye will shatter and float."

Her eyes rounded. "Float? Ye mean fly? Like a bird?"

At this, Esme guffawed. "No, silly, not physically, but it will feel as if ye're are indeed flying."

"It sounds delightful. No wonder ye always are in a hurry to drag Ruari to yer bedchamber," Catriona exclaimed. "I do not know that I can keep from insisting Ewan take me." Her face fell. "Does a couple have to be in love for these occurrences to happen?"

Esme frowned. "As long as there is attraction, I think it happens."

THE DAY DRAGGED by. Every hour seeming to take twice as long. During last meal, Catriona and Esme kept exchanging glances, each doing their best to keep from smiling.

Finally, Ewan turned to her. "What is so funny?"

"I do not know what ye mean," Catriona replied much too quickly. She bit her bottom lip at the mistake. "I have not laughed."

"Ye and Esme keep exchanging glances as if ye are sharing a secret."

"We are," she admitted. "An anecdote ye would probably not find humor in."

He let out a sigh and turned his attention back to his plate. Ewan was so utterly handsome, his dark hair framing a face that could only be described as beautiful.

And yet, he remained cool to her. Other than when they were in bed, he paid her little heed.

"Mother and my sister leave in the morning," she told him. "I will be sad to see them go."

He glanced in the direction of where her parents were seated. "I am sure they will return for a visit. I have extended an invitation to yer father."

She'd not considered he may have spent time with her father until that moment. "Ye and he spent time together?"

"Yes, a bit. We went for rides several times."

"Where to?" Not that it mattered, but she was shocked to know as her mother had not mentioned it.

"He wished to speak to me about ye and about the situation that may present itself. He wanted to make sure I was prepared, for instance, if ye go back into seclusion."

Her heart broke for her father. Of course, he was worried about her. After all, she'd spent an entire year sequestered in a small room after the attack.

"I hope ye reassured him."

Ewan gave her a droll look but said nothing. He knew what to expect as he'd been there when she was still reluctant to be around people. Had even gone so far as to attack those who'd participated in hurting her.

It was redundant of her to ask, and yet, she wished for her father not to have any worries. There was already much he'd had to endure.

"I assured yer father," Ewan said, meeting her gaze, "that I will never expect more from ye than ye can give and, in return, give ye all my faithfulness."

A vow. It was spoken, however, as if he were telling her the weather outside. Without emotion. Had he said them thus to her father?

Finally, it was time for them to retire. Any thought other than what she intended to happen that night instantly evaporated.

Could she do what Esme had instructed? Was it indeed possible to have enjoyable relations with a man who cared little for one?

It had been almost step by step and quite descriptive. Just thinking about it made her cheeks hot.

When he joined her in the bedchamber and prepared for bed, she'd already climbed into bed. She lay on her side facing his wardrobe and watched as he undressed. "Ewan, are we to leave for Tuath Avon as soon as my family departs?"

He looked over his shoulder at her. Unclothed from the waist up, the muscles of his back mesmerized her as he continued preparing for bed.

"There is no need for us to continue here. I must return. There are many duties awaiting me there. The people have been without attention for far too long."

"Yes, of course," she replied and then lifted up to her elbow. "I will need another day. Can we wait? I am going to ask Maisie and her brother to accompany us. She as my personal maid and he to work at the stables. Ye see, they are family and I do not wish to separate them."

His shoulders lifted and lowered. "Fine."

When he joined her in bed, Ewan seemed surprised that she looked at him with expectation. Every night before, she'd kept her gaze down, waiting for him to begin the routine of kissing, before he turned away and fell asleep.

For a moment, it was a bit awkward, but he leaned forward and pressed a kiss to her lips. It was a perfunctory kiss, not lingering or promising more. "Goodnight."

Before he could roll over, Catriona cupped his jaw and held it steady as she inched up and close enough to cover his mouth with hers.

Then as Esme had instructed, she allowed her fingers to trail just over his skin down the side of his neck. She let out a sigh and parted her lips.

According to Esme, he would take it as an invitation to push his tongue into her mouth. After which, she was to suckle it gently.

Her heart skipped when he did just that, and she let out a soft moan to encourage him. Then following her precise instructions, she pressed her own tongue against his while at the same time running her hand across his shoulder.

She wore her nightshift and he a light tunic, but the heat of his body seeped past the fabric when he pulled her closer.

They'd gone this far several times, so she was prepared for it, responding to his touch, the lingering of his hand on her hip. But instead of remaining still, as she'd done every night, this time she moved her midsection forward until their bodies touched.

For a moment, she thought she had failed in her attempt at seduction because Ewan stilled. His breathing caught when she broke the kiss and allowed her lips to trail to his ear.

"Make love to me," she whispered.

It was as if a dam was torn with a single hit, waters exploding forward without restraint.

Ewan took her mouth again, his wonderful body trembling with barely held back passion. He was holding back for her, doing his best not to bring her harm, while at the same time unable to stop from taking what was offered.

Inch by inch, his hand slid up her leg, past her thigh until her night shift was lifted to her waist on one side. She untied the fastenings and pulled the garment up over her head.

Ewan fumbled with his tunic and removed it until there was nothing between them.

Gently, he pulled her close until their bodies touched and then seemed to hold his breath. It was strange how soft his skin felt. At the same time, it was so firm and different. His sex twitched against her lower stomach and Catriona gasped.

Ewan rolled her onto her back. Lying beside her, his sex against her side, he maneuvered himself until his face hovered over hers.

Once again, he took her mouth. The kiss was hard, deep and passionate. At the same time, his fingers skittered across her skin. Each place he touched from the top of her thighs across her stomach was divine torture.

She lifted a bit when his hand lingered just above her sex. Esme had told her that one way a man prepared a woman for intercourse would be to slide their fingers down the center of her sex.

The anticipation made her squirm. Already, she ached for his touch, the heat pooling in her core uncontainable.

When his fingers touched her sex, Catriona let out a moan. "Yes," she whispered, encouraging him. "Yes."

Ewan needed no further encouragement. His hand cupped her sex, one finger pushing through the folds and into her wetness. "Ye are more than ready for me," he murmured.

When he lifted to climb over her, his gaze met hers. "If ye say stop at any time, I will."

Catriona couldn't fathom why she'd wish for him to stop. Instead of a reply, she placed her hands on his hips and guided him between her legs. If the man didn't hurry, she could not take responsibility for her actions.

Then as he took himself in hand and prepared to enter her, she held her breath. She waited for fear, for terror, but when he took her mouth again, all she could sense, feel and smell was Ewan.

And he was all things beautiful and good in her world. Their bodies came together in a way that was perfect, not with hatred or with intent to hurt.

"I will be gentle," Ewan said and prodded at her entrance. Once again, Catriona held her breath, then slowly released it, recalling what Esme had said.

"In the first moment, when he is about to join with ye, yer instinct will be to hold yer breath and be still. Do not. Instead, relax yer body and prepare for what will be just wondrous."

He pushed into her, ever so slowly, the entire time kissing and caressing her.

Truthfully, it was pleasant enough, but not as enjoyable as she'd been led to believe. Once fully seated inside, Ewan hesitated.

"Are ye well?" His gaze met hers. "Catriona?"

"Is this it?" she asked. "I thought it was supposed to be wondrous. It is a tight fit is it not?"

He pressed his lips together. She wondered if it was to keep from laughing. Finally, he cleared his throat. "I will begin to move and I believe ye will find that to yer liking."

"Oh," she said then, "oh," again when Ewan pulled out a bit and moved back inside.

The more he drove in and out of her body, the more she wanted him to continue. Every ounce of her being and every sense went taut with anticipation of whatever it was that floated just beyond her touch.

"Ewan," Catriona exclaimed and dug her fingers into his bottom. "Oh, my…"

She thought she was prepared for what was to happen. Goodness, Esme has been quite explicit, but there were no words, she now realized, for the elation that occurred.

"Ah!" she cried out when something inside her finally gave way and burst, sending tendrils of heat down her legs and up her stomach. Whatever happened, also sent her reeling, the world disappearing until all she could hear was Ewan's hard breaths and then his own hoarse cry.

He fell over her, still buried deep inside her. A moment later, he shuddered and she wrapped her arms around his waist, needing him to remain still.

They were both wet with perspiration and gasping for breath. Catriona closed her eyes, memorizing the moment. Mentally, she sorted each sound and scent. The soft breeze that fanned over them, the reverberations of the firewood crackling, barely audible over the heaves of their breathing.

The odor of their bodies was different than before lovemaking. It was to be their scent, she imagined.

Then she ran her hands up Ewan's back and then down to the swell of his bottom.

He lifted and pulled out of her. Then Ewan looked down at her, his face shadowed. "Was it enjoyable to ye?"

"Yes," she replied quietly. "I do believe it to have been wondrous."

"Wondrous?" he repeated the word, a touch of humor in the tone. "I agree."

When he pulled her over his chest and let out a long sigh, she couldn't help but wonder what he thought at the moment. Did he feel more for her than he'd insinuated? Probably not. According to Esme, lovemaking was a natural thing for men, unlike for most women, for whom it was more of an emotional occurrence.

She knew this, of course. Her sister often told her that even when angry, her husband would try to join with her. Catriona had not understood at that time. But now she figured if she was ever cross with Ewan, making love would be a good way to release emotions.

"Hmph," she said out loud, then hoped he'd not heard.

"Ye thinking of something?" Ewan asked, his words slurring with sleep.

Catriona let out a breath. "Aye, of things I was told regarding men."

"Ye should rest," he said. Then not even a moment later, she heard a soft snore.

The steady lifting and lowering of his chest gave Catriona a sense that Ewan had no worries, and no reason to doubt the days ahead. Sure, he was about to take on many duties but, for him, it was the culmination of his life.

As fourth-born, he could have never aspired to what had just been given to him. He was to be a leader of people and would assume the liability of the people that he was to govern over.

Like her husband, Catriona, too, was about to step into a role so much above her station, she could barely fathom it. Lady Ross was to be her title and, like her husband, her responsibilities were many more than what she could have ever imagined.

There was a shakiness to her breath as she exhaled. Tomorrow, her family would depart and the beginning of a new chapter of her life would begin.

⋙⋘

"WHERE IS YER husband?" Catriona's mother asked while wiping tears. "I wish to tell him what a precious gift we leave in his hands."

She'd not seen him since rising and now that her parents departed, she expected Ewan to be present. "I do not know. He must not be aware that ye are leaving at this moment."

"We should go," her father said, giving her a warm look before pulling his wife toward the carriage.

Already, Lady Fraser was in the front carriage, along with her companion. Her parents and Audra were to ride in a separate one. Coming to stand beside her, Esme took her hand. "It is always hard to see Mother off. Then once she's gone, I am relieved." Her giggle made Catriona smile, just a bit.

Her friend did her best to distract her from the slight of Ewan not being there to see her parents go. Even though she'd already scanned the courtyard, once again, she looked from one end to the other for a sign of Ewan.

They waited until the carriages disappeared through the gates before heading inside. "Do ye wish to go upstairs to see their progress?" Elspeth asked her, pointing to the ceiling. "From my balcony, ye can see for many miles.

"That would be nice," Catriona replied as they walked inside. Already, people were gathering for hearings with Laird Ross. She hesitated to scan the room. With an annoyed huff, she followed the women to the stairwell.

Just as she was to go up the stairs, she noted that a pair of maids headed toward her and Ewan's bedchamber.

"Excuse me for a moment, I will be up shortly," she said to Esme and Elspeth and crossed the great room. Upon entering the bedchamber, the maids were already packing Ewan's clothing.

"What are ye doing?" she asked and both jumped, staring at her with mouths agape.

"Miss…er, my lady," one stammered. "We were directed by Laird Ewan to pack his belongings."

Her eyes narrowed with annoyance. "And where, pray tell, is my husband?"

The maids exchanged curious looks. One swallowed visibly. "He left this morning, my lady. I believe to yer home."

Catriona tried hard to give the impression of nonchalance but knew she'd failed miserably when, once again, the maids looked to each other.

"Stop doing that," Catriona snapped. "He must have told me last night, but I didn't hear him. Yes, that is it. I am sure of it."

When the maids remained frozen, she waved them to continue. "Go on then. Were ye told to pack my things as well?"

They both shook their head.

Catriona whirled around and stomped to the kitchen. Surely Moira would know what had happened. Moira knew everything.

When she entered, the cook greeted her with a cheerful smile. "By the look on Laird Ewan's face this morning, I take it ye had a good night."

The woman winked and Catriona blushed even though, at the moment, she was very angry with said laird. "Moira, did my husband leave any word for me? He told me we had to depart soon, but I did not understand that he meant today, nor that he was to leave me behind."

"All he told me was that ye would follow in a couple of days. I asked if he wished his things sent with ye or earlier and he asked they be packed and sent right away."

"I see," Catriona frowned. "I suppose we must work on understanding each other better."

Moira nodded. "Aye, lass, men are not always clear."

Knowing it was best to push her ire away at the moment, she hurried upstairs, hoping to catch a glimpse of the departing carriages.

In the bedchamber, the women had lost interest in the departure because they sat about the room on different chairs and chaises talking.

Elspeth and her friend, Ceilidh, sat together on a long chaise, while Esme and Merida sat on chairs by the fireplace. Esme motioned to an empty one. "They disappeared already, but not before I said a prayer of protection."

"Thank ye," she said and lowered to the chair.

"What is the matter?" Esme asked, knowing her well.

Catriona looked around the room at the faces of women who, like her, had not so long ago married a Ross. "My husband left for Tuath Avon. He did not say farewell and his belongings are being packed. Last night, I asked that our departure be delayed by a couple of days. He replied 'fine', which I took to believe meant he agreed for both of us to wait."

There was a moment of silence before the women all began to speak at once. Then they all stopped talking, laughed and one by one began to tell her stories of miscommunications between them and their husbands.

An hour later, they were laughing so hard that most were in tears. Catriona held her stomach in an attempt to stop the pain all the laughter caused and blew out a breath.

"I think," she finally said, "I will miss all of ye greatly."

Esme sighed. "Ye are but a day's ride away. I promise to visit often."

"Actually, I believe it is two days," Merida said.

"Ye have not seen Esme ride," Catriona informed her. "She does not care for dalliance."

"Not in the least. I can make it to Tuath Avon in less than a day from my home," Esme added. "I have to be at archery practice. Would ye like to accompany me, Catriona?"

They walked out together, and Catriona followed Esme to the room she and Ruari were currently sharing. While Esme changed, Catriona paced the room. "When do ye leave to go to yer home?"

"In the morning, I suppose. Why?"

"I would like to travel with ye and then on from there to my own home. I must speak to my maid and invite her to come along with her brother, who works in the stables. Giles, I believe his name is."

"Ye should tell her right away," Esme said. "Go do it and meet me outside."

Catriona headed back to her bedchamber to find Maisie. Once that was done, she'd instruct the young woman to pack everything.

CHAPTER NINETEEN

THERE WERE NO tearful farewells when leaving Dun Airgid, especially since Catriona and Esme expected to see each other soon. The women of Ross Keep planned to visit the following week to see the house.

However, upon riding away, Catriona fought back the urge to cry. How strange to never leave one's birthplace and then suddenly be thrust into a different location altogether, not once, but twice.

By contrast, Maisie's face was bright with excitement. "I've never been away from Ross lands," she exclaimed, looking out the window. "I suppose we are still not leaving them, so I should say, I've not been so far from Ross Keep."

Her eyes never left the passing landscape as if she feared missing something new. "What are we to call our new home Lady Ross? It will be confusing to call it Ross Keep as well."

"Tuath Avon," Catriona replied. "I must say, I do love the name."

Maisie repeated the words, her tone solemn when memorizing her new home's name. Then her lips curved. "Giles is quite happy. He looks forward to helping set up the new stables."

After a moment, both fell into silence. Catriona considered her new responsibilities and all that would come after this day. Most of the staff had already settled into the home. She'd spent time with them when assigning duties and shopping in the nearby village with the cook. It had also given her a peek of what kind of people were there.

Although she'd only met those in the market square, they'd been friendly, but cautious, which she didn't blame them for.

As soon as they entered the courtyard at Tuath Avon, there was a flurry of activity. It was endearing to see the people who worked there were doing their best to make a good impression. Catriona exited the carriage, assisted by a guard. Just then, Ewan exited from the home.

He didn't smile, his expression more interested than welcoming. Immediately, a lump formed in her throat. But she'd made a decision. No one would see the vast chasm between her and Ewan. When it came to personal matters, they would keep it behind closed doors.

One of the most important lessons she'd received from Elspeth was to protect their privacy above all else. Allowing for gossip to run rampant would soon make things go out of control with rumors spreading to the villages and other lairdships.

She forced a soft smile toward him. Ewan approached and kissed her cheek in welcome.

Meeting his gaze, she pronounced loudly. "I am glad to be with ye, Husband, and to finally make our home here."

If Ewan was surprised at her declaration, he didn't show it. Instead, he nodded and took her elbow to lead her into the house. "I am glad that ye have arrived. I know the staff is more than ready for their mistress." His tone was not exactly warm, but not cool either.

Inside the great room, there were two lines of people. The kitchen staff that included the head cook and two helpers, a pair of scullery maids, three lads who would work as helpers and a chamber maid. Across from them stood the stable master and his pair of helpers, a gardener and a man who would look after the livestock and another man, whose responsibilities were to ensure any repairs needed to the keep were done in a timely manner.

Thankfully, Catriona had the opportunity to meet most of them on her previous trips, so she was able to address them by name. They'd not hired a housekeeper, as she'd decided the house was not large enough for someone to take on the duty. Catriona would oversee the staff and ensure they completed all the work.

She looked to Ewan. "Have ye decided who will be in charge of the outdoor staff as yet?"

He nodded and motioned to an older man. "Aye, Owen. He will ensure all duties are completed as necessary."

The man, who was also the gardener, gave her a toothy smile. "I am most honored, my laird and lady."

The choice seemed strange to Catriona, as she'd expected it to be given to the stable master, but she kept her opinion to herself and gave Owen a warm look. "I am sure ye will do an outstanding job."

The rest of the day was spent ensuring all her items, as well as Ewan's, were unpacked. By the time last meal came, she'd barely had an opportunity to breathe.

"Lady Ross," Maisie said as she pinned the last tendril of hair up. "Ye look like ye are about to fall over."

Catriona looked at herself in the mirror. There were dark shadows under her eyes and her face was drawn. "Thankfully, there are no visitors tonight. I would make a horrible impression."

"Ye should rest well because, on the morrow, my laird has invited local dignitaries and their wives. All eyes will be on ye."

When Catriona groaned, Maisie giggled.

THE NEXT SENNIGHT at Tuath Avon passed without incident. Thankfully, Catriona and her cook, Iona, worked well together and soon had a good system going when it came to meals and such. The maids all seemed to get along well, and Maisie soon became well versed in the household gossip. She kept Catriona informed of all the goings-on, which she didn't discourage as it helped to ensure she could keep potential problems in check.

However, the situation between her and Ewan was not as smooth. Most nights, he stayed away until late, and when she woke, he was either already gone or continued to sleep. Other than a perfunctory kiss, he kept his distance from her when they were alone. In public, when there were visitors, he acted every bit the attentive husband.

So much so, he even fooled Esme, who was currently visiting. "I must say, ye and Ewan have the best run home I've ever been to," Esme said with a wide smile. "Ye are an amazing mistress."

"There is really not that much to do. The house is much smaller than Fraser Keep and although the staff is small, they are quite eager. For most of them, it is their first time in service, and they are very grateful for the wages."

"It shows," Esme said as they settled into chairs in Catriona's sitting room. "Ye must make friends. I hate to think of ye alone all the time."

Catriona gave her friend's comment some thought. "Several women have visited, but I have yet to find anyone particularly interesting."

Esme threw her head back and laughed. "Ye always have been hard to impress."

Just then, there was a clearing of throats at the doorway. Both Ruari and Ewan entered. Immediately, Catriona could not draw her eyes away from her husband. He seemed to grow more handsome every day and standing next to his cousin, with their identical hazel eyes, he looked every bit a warrior.

His gaze lingered on hers for a moment before moving to Esme. "I've come to issue a challenge," Ewan said.

Esme leaped to her feet, her eyes bright with excitement. "Archery?"

"Aye," Ewan replied, his lips curving. "At twilight."

It was the perfect time. No shadows to distract from the target. Catriona only knew this because of her many years of friendship with Esme.

"One arrow at a time," Esme quipped, lifting an eyebrow. "No trickery."

"Ye wound me," Ewan said, attempting to look serious, but then his lips curved. "I agree."

When the men left, Catriona looked to Esme, who studied her with interest.

Her friend remained silent, all the while scrutinizing her. At a loss for what to say, Catriona leaned forward, picked up her cup and drank the sweet cider.

"There is something in the air," Esme finally said, her eyes narrowed toward Catriona. "Tell me, what is it?"

There was no question that if she spoke, the dam would break and Catriona was not prepared to tell Esme that her marriage was not a love match. It was barely a friendship if she were to be honest. They didn't speak when alone, if they ever were. Ewan seemed to go out of his way to avoid her. It was only the one time that she'd initiated it that they'd made love.

"Fine, do not tell me now. But ye will before I leave." Esme picked up a sketch book and charcoal. Soon, the sounds of scratches on the paper filled the empty air between them.

"My marriage is not what I expected in the least," Catriona finally said. "Ewan does not care for me and goes out of his way to avoid me."

Her friend searched Catriona's face. "I can hardly believe it. He seems so demonstrative."

"In public, yes. If not for the fact I do not want the staff to talk, I would slap his hands away."

"What are ye going to do?"

Catriona gasped. "Me? Why should I be the one to do something?"

"I can speak to him, if ye wish me to." Esme crossed her arms. "I will not have ye unhappy."

If she were to be honest, she'd been too busy to consider herself unhappy. Yes, the situation with Ewan saddened her but, at the same time, she'd had plenty of time to grow accustomed to solitude.

"I am not unhappy. I am not content, either. Ye can say I've accepted my lot and am indifferent to it."

Esme huffed. "That will not do. Not in the least. I know that man cares for ye. His gaze follows yer every move. Even his countenance changes in yer presence. I will never be convinced Ewan Ross does not love ye."

"Love is a stretch," Catriona said with a halfhearted chuckle. "He can only just barely tolerate me."

CHAPTER TWENTY

"DO NOT BE a fool like I was," Ruari said.

They'd been riding for over an hour. Ewan was anxious to show Ruari his lands. Ban shook his head, the mane flying side to side and Ewan knew his steed tried to impress Ruari's huge warhorse.

"I cannot bear to be alone with her," Ewan admitted. "It will not take but a look from her and my armor threatens to fall away."

Ruari slid a sideways glance to his horse. "What is that animal doing?"

"He is trying to impress yers."

"Make him stop. He does realize my horse is male."

"My horse is indifferent to another animal's sex. He wishes to be loved by all."

"Does he mount yer enemies' horses while ye go to battle?"

"Not yet. If he does, it could be helpful, an unexpected surprise tactic."

Ruari laughed. "Ye and yer horse are both fools. There is nothing wrong with admitting loving yer wife. She is a good woman."

"I know she is. However, she turned me away before." He blew out a breath. "I do not wish to speak of it any longer."

They rode for a while longer. By the time they returned, it would be dusk and time for him to compete against Esme. Ewan doubted he could beat the woman, but he hoped to at least do as well as she did.

"Ye know Esme will beat ye today," Ruari began. "How will that look to yer people?"

Ewan raised a brow. "I am as competent as she is. I believe I can best her."

When his cousin chuckled, Ewan wondered if Esme would allow him to win so that he did not appear weak in front of those gathered. Then again, the only people he expected to be there were his guardsmen and a few from the village. The latter could, of course, return and spread news of his loss. He frowned and considered if he'd been hasty in challenging the woman.

"No, she will not lose to make ye look good," Ruari said before he could ask.

"I do not expect her to," Ewan snapped.

THEY RETURNED EARLIER than planned, as Ewan had lost his enthusiasm for the surroundings he'd been showing to Ruari. It turned out to be a good thing, because the newly assigned village constable, his wife and his brother had arrived.

Both the constable and his brother were men about Ewan's age. Although the brother seemed just a year or two younger.

The men were invited to sit at a table in the great room so they could speak of whatever issues they'd come to speak about.

Catriona appeared, dressed appropriately to spend time outside. Her dress had dark tones of green with a mixture of burnished brown. When she approached, the constable's wife acknowledged her and introduced her to the man's brother.

The constable's brother could not disguise his admiration for Catriona. Even when Ewan cleared his throat, the man had yet to look away from his wife.

Even more annoying was that Catriona didn't seem to notice. If she did, it was obvious she didn't mind. He'd feared meeting new men would affect her negatively, but his brave wife continued forth with ease. She welcomed the constable and his brother, who fawned over her and the constable's wife.

When she invited the woman to another table for a sip of honeyed mead, to his chagrin, the constable's brother invited himself along.

"Does yer brother live in the village as well?" Ewan asked the constable.

The man looked to him as if confused for a moment. "No, my laird, as I told ye, he visits from another village, north of here."

Obviously, while he'd been watching the younger brother with Catriona, he'd missed that part of the introduction. "So, he has a family there then?"

This time, the constable did not bother hiding his confusion. "He is considering moving to our village."

Ruari spoke to the constable. "I noticed yer horse. I do not believe I know the breed."

Thankfully, the question worked as the man began to tell Ruari about his horse's lineage.

"If there is nothing pressing, I must change. I have challenged Ruari's wife to an archery competition," Ewan said, standing.

The constable grinned. "No, my laird, I came only to introduce my brother. He wishes to ask for a position here as a guard, if one is available."

"He should be here speaking to me instead of there," Ewan said in a flat tone, looking to the table where the man spoke to Catriona.

This time, both men looked at him as if he'd grown a second head. "The constable asked if his brother could remain to speak to ye and ye said no," Ruari said. He followed with, "Are ye unwell?"

"I was distracted. There is something I must take care of. I apologize," he said to the constable. "Please remain for the night so that we can discuss more tonight."

The constable beamed. "My wife will be most pleased."

By the time he'd changed and hurried back down the stairs, everyone was already outside. He stalked to where the targets had been set up, annoyed that Catriona had not waited for him.

Being they had little to no communication, he couldn't blame her for not knowing what he wished. However, in his estimation, she should have considered that it would look good for them to walk out together.

Esme stood with Ruari. Whatever was said between them must have been private because he nuzzled her neck and she pretended to be annoyed. By the flush of her cheeks and her smile, she was anything but.

With a critical eye, he studied the targets, and then looked to where some benches had been set up for the spectators.

There were more people than he'd expected. Not only had a small crowd of villagers gathered, but also the servants and most of the guardsmen. He frowned at noting what looked to be bets taking place and wondered if most bet against him. If Esme's reputation had reached their ears, then most would probably side with the female archer.

At first, he could not find Catriona. But finally, he caught sight of her. She sat with the constable's family. To her right was the man's wife and on her left was the irritating brother. At the moment, she had her head bent toward the woman listening to something.

Meanwhile, the constable's brother hovered like a damned predator. A vulture would be a more apt description.

"I will go first," Esme announced, holding her bow up. The small crowd cheered. "Best out of five."

Ewan scowled. "We have not yet discussed the rules of the game or the prize."

"True," Esme said, her eyes scanning the surroundings until landing on his wife. "If I win, I wish ye to spend the night with Catriona outdoors, no shelter, only bedding."

"That is a stupid prize to ask for," he growled.

"Fine," Esme then said. "If I win, I wish for ye to remove all yer clothing and run around the entire keep with nothing but a hat on yer head. Hat of my choice, of course."

Ewan looked to where Catriona sat. They could not hear what was being said, but she watched them with ill-concealed curiosity. Just then, the damned vulture leaned into her ear and she smiled at whatever the idiot spewed. "I will sleep outside if I lose."

"With yer wife?" Esme asked.

"She will be angry with ye. But very well."

"What do ye wish for a prize if ye happen to win?" Esme asked, daring in her gaze.

"That ye ride on a horse facing backward the length of the field." He pointed over to a wide field.

"I would fall," Esme said with an astounded expression. "I am an able rider, but I must admit that I've never attempted to ride back-ward."

He waited until she finally met his gaze. "No matter. I do not in-tend to lose."

When they stepped up to the marks, the crowd silenced. Esme looked to him and gave him a narrowed look. She then turned to the target and shot. The arrow hit almost center, but just to the right.

Ewan grinned. It wasn't like the woman to ever miss. Perhaps she was a bit distracted.

Letting out an exhale, he stared straight then took his shot. He also missed, hitting to the left of the center.

There was a hush in the crowd as two guards who'd been appoint-ed to be impartial went and inspected the target.

They held up Ewan's arrow and the crowd cheered.

Esme huffed loudly and walked up to the mark. "I am not toying with ye any longer."

She pulled back, stood utterly still, then loosed the arrow. This time, she hit the target dead center, and then to everyone's glee, performed a happy little dance. Those gathered clapped.

Ensuring to keep his breathing even, Ewan stepped up to the mark. He let out a long breath, pulled back and released his arrow. It hit the target at almost the precise place as before.

The two guards inspected the target and held up Esme's arrow.

It was a tie.

They shot twice more. Ewan edged a win first, barely, and then Esme beat him. It finally came down to the last shot. Whoever hit closer to the center would win.

There was a hush, followed by murmurs as Esme went to stand at the mark. Ewan saw it then, a strange stillness about her. She didn't move, her feet planted perfectly, back straight. When she let the arrow fly, he didn't have to look to know she had hit the target perfectly. Dead center.

There were loud gasps from the crowd followed by claps. Then when he went to the mark, everyone once again silenced.

It wasn't that losing would be so awful. He would, of course, not mind spending time outdoors with Catriona. It was the consequences he feared. For days on end after making love with her, he could think of nothing else.

Every waking moment, he saw her face, heard the sounds she'd made when they'd made love. If he were to be alone with her, could he keep from taking her again?

He was close to losing control of his emotions. His heart ached for her, his body demanded her.

Ewan could not lose the match.

His booted foot on the mark, he stepped back with his right and pulled the bow taut. Concentrating on his breathing, he focused on the target, his vision directly on Esme's arrow.

On his exhale, he released the arrow.

There were exclamations, cheering and laughter. When he looked to the target, his arrow was not there.

"Ye lost on purpose," Esme challenged. "Ye missed the target altogether."

"Impossible," he said, stomping to the target. "Where did my arrow go?"

When he got close to the target, several of his guards ran out and began slapping him on the back. One laughed. "I would lose, too, if I was forced to spend the night outdoors with a beauty."

He looked over to Catriona, who'd paled. The constable's wife was obviously telling her about the bet he and Esme had made.

When she met his gaze, she quickly turned away, but not before he caught the look of something like disappointment.

Then she turned to the constable's brother and said something.

Perhaps they'd planned to steal away and now his win had dashed the plans. No. Catriona would never do that. Ewan instantly felt horrible for allowing his jealousy free rein.

Jealousy? Yes, that was exactly what he felt. It ravaged through him, especially when Ruari rushed to Esme, picked her up and turned in a circle. The couple was laughing wildly as if they were alone in the world.

"I am sorry ye lost." Catriona had come up to stand beside him. "Ye did well until the last one," she continued and lifted to her toes to place a chaste kiss on his cheek.

The people in the stands began to stomp their feet, calling out for a full kiss.

Ewan pulled Catriona into his arms, leaned her back and as he lowered to take her mouth, looked to where the constable's brother watched them.

The man smiled. Obviously, he'd not expected to spend time alone with Catriona.

He kissed her fully as those around them began to cheer loudly.

When they straightened, Catriona was flushed. She smiled shyly toward the where the people were, but never looked at him.

She walked alongside him as he went to greet the people. Since it seemed he'd lost on purpose, they could not gossip about his lack of ability. In a way, this was the best conclusion.

"Outdoors. In the courtyard? Or out in the field?" Her expression was sullen.

He shrugged. "Esme didn't specify. I suppose we can sleep in the garden."

"Very well." Catriona remained for a few moments, chatting with people that were visiting. Most were invited to remain for last meal. She then went toward their home. Probably to prepare for the meal, and for their night out.

It could also be his wife was about to give Esme an earful. Although, Ewan doubted she'd find the couple since they'd suddenly disappeared.

CHAPTER TWENTY-ONE

CATRIONA STOPPED SHORT of knocking on the door of the bedchamber Esme and Ruari were currently using. And using it they were. For a moment, she stood still listening to the sounds of their lovemaking.

If only she and Ewan had the same passion. There was no mistaking the attraction between Esme and her husband. They seemed to fight for privacy every moment they were together. As happy as she was that her childhood friend had found the perfect match, her heart ached each time she witnessed their devotion.

Turning away, she decided it was best to prepare for last meal. Once that was done, she'd have to be ready to sleep outdoors.

Only Esme would try to do something that would force her and Ewan to spend time alone. Then again, without the distraction of others, perhaps they could finally talk.

Catriona was not a fool. She was fully aware her husband did not love her. As a matter of fact, he acted as if he didn't particularly care for her in the least.

Most days, she was lucky to catch a glimpse of him any time other than at last meal. True, there was much to do and his duties as laird were many but, to her, it seemed as if he invited more work.

Just two days earlier, there had been a large group of farmers who he'd invited to come and share about their crops. The group, along with wives and children, had filled the great room to capacity.

Next was the archery tournament. The house would be filled with villagers. Afterward, Ewan was to leave with Esme and her husband to spend time with Ruari learning about warhorse breeding. Although Catriona had been invited to come along, she was forced to remain behind as the wife of a McLeod was scheduled to come for a visit.

In truth, she was excited to meet Paige McLeod, who'd married Alec, the laird's first-born son. According to Elspeth, she and Paige had much in common. Paige had been a village girl who'd stood up to both the McLeod and the Ross to defend men she loved.

When Catriona changed to look more presentable for last meal, she entered the great room and, as expected, Ewan was surrounded by men who seemed to be picking on him good-naturedly about losing to Esme.

"It was obvious he lost on purpose," Esme said, coming up behind her and weaving an arm through Catriona's. "Yer husband could not help it. Spending the night outdoors in the fresh air with his beautiful wife is not a consolation, but a prize."

"Ye are incorrigible," Catriona replied. "I cannot say I look forward to sleeping outdoors."

"Where are ye to make yer bed?" Esme asked with a smile. "The woods, the creek or perhaps atop a tree?"

"In the garden," Catriona said and had to smirk at Esme's crestfallen expression.

Her friend frowned. "Right outside the kitchen?"

"I suppose it is." Catriona had not thought about all the people coming and going, passing by while they tried to sleep. "No, I think the other side garden would suit best."

"I should have specified outside the keep," Esme said, but didn't seem overly disappointed.

THE MEAL WAS long until, finally, Catriona leaned closer to speak into her husband's ear. "I am not sure exactly how to prepare for tonight," she admitted.

Already, bedding had been set up for them in the back of the house, between a wall and what was to be a garden once Catriona had time for it.

"I would wear something warm," Ewan said, giving her a side glance. "Perhaps one of those heavy shawls ye prefer in the winter."

A shawl and a heavy dressing gown. Perfect, she'd barely be able to move. With a soft huff, she stood and walked to the stairs. If her being bundled up is what he wanted, she would do the opposite. She was growing tired of whatever the game was that he played.

He pretended that she barely existed.

Two could do the same.

"WHERE ARE WE going?" Maisie asked, running after Catriona, who hurried through the home to a door that opened to the back garden. Servants were still there making what looked to be a love nest. Thick blankets had been spread along with decorative pillows and even some sort of posts on each corner with fabric spread laterally. They followed the instructions for there not to be a cover over them and had gotten creative to ensure them privacy and a bit of protection from the breeze.

"Very nice," she said primly. "Now, put another, smaller bed over there." She pointed to a space next to the wall.

The maids looked to one another. One finally spoke up. "We do not have any more bedding, my lady."

"Take this." Catriona pulled one of the blankets from the fancy bed. "Use that and a pair of these pillows." She stood still as they placed a thick layer of hay down and added the blanket she'd given them.

Maisie shifted from one foot to the other. "Am I to sleep here?"

"What?" Catriona turned to her. "Do not be silly. Ye will sleep over there with me," she said, pointing to the larger bed. "The laird will sleep here."

"Oh." All three maids froze and turned to her with wide eyes.

"I cannot possibly," Maisie said. "The laird will not be pleased."

"He cannot say much if we are already asleep. Now, come hurry. Take off yer shoes. Let us rest."

Thinking it a great game, the maids laughed.

⫸⫷

EWAN WAS A bit in his cups by the time he staggered out the back door to find his bed. Although Esme had been creative in her request, she'd not given enough specifics. He figured Catriona would be asleep and there would be no need to talk to her, or worse, compelled to kiss her.

Once outside, he stopped at seeing what looked to be a proper bed. The servants had certainly gotten creative.

He lifted the torch to get a better view, which he really didn't need as there was a full moon and enough light.

There, in what he assumed was to be where he'd lay his head, were two women, fast asleep.

Catriona on her side facing him and the maid, Maisie, rolled into a ball with her back to where he stood.

"Where in the devil am I to sleep?" Ewan muttered and then he saw it. A slim bedroll.

His wife, it seemed, was just as anxious not to spend time with him.

He'd show her. Ewan crept to the opposite side of where Catriona slept and not-so-gently scooped up the sleeping maid, who barely stirred.

He then placed her on the slender bedroll and pulled a blanket over her.

After, he lowered to the ground, removing his boots and breeches. Doing his best not to wake Catriona, he slid between the blankets and was immediately surprised at how comfortable the bed actually was.

He lay on his back for a while, looking up at the starlit sky. It certainly was stunning. He'd have to remember to thank Esme for giving him the opportunity to see the beauty of a night sky.

Catriona stirred and rolled to her back. In slumber, she was a masterpiece of beauty. Her long lashes fanning down over her cheeks, pink lips pursed demanding to be tasted.

His loins stirred and Ewan took a deep breath, forcing his gaze back up to the sky. But then she let out a soft sigh and he turned to her again.

Whatever she was dreaming of brought a slight curve to her lips. Probably thoughts of besting him that night.

His own mouth softened, and he chuckled. In truth, he missed their friendship. He missed the many many days they'd spent talking about inconsequential things while he tried to bring her out of the shell caused by the attack of Mackenzie guards.

She rolled back to her left side, her back to him.

Perhaps, it was time to begin again, to rekindle the friendship. Avoiding her and acting like an idiot was hurting the marriage.

Ewan rolled to his side and pressed a kiss to her shoulder. Then when she didn't wake, he wrapped his arm around her waist and pulled her against him. He nuzzled the back of her neck and pressed his erection between the orbs of her bottom.

What happened next was something he'd never seen before. Catriona let out a low guttural sound. It was animalistic, like a painful groan.

Her entire body shook so hard, he let her go. Then she began to kick and scratch her own skin. Sobs racked through her and she dragged herself away. The entire time, her eyes were squeezed shut. "No. No."

She gasped for air, almost as if it were impossible to get enough.

In the next moment, she was on the dirt, crawling to the corner where the short walls of the garden met. Once there, she began to mewl, her arms wrapped around her bloody legs.

He wasn't sure how much the maid had seen, but now Maisie sat up, her wide eyes taking in what was happening.

"Do not approach her," Ewan said. "Go inside and find Esme Ross. Do not alert anyone else. Hurry."

The maid scrambled away, and he went just a bit closer to Catriona, leaving enough distance between them not to scare her more.

"Catriona," he whispered. "It is me. Ewan."

She cried out and wildly batted the air between them with both arms. "No, no, no, no."

Her face was a mixture of blood, mud and tears and she looked so pitiful, he wanted to cry himself.

What had he done?

"What happened?" Esme and Ruari burst out of the side door. At once, Esme hurried to Catriona, lowering next to her and whispering in his wife's ears. Immediately, Catriona dissolved into heart-wrenching sobs and clung to Esme.

Esme looked to him with obvious pity and mouthed. "Go."

The dimness of the interior of his home fit his mood perfectly. He didn't bother with light and went directly to pour whisky into a glass and drank it down in two gulps. The whisky felt like a rock when it hit his gut and instead of the calming effect he expected, it was the opposite.

The mixture of the ale he'd imbibed earlier, the food and now the whisky bubbled in his gut until he had to run back outdoors and empty the contents of his stomach.

When he straightened, Ruari stood before him with arms crossed. "Are ye finished?"

Although Ewan was a large man himself, no one could compare to

Ruari. The huge warrior was broad of shoulders, muscular beyond compare and, at the moment, had a dark fury in his eyes that made Ewan want to take a step back.

Instead, he swallowed and waited to see if his stomach was settled enough for him to speak.

"Finished with what?"

"Acting like a fool. Pretending at marriage. Mistreating yer wife."

Fury boiled and he held an arm pointing in the direction of the garden. "I did not attack her tonight. What happened is a result of before…"

"I am not speaking just of tonight," Ruari snapped. "But of how ye have acted toward her. How in the bloody hell is she supposed to feel comfortable with ye? Do ye really think yer current actions are not what brought this to happen?"

When his stomach protested to his standing upright, Ewan threw up again. It was not the whisky nor the food that had him feeling sick. But seeing Catriona in such as state. Dirty and bloody, hair plastered to her face with the wetness of her tears. Surely, it had to be what she'd looked like when she was held prisoner.

Tears welled and he gulped back a sob. "What have I done?" He stumbled away from the house without a sure direction. "My God."

He bent over, attempting to settle his stomach with long breaths.

Ruari's feet appeared below and he realized that both of them were in bare feet and half-dressed.

"Ye are going to either vow to repair this, or she comes to live with us." Loathing dripped from each word uttered.

Ruari walked away.

CHAPTER TWENTY-TWO

A TRICKLE OF sunlight did little to brighten the room, but it was just right in Catriona's estimation. For a few precious months, she'd been back to herself. And now the thought of stepping past the doorway terrified her.

In the three days since the garden, she'd only seen Esme and Maisie. A messenger had been dispatched to McLeod Keep postponing Paige's visit, citing illness. It bought Catriona a couple weeks to regain control. Hopefully, it was long enough.

"That will not do at all," Esme said, plopping down on a chair next to her. "The color is horrible."

Catriona had been attempting to sketch but, in truth, her heart and mind were elsewhere.

"I think it matches the view perfectly." She was drawing the window, dark curtains pulled aside, fabric pooling onto the floor.

Esme sniffed. "I suppose the view is dreary."

Despite the sadness that pooled inside, Catriona managed a smile. "Ye do not like my taste in décor then?"

"I do," Esme began. "But not in this room."

They were in a small guest room, which is where Esme had directed she be brought from the episode in the garden. A small space would not be as jarring for her when in a fragile state. And although Catriona agreed, now she wondered if it would have been better to return to her own chambers.

"I am going to move to another bedchamber tonight, a larger one. I wish to speak to Ewan."

For the last few days, he'd asked to speak to her, and she'd not been willing, considering her husband did not love her and had no interest in her other than her duties as wife. Some of her duties anyway. Those that did not include intimacy.

Esme gave her a concerned look. "There is something I must tell ye."

There was no reaction in her mind or body. Catriona had stopped caring again. "What is it?"

"Ruari told Ewan that ye are coming to live with us," Esme said, holding her chin up a notch. "I agree with him. It would help in yer recuperation."

"I do not agree."

"Ye must," Esme replied. "It may be for the best."

Considering all the plans she'd had for her new home, Catriona wondered what would happen if she left. "This is my home, Esme. I may be in a loveless marriage, but I took vows, and it is my duty as Lady Ross to complete my tasks. Many couples live separate lives in the same home. I will survive well enough. This episode...well, it was bound to happen."

Moments later, after a rap on the door, Ewan entered.

She'd not seen him looking so poorly since he'd been injured and she'd nursed him to health. His jaw was bearded, there were dark circles under his eyes and his hair was uncombed. She paused for a moment, taking in his rumpled clothing.

"May I sit?" he asked, nearing hesitantly.

Catriona motioned to a chair. "Of course."

He reached for her hand, but then pulled back. "I am sorry. So very sorry for what I caused."

"Ye did not cause it, Ewan. It was inevitable. We both know what I've been through. Yer attentions caught me off guard and brought it on, but that is not yer fault."

"It is," he insisted. "For the way in which I've been treating ye. So distant. To suddenly thrust myself upon ye had to be...jarring."

Past the window, a flock of birds flew by, their wings in symphony, communicating with steady chirps. The day had become cloudy. Catriona wasn't sure if it was afternoon or evening. When one stayed in one place too long, it became harder to tell the passing of time.

"Do ye wish me to go with Esme? To live there? That way, ye do not have to work so hard to avoid me."

Silence was followed by the sounds of footsteps in the hallway. Servants hurried past as they went to start preparations for whatever mealtime it was.

"That is precisely what I wish to speak to ye about." There was sadness in his gaze. "I have been a bloody fool."

A question was on the tip of her tongue, but Catriona refrained and, instead, waited for him to continue.

"I have kept my distance because of fear and because of my foolish actions. I have caused ye and our marriage so much harm." This time, he did take her hand in his. "Do not leave me."

Catriona closed her eyes, hating the loss of the bond they'd once shared. "If I remain, I wish to move into another bedchamber. I do not wish to leave ye. I have duties, responsibilities here."

"Will ye stay in our bedchamber for a few days? Give me an opportunity to gain yer trust again?"

She'd been missing their comradery, the way she felt secure and comforted when he was with her. Was it still there?

Catriona stood. "Hug me." The words sounded hollow because, in truth, she didn't expect to feel anything. "I wish to see what I feel when ye do."

Her husband was hesitant, and she almost told him to forget it, but then he spoke. "I haven't bathed. Ye may be repelled."

Opening her arms, she waited for him to close the distance between them. Ewan came then, pulled her into his arms and held her tightly against him.

At once, the sensation of safety enveloped her. She clung to him and put her ear to his chest, listening to the steady beats of his heart. Everything seemed right in that moment. It was as if nothing could harm her, nothing could penetrate the invisible safety.

"I love ye, Catriona."

The hoarse words echoed against the ear she had to his chest. Catriona held her breath, unable to fathom that what he spoke was real or sincere for that matter.

"What?"

He pressed a kiss to her temple. "I love ye and I have been foolish in my attempts to keep it locked inside. I fear the pain of being rejected, of what happened in the past. But I have to be a man about it. I have to admit the truth and let what happens from now on come as it may."

It was not the most romantic declaration of love. That he declared his fear along with it, though, made it sincere and heartfelt.

"Ye should not fear," Catriona said. "I would never, ever betray ye."

"And I have done nothing but hurt ye," Ewan said, once again kissing her head. "I have failed as a husband."

She pushed again because, in truth, it was becoming hard to breathe and avoid the smell of his unwashed body. "We have only been married a short time. There is plenty of time to repair things between us."

"What about the other night? What if I cause it to happen again?" Ewan let out a breath and a distraught expression crossed his face. "Esme won't be close enough to help."

There was no way to tell how or when the next episode would happen. Catriona would not fool herself into thinking it would not reoccur. It was a part of her now, a burden she would have to live with.

"We will have to deal with it on our own. I will have a long talk with Maisie and tell her everything. It is possible she can help. After all, she's been through some horrible things herself. The death of her family during an enemy attack on her village several years ago when the Mcleods and the Ross Clan were at war."

Ewan studied her face for a long moment. "It's best I go wash up. Last meal will be served shortly. Will ye accompany me?"

"I will," Catriona replied. "First, I must speak to Esme."

THAT NIGHT, WHILE preparing for bed, a peace enveloped Catriona. She met Maisie's gaze in the mirror. "Tomorrow, ye and I must speak about what occurred to me when I was captured. There are things ye must know in order to help me should it happen again."

"Of course," Maisie replied, her expression reassuring. "I understand ye, Lady Ross."

Catriona believed the young woman did. "Now, go and get some rest. My husband should be here shortly."

When Ewan came in, it felt a bit awkward. He went to a side table and poured them a glass of honeyed mead.

Catriona sat in front of the fireplace and waited for him to join her. He handed her a glass and lowered to the other chair.

"Ye must feel better after bathing," Catriona teased to relieve some of the tension in the room.

"I do," Ewan said. "I am not sure how the others could stand being around me."

"The privilege or, in some instances, sadness of being leader is that others are forced to deal with ye regardless of things like that."

His lips curved. "In this case, quite a sad thing."

Their gazes met and Catriona took a sip of her mead. "I will be sending a messenger to McLeod Keep reissuing my invitation to Lady Paige to come visit."

Ewan nodded. "I am glad to hear it. I know ye were looking forward to learning about herbs from her."

"Ye knew that?"

"I kept myself informed of what ye did. Although I kept a physical distance, I wished to know everything."

She was surprised to hear it. At the same time, it made her feel so much better that when she thought he barely cared, he was, in fact, involved.

When they finished the first cup of drink, he refilled them. If there was something he wished to share with her, Catriona would be patient.

"When will I meet yer family?" she asked in a quiet tone, her fingers fiddling with the edge of her robe's sleeve. "I hope they will like me."

When he didn't answer right away, she looked up to meet his gaze. His face was soft. "They will like ye very much. I believe my eldest half-brother will travel here soon. He wishes to meet Malcolm and get to know this part of the family since I am to be laird here."

"I will make sure to have everything prepared."

"Good," he said, then took another sip of his drink. "There is something I wish to share with ye."

A shiver ran down her spine. Catriona took a shaky breath. "What is it?"

"My past and the reason I did my best not to love ye."

She waited as he looked to the fire for a long moment before speaking again. "I caught the woman I married in bed with my own father." He hesitated briefly when she gasped but did not look at her.

"I beat him half to death. My brothers had to pull me away. It was then he banished me from our lands, and I left. I demanded that our marriage be dissolved but wasn't sure until I returned if it truly was."

"What of bairns?"

"My wife had one child, a son, while we were married. He is not mine. I was gone to train in archery with a master for several months. When I returned, it was only a few days later that she claimed to be with child. The boy was born six months after my return. She claimed he was early, but he was well formed and healthy."

The tone of his voice was flat, without emotion. However, the bitterness in the undertone was very evident to Catriona. "I am so sorry, Ewan. I cannot imagine."

"To be cuckolded by one's own father is horrible enough. That he banished me and kept the whore there, living under the same roof as my mother...that, I could never forgive him for."

"Was she still there?" Catriona asked.

Ewan shook his head. "No. Upon my father becoming ill, my brothers threw her out. However, my father had suspected they would and had a house built for her. He paid for servants and left a large amount for her to live well."

To Catriona, it sounded like the man had been deeply in love with Ewan's wife. He'd preferred her to his own wife and son. It was a horrible thing.

"What about yer mother?"

"Honestly, she has fared the best of all of us. I do believe she and Father came to the point of barely tolerating one another long before this all began. They kept different chambers on opposite sides of the keep and rarely spoke to one another."

"Still, it had to be humiliating," Catriona said. "I would not have stood for it."

Ewan's lips twitched. "Is that so?"

She lifted an eyebrow, meeting his gaze. "If I ever hear of ye consorting with another woman and it is proved to me, I will leave."

"I am glad that ye made that clear. I will not issue the same warning to ye."

Was he trying to confuse her? "Why?"

There was a combination of warmth and heat in his eyes. "Because I have no doubts about ye. I know in my heart ye would never be unfaithful."

Catriona could not stop herself from dropping the cup in her hand and throwing herself into her husband's arms. Wrapping her arms around him, she inhaled deeply, loving the scent of him, the feel of his solid body against hers.

"I love ye, Ewan, and I stand by my vows to ye. I will never, ever be untrue to ye."

When his mouth took hers, she let out a sigh of relief. Then she whispered into his ear, "Take me to yer bed, my laird."

The crash of his own cup to the floor was followed by his scooping her up and stalking to the bed. Catriona giggled when he dropped her on the bed unceremoniously so that he could undress.

She sat up, her legs draped over the side of the bed, and stripped away her own clothing, too anxious to be joined with him to attempt at any kind of modesty.

From his wide shoulders to his well-formed chest, Catriona allowed her gaze to take in every inch of him. His stomach rippled when she looked at it. Then just below a patch of brown hair, his erect manhood made her inhale sharply.

"I want to be gentle," he said, closing the short distance and lowering above her. "But I am not sure I can be." His mouth closed over hers before Catriona could say anything.

The kiss was hot, impassioned to the point it took all her breath. Catriona gripped his shoulders and tried to pull him over her, but he resisted.

He lifted her legs. "Wrap them around me," he instructed.

Catriona watched through a daze as Ewan took himself in hand. The sight fanned the flames of heat that had pooled between her legs and she wanted nothing more than for him to plunge fully in.

His gaze met hers and then with one solid thrust, Ewan filled her completely.

"Oh," Catriona gasped out. "Oh."

Thankfully, he began moving, pulling out and then pushing back in a steady rhythm. It was what they needed. A proclamation of their bodies joining in a fashion that left absolutely no doubt about the depth of their feelings for one another.

Once again, Catriona reached for him, but Ewan had other plans for their lovemaking. He shook his head, a wicked smile to his lips. And then, to her utter dismay, he pulled out.

"Move up onto the bed," he said, helping her settle. Then he climbed onto the bed and studied her for a moment.

His gaze fell on her wet sex and Catriona shifted, too full of want to be patient. "What are ye doing?"

"I want to take ye fully, deeper. Here, put yer legs over my shoulders."

Despite not being sure what exactly would happen, she did as he instructed when he leaned forward and scooped her bottom off the bedding.

When her legs were over his shoulders, he moved over her effectively bending her practically in half.

When he drove into her, he was indeed deep. Catriona cried out at the satisfaction that ensued.

She pushed up against the headboard to keep from hitting her head when Ewan's thrusts became more and more energetic. With each thrust, he sent her higher and higher to a place she never would have imagined existed.

Their moans intertwined with the slapping sound of their bodies coming together over and over again. Catriona could not withstand it any longer. She flailed under him as she shattered into pieces, any grips on reality slipping into a fog.

As she fought not to lose herself too fast, Ewan lowered her legs from his shoulders and continued his vigorous movements, his fingers digging into her hips as he fought to find release.

Catriona cried out once again, her body convulsing with a second climax.

Still, he thrust in and out, so fast now, he gasped for air. His large body dripped with sweat as he finally let out a low growl, shuddering in a release so hard that he shook.

Collapsing over her, he gasped for breath, gulping in air while murmuring a strange string of words.

Catriona herself could barely breathe, but she managed to wiggle from under him and gulped in a full breath as he did the same.

"It has never ever been this good." He grinned like a loon. "Never."

CHAPTER TWENTY-THREE

Two months later – early autumn

ATOP HIS STEED, Ewan rode ahead of the party that headed to Dun Airgid. His half-brother would be arriving in the next day or two and they'd agreed to first meet at Malcolm's home.

Although Ewan and Catriona had a large home, depending on how many people Darach traveled with, it could be that there would be too many to accommodate comfortably.

He looked over his shoulder to the carriage in which Catriona and her faithful companion, Maisie, rode and his lips curved.

Two years ago, upon arriving at Ross Keep from Uist, never would he have imagined a life like he had now. A lairdship, people to oversee, a large family that supported him and, above all, to be married to the love of his life.

Everyone in the keep had adjusted to their lifestyle now. Usually, he and Catriona were not expected to rise early, as they'd come to an agreement to spend evenings alone getting to know one another.

They often stayed up until the wee hours of the night, talking about anything and everything. She'd become his confidant and adviser.

When first meeting her, he recalled that Esme had told him about

Catriona's intelligence and sensible way of seeing things. It was true...she often guided him to make decisions in a way that soothed people's ire.

Their lovemaking had turned into an art form of discovering each other's body and learning what satisfied each of them best. Ewan did his best not to think of bedsport with Catriona when not alone as it could be embarrassing.

Even then, he shifted in the saddle and looked across to a guard.

"Riders in the distance," the guard said. "It is not our scout."

Immediately, they called for a halt and the accompaniment of guards surrounded the carriage.

"Ye should get in the carriage as well," the guard instructed.

"I will not cower," Ewan protested.

"Laird, ye must." The guard left no room for argument.

After guiding Ban to the back of the carriage, Ewan dismounted and went to the carriage, grumbling under his breath.

Catriona gave him a worried look. "Why have we stopped?"

"Our scout is delayed. We will move with more caution until he meets us."

"Oh," she replied, paling. "I hope nothing is amiss."

Maisie met his gaze and turned to Catriona. "I hope they didn't send Giles. The boy will stop and talk to a tree and is always late for everything."

The scout was not Maisie's brother, but Ewan didn't clarify it to Catriona. "If it is Giles and he causes us to be delayed, he will be banished back to the stables."

Maisie giggled. "He would hate that."

Their interchange seemed to calm Catriona. Ewan leaned sideways to look forward. So far, there didn't seem to be any kind of threat.

Just then, they came to a stop and one of the guards came to the door and opened it. "Laird, we are being greeted by Munro warriors."

Ewan met Catriona's gaze. "Gisela's family. No need to worry."

"Gisela's family?" Catriona peered out. "I'd like to meet them as well."

"This is not her family now," he clarified. "They are her family's guardsmen."

Upon exiting the carriage, his horse was brought forward, and Ewan mounted. He wore the Ross colors with the crest pinned on his chest. Flanked by four warriors, he rode to where the group of six Munro men formed a line.

"I am Ewan Ross, new laird of the Ross northern lands. I am sure yer laird has been informed as he attended the festivities on my behalf."

One man, who he assumed was the leader nodded. "Aye, Laird, we are aware. We are not here to threaten ye, but to help escort ye across our lands. We are currently at odds with a neighboring clan and do not wish any harm to come to ye or yer people while in our territory."

He wasn't used to special treatment. In all the times he and others had traveled through Munro lands, they'd not been stopped. Several times, he himself had seen Munro patrols. They'd always remained friendly.

"Who do ye fight?" he asked as they continued forward toward Malcolm's land border.

"The Mackay," the man replied. "Nasty bastards they are."

Moments later, fearing for his wife's reactions to this unexpected interruption in travel, he returned to the carriage to reassure Catriona.

Surprisingly, she seemed serene when he opened the carriage door and peered in. "They are, indeed, from Clan Munro and have asked to escort us through Munro lands. It seems they've been having problems with the Mackay."

"That is good then," Catriona replied, meeting his gaze. "Be with care."

Not caring that Maisie sat next to Catriona, he leaned forward and kissed her soundly. "I will. Soon, ye will meet Darach. Be prepared for him to tell ye stories of my childhood mischiefs. Do not believe a word he says," Ewan told her with a wink.

The rest of the journey went without incident. Upon reaching the Ross land border, the Munro patrol turned back to their own lands.

While thanking them, along with sending greetings and thanks to Laird Munro, Ewan informed them of their plans to return back through their lands the following week. The men seemed certain there wouldn't be any issue but promised to keep an eye out for them.

Ross Keep came into view and Ewan let out a long breath. He expected that his half-brother would travel with perhaps another of his siblings and their mother.

Although he was extremely proud of his family, he wondered what their true feelings were of him becoming laird. His mother had seemed happy for him, but sad that he was to permanently live so far away.

As far as Darach went, his half-brother was not one to ever show emotion. On the other hand, one never had to wonder what Darach thought as he was quite blunt. It mattered little to Darach if feelings were hurt. At the same time, he was forever honest.

⤜⤜⤜✦⤛⤛⤛

THE DAY AFTER arriving at Ross Keep, Catriona felt as if she'd barely gotten her breath when the announcement was made that the travelers from Uist were to arrive.

She, along with Elspeth, hurried to the front entrance of the home, while Malcolm and Ewan stood just in front of them.

The party consisted of four guards in the lead, then two men on horseback, followed by a carriage and behind that a small contingent of what Catriona assumed were warriors and archers.

Once the entire party entered, two riders and the carriage came to a stop. The guardsmen were guided to line up behind it.

The two men dismounted. By their size, they were definitely Ross men.

When Ewan, Malcolm and Tristan greeted the newcomers, Elspeth leaned to Catriona's ear. "Ross men are certainly attractive are they not?"

"Very much so," Catriona said, her attention on one of the visitors.

One of the men stood out from the others.

Of all the Ross men she'd met up until this point, none were like him. The sun brought out the light shade of his hair, the wind blowing the golden tresses sideways as he spoke to the others. He was tall of stature, about the same height as Ewan.

The other brother, who was of the same coloring as Ewan, was greeted by Tristan with hands on shoulders. It was as if two giants faced off.

Unlike the greetings with the Ross cousins, the golden-haired man hugged Ewan, which led Catriona to believe he had to be the eldest, Darach Ross.

"Do ye think he is the eldest, Darach?" Catriona asked Esme, who'd come to stand next to her while Ruari walked over to join the other men.

"Who?"

"The golden one."

"He reminds me of a lion," Esme said, eyes narrowed. "It is hard to tell. Both of the men who just arrived are wearing both a tartan and crest. However, the blond one does act like a leader. Look how he and Malcolm stand. Yer husband as well."

"The stance of lairds," Elspeth proclaimed. "If they do not come to make introductions soon, I say we go inside."

It was as if Malcolm heard her, which was impossible, but he looked over and motioned to the golden one toward where the women stood.

The other newcomer hurried to the coach while Ewan, Malcolm

and the golden-haired man walked toward them.

"Ladies, I present Darach Ross, Laird Ross from South Uist," Ewan said. "The other, who's gone to see about our mother is my brother, Stuart." He then proceeded to present first Elspeth, since she was the lady of the house, followed by Catriona and, lastly, Esme.

Darach was astonishingly handsome, with mesmerizing eyes a color that made it hard to pinpoint. At one point, Catriona thought them green, but soon decided perhaps blue. He seemed to find her interesting as well, his cool gaze moving over her face.

"Lady Catriona, I am pleased to meet ye. If ye find Ewan lacking in any manner, do not hesitate to inform me." His demeanor and tone remained formal, but there was a glint of humor in his eyes.

Just then, a woman neared, Scottish through and through, with bright green eyes and red waves that had been pulled up into a loose hairdo.

"My mother, Lady Mariel Ross," Ewan said. Upon their gazes clashing, Catriona immediately loved her.

CATRIONA KEPT NOTE of everything Elspeth did. Visitors were seated based on their ranking and with there being three lairds present, it was quite a production.

At the high board, Malcolm's right side was ceded to Darach. Elspeth, Ewan and Catriona on the left.

Catriona was glad to have Ewan's mother on her side. Lady Mariel Ross was gracious and beautiful, making Catriona wonder why her husband sought another woman to consort with.

As soon as the meal was over, Lady Mariel asked about her bedchamber, claiming exhaustion from the travel.

"I will show ye," Catriona said and stood. Upon reaching the doorway of the guest room, Lady Mariel insisted Catriona come inside with her.

The woman seemed to gain energy. She went to the bed and

dropped her shawl and then pulled pins from her hair, shaking the red strands loose. "I cannot stand to have my hair pinned up all the time," she grumbled.

"Come sit with me for a bit," Lady Mariel said, motioning to a pair of chairs.

As soon as Catriona sat, Lady Mariel smiled broadly. "I wish to tell ye how happy I am to see my son married. It is obvious to me in the short time I've been here how well suited ye are."

"He is a good husband to me," Catriona said. "We love each other." Her cheeks heated at disclosing this to her husband's mother. However, in Catriona's opinion it was important to soothe the woman's worries about her son being hurt again.

"I am sure ye will both be very happy. I am anxious to see yer home."

"And I am as eager for ye to spend time there with us."

Catriona was surprised when the woman caressed her cheek, a glint of tears in her eyes. "My son has been through a great deal. He needs a good strong family. Ours is still reeling from the loss of my husband and all that occurred in the last years of his life."

As much as she wanted to know more, there would be more time as they were to visit for a fortnight.

"Yer son Darach, he seems a good strong leader," Catriona imparted. "I am sure he will rebuild the clan."

Lady Mariel nodded. "Aye, he must." She chuckled. "I am so very proud of my son." Looking to Catriona, she smiled warmly. "He is not my son by birth. His mother died the night he was born. When I married the late laird, Darach was but a few weeks old. I fell in love with him immediately."

It explained why Laird Darach Ross looked so different from the others.

"I cannot wait to have bairns, many of them," Catriona said to lighten the mood.

Ewan's mother laughed. "Beware of bearing too many sons. They can make ye ponder how boys ever survive to adulthood."

Catriona laughed. In that moment, she was saddened not to live closer to her husband's mother.

Chapter Twenty-Four

Fraser Keep

"WHAT ARE YE doing?" Ava Fraser walked to where Flora hid beside a tree. "Who are ye hiding from?"

"No one," Flora whispered and yanked the woman unceremoniously behind the tree. "Lower yer voice."

Flora then peered around the tree to where a couple walked. Broden was walking with a woman. They were deep in conversation. Surely any moment now, thinking to be alone, they would show their intention for wandering away together.

"Who is she?" Ava asked, looking to where the couple now stood, their backs to them.

Flora shook her head. "I do not recognize her. They are too far away."

"What is going on?" Eileen, the cook, walked out with a basket. "Who are we spying on?"

The older woman came to stand next to them and narrowed her eyes toward where Broden and the woman were. "Ah, yes, this is very interesting. I wonder what excuse she will give for abandoning him so long ago."

"His wife?" Flora asked, her chest tightening. "Why did I not know? He kissed me…"

"His mother," Eileen clarified. "She left him and his father when Broden was but a wee lad, perhaps five. She has returned now, over twenty years later, with a new husband and family. The nerve of the woman. Poor Broden's been avoiding her, but she appeared this morning, insisting to speak to him."

Just then, the woman reached for Broden and he took a step back, holding both hands up. Evidently, he didn't seem to want anything to do with the woman.

"Who raised him then?" Flora asked, not taking her gaze from Broden.

"His father and aunt. Broden had a good childhood. He was a bright, well-liked boy."

"Good," Ava said, and then huffed. "We should ask that woman to leave."

"We?" Flora and Eileen asked in unison.

Ava nodded. "I could send a guard to send her away."

"That would be strange," Flora mused. "Broden can take care of himself."

"Did ye say he kissed ye?" Ava asked, and Flora swallowed.

Why had she blurted that out? In her distress, her tongue had loosened. "It was nothing, just that one night we found ourselves alone, in the corridor…I was caught off guard."

"I bet," Eileen said with a chuckle. "Accidently pressed yer lips to his in yer confusion?"

Ava giggled.

"We should go inside and give Broden his privacy," Flora said, but then turned back to look.

Broden said something and stalked away. The woman's head fell forward and she covered her face with both hands.

"Forgiveness is not so easy to get as some people would think," Eileen mumbled and headed toward the woman.

Flora and Ava didn't bother to hide. Instead, they stood side-by-side, watching as Eileen went up to the woman. Whatever the cook said made Broden's mother nod. Then they walked closer.

Broden's mother looked drawn and pale. Her reddened eyes flicked to Flora and Ava for only a moment before she pulled her shawl over her head and went to a cart. She climbed onto the bench and snapped the reins.

The three of them watched as the woman rode out through the gates.

"What did ye tell her?" Ava asked.

"I told her she should leave, that unless Broden welcomed her, she was not to come here again."

"Good," Flora said.

Ava looked to Flora. "Ye should go find him. He may need someone to speak to."

FLORA FOUND BRODEN in the area beside the stables. It was a place people often went when needing time alone. The space was blocked from view which gave privacy. There were only rain barrels and some benches that were pulled out when festivities occurred.

He stood looking out toward a field where sheep lazily grazed, his back straight, arms down at his sides.

"Broden," Flora said, nearing. "Do ye need to talk?"

When he turned to her, Broden sighed. "I am not sure if I will be good company right now. It would be nice for ye to stay for a moment."

Flora walked to stand next to him and looked out to the field. "It is easy to be envious of the obliviousness of animals."

Broden remained silent but nodded.

"Do ye miss him?"

The question caught Flora by surprise. He spoke of her dead husband, of course. Instantly, the familiar stabbing of pain hit her. "Very much. Every day."

"How do ye continue?" He gave her a curious look. "How are ye so strong?"

Flora smiled. "I have to be. I have a son and my mother to look after. Death and life are both realities we must deal with. Ye, too, have suffered a great loss. When yer mother left, she may as well have died."

He swallowed. "It is not the same. Yer loss is much greater."

"Loss cannot be measured. Ye continued, made yerself into a good man. Do not belittle it." Without realizing it, Flora had taken his hand. When his fingers tightened around hers, she gasped.

"Thank ye," Broden said, not releasing her hand.

There was open sincerity when he pinned her with a direct look. "I spoke with Lady Fraser about ye. I have been watching ye and find ye to be admirable. I know this is sudden, but I would like to ask that ye consider marrying me, Flora."

Her eyes widened and she swallowed. After just admitting to missing her husband, how could Broden accept her knowing a large portion of her heart would never be his?

"I do wish to…" she began. "I find ye most attractive."

His lips curved. Then, suddenly, he pulled her close. They kissed, not a gentle one of two people who'd only recently begun to explore possibilities. No, this was a kiss of two lonely souls finding one another.

Flora threaded her fingers through his hair, while pressing herself against the strong man. For months, she'd pretended not to need him, but no longer. It was time to admit what everyone had been telling her. She'd found love again. She was madly in love with Broden.

"I want ye, Flora. As my wife, as my lover."

Flora pulled away and met his eyes with daring. "Take me then."

He pushed her against the building and she clawed at his breeches, while he fumbled with her skirts. Both were desperate with want, need and passion.

Lifting her to wrap her legs around him, Broden drove into her, his thick sex invading her thoroughly. Flora buried her face into his neck to stifle her scream.

Each thrust brought so much fulfillment, she could barely keep from cresting. But within seconds, Flora lost control, her entire body shuddering in release.

Broden's powerful body continued to seek reaching a climax. His masculine grunts filled her ears as she held on to his shoulders, urging him to completion.

Abruptly, he pulled out and spilled into his hand, his body jerking in release.

Flora straightened her skirts, attempting to catch her breath. How could she have allowed things to go this far? He certainly wouldn't marry her now.

"Ye do not have to…"

Broden smiled widely at her, then pulled her close, covering her mouth with his. "Thank ye, beautiful Flora. I will take ye allowing us to go this far as a very certain yes."

Unable to keep from it, Flora pushed back and grinned up at him. "Yes, Broden McRainy, I will marry ye."

He lifted her up and twirled in a circle. "Ye turned this day from one of the worst to the best one yet."

When he lowered her, she looked up at him. "What did ye tell yer mother?"

His eyes darkened, a furrow appearing between his brows. "That I never wished to see her again. I no longer considered her my mother. I thanked her for giving me life and for leaving me to be raised by a caring woman, who was my true mother."

"Good for ye," Flora said as he guided her to walk back toward the house. "I am proud of ye."

Broden slid a look to her. "Proud enough to marry me with haste? I do not think I can resist time apart."

When they came out from around the building, Ava and Eileen

stood just a few feet away, pretending interest in a lad milking a cow.

Flora pushed from Broden and hurried to them. "Were ye spying?" Her face was so hot, she knew it was bright red.

"Of course not, dear," Eileen said with a scoff. "Why would we want to spy on a couple in the throes of lovemaking?"

Ava burst out laughing and grabbed the cook's arm. "We really should finish picking vegetables from the garden for last meal."

"What is so funny?" Broden came to walk alongside Flora, who looked anywhere but at him.

"Whatever they think is funny, is not to me." Flora turned to him. "I must speak to Mother and inform her of our plans. When should I plan the wedding for?"

"Whenever ye please. Just do not make it too far into the future." Broden pressed a soft kiss to her lips. "I will go inform the laird."

They parted ways next to the back entrance, Broden heading inside and Flora walking to the garden where her mother stood with both Ava and Eileen.

When she approached, her mother smiled and immediately hugged her. "I am so very happy for ye."

"For us," Flora said, hugging her back. "God has, indeed, smiled upon us again."

War had taken her husband, the man she'd never stop loving. But somehow, Flora realized, Broden was to fill the void and take the other half of her heart.

Flora turned to Ava and Eileen. "I will require yer help planning the wedding. I presume it will be at the village."

"Nonsense," Lady Fraser said, appearing from beside the shed. "I think our clan needs a reason to celebrate. It shall be held here."

Ava and Eileen exchanged guilty looks. Obviously they'd been informing the laird's wife and her mother of the goings-on prior to going to spy on her.

It was hard to remain angry. She laughed and shook her head. "I sense there will never be any secrets between all of us."

CHAPTER TWENTY-FIVE

Two days later, Tuath Avon

E WAN AND HIS brothers walked out into the silence of the night. The sky was clear, making it easy to see the multitude of stars. The scent of the nearby creek was carried in the air by the soft breeze that blew steadily across their faces. By the slight chill, the leaves would soon change and drop to the ground, turning it into a colorful tapestry of brown and golden hues.

"This is a fine home," Darach said, his gaze out toward the forest. "I will forever be grateful to Cousin Malcolm for bestowing this grand gift upon ye."

Pride filled Ewan as he looked about, seeing what his brothers saw. A thick forest, filled with game, rich lands for farming and a source of water to replenish fields and livestock.

"Is it not strange that destiny would make me a fourth-born laird?"

Darach studied him. "Are ye happy here?"

The question startled him, and Ewan did not reply. He considered that there was absolutely no reason not to be.

Thankfully, Stuart interrupted by giving him a wide smile. "Yer wife is beautiful. Tis too bad she didn't see me first."

"She would have hidden in horror," Ewan teased.

His younger brother gave him a warm look. "In all honesty, Brother, ye have done well. I am happy for ye."

"How is it?" Ewan asked Darach. "Taking over for Da?"

"Not easy at all," Stuart interjected. "Darach has a lot on his shoulders."

Ewan studied Darach. "Father did a great deal of damage, I assume."

"Against both the MacNeils, the Uisdeins and the Macdonalds, I'm afraid," Darach replied. "I have to find a way to make repairs, else we will find ourselves at war."

"The MacNeils?" Ewan asked. "Surely they will take our side. Mother is a MacNeil, after all."

"We will see," Darach said, placing a hand on Ewan's shoulder. "Do not worry. I am sure all will be well."

Despite Darach dropping the conversation, Ewan sensed the tension. All was not well. "If ye need help at any time, send word. I will come immediately." Then he continued. "And Malcolm has hundreds of warriors. He will not hesitate to send help."

Darach nodded. "Aye, he has given his word to support our cause. For it, I am grateful. I do not foresee needing it."

"Why?" Ewan asked, intrigued.

"Because, as ye know, our numbers are almost the same as the three of them."

"They can be strong if they combine," Stuart said. "Ye should plan to ask Malcolm for support."

>>>><<<<

WHEN EWAN WALKED into the bedchamber, he was exhausted. The days his family would remain there would fly by and he wasn't sure he'd be ready for them to leave. However, he had a new life, people's needs to see after and a wife and household to maintain.

Catriona stood and greeted him with a tight hug. It seemed his wife was in need of reassurance.

"Does something bother ye?" he asked after pressing a kiss to her lips. They remained standing, arms around each other's waist. "Tell me."

She frowned. "I love yer mother and yer brothers. They are nice as well."

"Why, then, does a frown mar that beautiful face of yers?" Ewan asked and kissed the crease that formed on her brow.

"It could be that we should have gone to Uist upon marrying instead of remaining here. We are both so far from our homes here."

Ewan chuckled. "I am glad ye care for my mother and brothers. However, I have given my word to Malcolm to take over this lairdship. I plan to fulfill my vow and so should ye."

She lifted her chin and gave him a challenging look. "Ruari and Esme would do well here. Perhaps better. She is much more suited to be a laird's wife than I am."

Ewan thought about what Catriona said. A part of him discounted each word. However, as a dutiful husband, he considered what life would be like if he were to return to Uist.

"We would live in a humble home on the isle. I would return to archery and ye would have only Maisie to help ye. Our meals would be taken at the keep and ye would fall under whoever Darach marries."

She kissed him, her hands sliding down the sides of his neck. "Sounds divine."

EPILOGUE

A NEWBORN'S ANGRY wails filled the air and Ewan could not stand it any longer. Why hadn't the midwife come for him as yet? Was something wrong?

Unable to stand it any longer, he stormed into the room and all the women surrounding the bed turned to him startled. Breath left his body and he struggled not to fall sideways and crumple to the floor.

"What is happening?" he asked in a whisper.

The bairn cried again and everyone parted to allow him forward.

In the bed, Catriona beamed up at him. In her arms was a red-faced, quite angry babe. "He seems none too pleased to be taken from his warm place," she said.

"Why was I not called in?" he snapped at a wide-eyed Maisie. "I thought something was wrong."

"I asked them to wait until I was a bit more...presentable," Catriona said, looking to the midwife. "I should have known better."

Rounding the bed, he kneeled beside it and peered at his wife and newborn child. "Next time, I am staying in the room," he said, unable to take his eyes from the bairn.

"Is he?"

"He's perfect," Catriona replied. "Exceptional."

His mother smiled at him. "Ye will have to give him a good name, befitting of a strong man."

Catriona's mother nodded and added. "A name befitting a leader."

"I agree," Darach said from the doorway. "The first grandchild to be born. He will always have a place of honor in our family." Their gazes met. "Congratulations, Brother."

When Ewan placed his hand on the child's chest, the babe quieted, and he smiled. "He knows me, ye think?"

"Of course, he does," Catriona replied. "He has heard yer voice all these months."

The room emptied to give the new family privacy. He could tell Catriona was exhausted and would soon fall asleep.

"Once our home is complete, we shall move. For now, I want ye to rest. Maisie and our mothers will ensure ye do not leave this bed. They were already arguing over who will mind the bairn first."

Her sleepy gaze moved from the child to him. "I will rest. Ye must do the same. I can tell ye were up all night as well."

Indeed, all night, he'd paced the corridor, praying for both his wife and child. A part of him wished to demand they not have more. However, Catriona had insisted she wished for a large family. Besides, it would be impossible to keep away from her. Ewan found her completely irresistible.

"Sleep, Wife. I will get rest as well."

"Not in here," Catriona said. "Ye must sleep elsewhere."

Although he'd not planned on sleeping there, he asked. "Why?"

"I wish it," she replied with a haughty smirk. "I do not want to worry about ye flopping about."

"Flopping?" He pretended to be insulted. "I assure you, that I do not flop."

She giggled. "Go."

"Very well." He leaned forward, placed a kiss on the slumbering child's head and then kissed Catriona on the lips. "I love ye, Catriona, and thank God for ye daily."

Her eyes misted. "I feel the same about ye."

Ewan could barely make it out the door as their mothers hurried in to take the babe. He walked out past the great room and up the stairs. Then he went out to the balcony of the bedchamber he would be sleeping in.

The sun had fully risen, its rays casting bright streaks atop the sea's surface. The fresh scent of the ocean blew across his face, salty and cool.

He'd come home to Uist and, this time, he'd remain.

The End

About the Author

Most days USA Today Bestseller Hildie McQueen can be found in her overly tight leggings and green hoodie, holding a cup of British black tea while stalking her hunky lawn guy. Author of Medieval Highlander and American Historical romance, she writes something every reader can enjoy.

Hildie's favorite past-times are reader conventions, traveling, shopping and reading.

She resides in beautiful small town Georgia with her super-hero husband Kurt and three little doggies.

Visit her website at www.hildiemcqueen.com
Facebook: HildieMcQueen
Twitter: @HildieMcQueen
Instagram: hildiemcqueenwriter